THE
FIGHTER

TARA CRESCENT

THE
FIGHTER

Editing by Molly Whitman at Novel Mechanic, www. novelmechanic.com

Cover Design by Bookin It Designs, www.bookinitdesigns.com

v. 20240630

*To finding a partner who will always, **always**, fight for you.*

1

ALINA

I am the queen of bad decisions.

If I said that to my friends, they would tell me I was being too harsh. Rosa, who trains at my gym, would cluck her tongue and scold me for being so down on myself. Annie, the ESL teacher who lives in the building around the corner, would grab a piece of paper and start making a list of all the smart decisions I've made to counter the narrative.

But they're my *friends*—being supportive is in the job description. I know what I know. As evidence, I present my useless, waste-of-space partner in this gym, Simon Groff.

I met Simon two years ago, just after my mother died from a long and debilitating fight with earlier-onset Alzheimer's. When she passed away ten days before Christmas, I was simultaneously relieved that her suffering had come to an end and also more than a little shellshocked.

I had been her primary caregiver, and until the very

end, my days had been full of all the things I needed to do for my mom. Then she died, and I had nothing to distract me from the emptiness. Everything in the apartment I shared with her was a reminder that she was no longer around. I taught part-time MMA classes, but the gym I worked at was closed until the new year.

Rome was cold, damp, and miserable, and I just wanted to escape. I wanted to run away from it all and spend a week in the sun, drinking margaritas on a beach while I figured out what I wanted to do with the rest of my life.

So I did.

I took a plane to Tenerife on Christmas Day, and I met a guy as soon as I arrived at my resort.

The years of caregiving had worn me out, and I felt pale and invisible. But Simon flirted with me. We spent a lot of time together. We were the only two regular attendees of the early morning yoga class the resort offered. We drank margaritas on the beach, and of course, we slept together.

That, by itself, wasn't the bad decision. Vacation flings, I understand.

I even forgive myself for confiding in Simon, telling him about how I felt stuck and in a rut. Simon was, in those days, a good listener. "What do you want to do with your life?" he asked. "What is stopping you from living the life of your dreams?"

I considered his question seriously as I sipped my third margarita, and the answer seemed to come to me out of nowhere. "I want to move," I replied. "I want to leave Rome and move to Venice." My mother would take me there every year. One of my earliest memories is of chasing pigeons in la Piazza San Marco, laughing as they took to the air to avoid the chubby toddler intent on cuddling them.

"I've been to Venice," Simon replied, a frown on his face. "*Once,* and that was enough. It's not as magical as the tourist guides make it out to be."

"I know." Yes, the city was always jammed with tourists, and truly good restaurants were few and far between. People also had an unfortunate habit of dumping garbage in the canals when they thought nobody was looking and then complaining about the smell.

But despite its many flaws, I loved it. Venice always felt magical to me, and more importantly, *it felt like home.*

"What would you do there? Work in a gym?"

"I'd open my own," I replied. *Like a fool.* "My mother left me some money. Enough to buy a building and survive the first year." The money was a shock. I didn't think she had any, but when I went to the bank after her funeral to attend to the details, a million and a half euros was sitting there. "She never wanted to invest it," the branch manager told me. "She was insistent it should always be available in case she needed it in a hurry."

Simon's eyes were suddenly alert. He sat up on an elbow and stared at me as if he were properly seeing me for the first time. "Want to do it together?"

I knew nothing about Simon. I should have either turned him down outright or, at the very least, done my due diligence by looking into him first.

But I did neither of those things. Instead, fueled by tequila, hope, and sweaty, if not particularly good sex, I said yes.

Queen of bad decisions.

IT'S SATURDAY, and the aforementioned bad decision has blown off the class he's supposed to teach for the second time in two days. I grit my teeth and pray for patience as a cluster of over-muscled, protein-chugging men crowd around my desk, demanding to know where Simon is.

'How should I know?' is what I want to say. Simon's interest in our gym has steadily tapered off to the point where he is now doing the bare minimum. No, not even that. He's gone from teaching ten classes to eight, then five, until he settled at two. Just two classes a week, and he hasn't bothered showing up to either of them this week.

He tells me that he's pulling his weight by keeping the books and doing routine maintenance, yet we're still paying a bookkeeper, and the bathroom taps have leaked for *months*. He was responsible for finding a contractor to renovate the women's changing room, and the guy he hired was completely inept. Marcelo did half the work badly, and to add insult to injury, he's refusing to come back and fix the mess.

Two months ago, I confronted Simon and asked him what the hell he was doing to justify his share of the profits. "I am out finding us new members," he replied loftily.

Of course, that's bullshit too. Enrollment isn't up—it's down. Probably because Simon leers at every woman that trains here until she becomes uncomfortable and quits.

"I'm so sorry," I tell our annoyed customers. "Simon

4

must have had an emergency. We'll comp this class, of course."

That does not mollify them. "Will you also comp the babysitter I paid for so I could attend this class?" one of the customers, Gerald, asks snidely. Gerald is a finance influencer whose advice comes with a heaping dose of poverty shaming, but as much as I violently disagree with every one of his opinions, he does have a point here. People made time in their schedules and showed up for their class. Unfortunately, their instructor couldn't be bothered to do the same.

"I'm really sorry," I say again. "The best I can do is comp your next class as well." And there goes our profit margin for the week. It's a good thing Simon isn't here because if he was, I'd be tempted to wring his neck.

The guys continue to grumble but eventually disperse. Fifteen minutes later, my phone rings. Shocker of shockers: it's my missing partner.

"Where have you been?" I demand, too angry to hide it. "You didn't show up to your class today, and you were a no-show yesterday as well. What the hell, Simon?"

"I was in the hospital," he huffs. "That's why I couldn't call you. I have two broken wrists."

I roll my eyes as I doodle on the notepad in front of me. Two broken wrists—that's a likely story. He couldn't even be bothered to think up a decent excuse. "Both your wrists are broken?" I ask skeptically. "How did that happen?"

"It was an accident," he says evasively. I grind my pencil on the sketchbook so hard that the point snaps. "But that's not why I'm calling. I'm leaving Venice and moving back to London."

I set down my pencil. "You're doing what now?"

"I'm out, babe," he says. "Arrivederci to the canals, the ombre, and the fucking tourists. I'm in London already, and I'm not planning to come back."

My heart starts to beat very fast. For eighteen months, I've been trying to get Simon to sell, but his asking price has always been ridiculous. He wants a million euros for his share of the business, and even if it were worth that much—it isn't—it's not money I have.

But now?

This is the opening I've been waiting for.

And you know what they say about opportunity. When it knocks, you don't just open the door. You kick the damn thing down.

"What about the gym?" I ask, doing some mental calculations about how much money I can access in a hurry. "I hope this means you're finally willing to quote me a reasonable price, Simon, because if you think you can do your part from the UK, think again. Both of us need to be here every single day, teaching classes, unplugging toilets, pulling hair out of drains, and doing whatever else is called for. You're already not pulling your weight here, and in fact—"

"You make it sound so attractive," he sneers, cutting off my rant. "But you're too late. I already sold my share of the gym."

For a long instant, his words don't register. When they finally sink in, I see red. "You did what?" I say slowly. *Carefully.* I'm on the verge of exploding in sheer rage, but I have to keep it together for the customers. "Simon, you can't sell your share of the gym to anyone else. The contract we both signed says that I have the right of first refusal."

"Well, it's a done deal," he says, as if that somehow makes it okay. "The guy who bought my share said he'd drop by the gym sometime this weekend to meet you. You can discuss the details with him. Bye, Ali."

Then the jerk hangs up.

As if on cue, the door opens, and a man walks in.

2

ALINA

My first impression of the man who just walked in is that he's lost.

He's tall and lean, and his navy suit fits so impeccably that it has to be bespoke. This guy doesn't belong in my gym, where the air is laced with testosterone, and the men are sweaty and muscled. He's too clean. Too manicured. He looks like he belongs on a runway somewhere or on the cover of a fashion magazine.

Not my type at all.

He walks up to the desk, his strides sure and unhurried, and as he nears, I get a better look at his face, and wow. *He's gorgeous.* His dark hair is ever so slightly tousled, as if a woman's been running her fingers through it. A smile dances on his full lips, but when he reaches the front desk and I look into his gray eyes, there's no answering smile there.

A frisson of warning rolls down my spine.

"Il Doge is two doors down," I tell him. The trendy

restaurant doesn't have a sign or any other indication that it's a commercial establishment. For reasons I am too unsophisticated to understand, it's supposed to be difficult to find. I've never eaten there, but I've heard the menu doesn't have prices either. If you need to ask how much the food is, you don't belong there. It's not my kind of restaurant at all, but Mr. Bespoke Suit would fit right in. "It's the one with the black door and the doorknob in the shape of a lion."

He quirks an eyebrow. "I'm not looking for Il Doge," he replies. His voice is gravelly, and his Italian has just a hint of an accent. Sexy. "Mediocre food in a pretentious atmosphere. No thanks."

Up close, he's not quite as manicured as I thought. There's a hint of stubble over his cheeks and a spiderweb tattoo on the back of his left hand, the combination giving him a bit of an edge. Enough of an edge that I find myself wanting to engage in conversation with him. "You think so?" I ask, a wicked urge seizing me. "It's one of my favorite restaurants."

Hello, Ali? Why are you trying to flirt with a perfect stranger?

He doesn't miss a beat. "I've put my foot in it, haven't I?" His lips tilt up charmingly. "Let's start over. I love Il Doge. The food is truly exceptional. As for the decor—"

I have to fight not to laugh. "I'm going to stop you there," I tell him. "I've never been to Il Doge; I was just messing with you. How can I help you?"

He holds out his hand. "My name is Tomas Aguilar. I just purchased Simon Groff's share of this gym."

The words are like a bucket of cold water, and any attraction I'm feeling instantly evaporates. This is the guy that Simon told me about. I stare at his outstretched hand. His fingers are long and elegant, his fingernails neatly clipped, and I'm sure that his handshake will be firm, straight out of a Business 101 book.

When Simon told me he was done with Venice, there was a moment when I was *almost* hopeful that the gym could finally be mine.

This is the guy who destroyed those dreams. Tomas Aguilar, with his fancy suit and his smug smile.

"Alina Zuccaro," I reply, my voice clipped. This situation might not be his fault. I wouldn't put it past my former partner to hide the relevant details from a potential buyer. "Simon signed a contract with me, Signor Aguilar. I'm afraid he was in violation of it when he sold his share to you. I had right of first refusal." Maybe he'll be willing to listen to a reasonable offer. He's looking around dubiously, and it's obvious he's out of place here. "I'd like to resolve this amicably. If you tell me how much you paid—"

"A million euros."

Disbelief fills me, followed swiftly by disappointment. Tomas Aguilar wildly overpaid Simon. There's no way I can offer him anything close to that much money. I'm about to admit that to Tomas when he looks around dubiously and adds, "I can't believe I paid that much for this dump."

He called my gym a *dump*.

Fury fills me. Yes, the couch in the lobby is worn and sweat-stained. The reception area badly needs a new coat of paint—another thing Marcelo was supposed to do— and the smoothie machine has been broken almost since the day Simon bought it. *But still.* How dare he walk in here and insult my business? Who the hell does he think he is, anyway?

"Why the hell would you pay Simon his asking price?" I hiss, hot rage sparking under my skin. "Are you insane? It isn't worth anything close to that."

"Yes, that much is clear," he replies, giving the gym another disdainful glance. "Your drywall looks like it's water damaged. And is that mold I see?" He shakes his head. "It's a miracle the authorities haven't shut you down."

"Our contractor has been giving us the run-around, not that it's relevant to this discussion," I say through gritted teeth. Tomas Aguilar was never going to be my favorite person—he bought Simon's share of the gym from under my feet. But after the repeated insults? I don't just dislike him—this is *hate.* "Nobody asked you to be here," I bite out. "And Simon shouldn't have sold his share to you; he should have offered it to me first. It's a clear violation of our contract. I should take you to court."

He doesn't seem disconcerted by my antagonism. In fact, he has the nerve to smile as if my fury is amusing to him. "Let's say he did offer to sell to you," he says calmly. "You would have had a week to come up with a million euros. But you clearly have no access to money. If you did, you'd have already used it to fix this space. We can pretend, if that'll make you happy. Would you like me to offer to sell my share to you, then come back in seven days to have this exact conversation again?"

Trust someone wearing a custom suit that probably costs more than I make in a year to throw my lack of money in my face. Asshole. Smug, conceited, supercilious *asshole.* "You think you're funny?" I demand. "You think it's a joke that you've waltzed in here to trample all over my livelihood?"

Someone clears their throat. "Tomas, play nice," another suit-clad man says. I didn't even see him enter. He comes forward and offers me a warm smile. "My name is Daniel Rossi," he says. "I'm acting as Tomas's lawyer." He gives the other man a wry look. "Apologies for the way Tomas delivered the news. My friend frequently forgets that some of us have emotions. If he had his way, we'd live our lives with Vulcan detachment."

I give him a blank look. "*Star Trek*?" he says. "No? Never mind. What Tomas meant to say was that, yes, Simon Groff should have offered you the first right of refusal, and he didn't. You have a legitimate cause for complaint. *Against Mr. Groff.*"

"Let me guess," I say bitterly. Daniel might be smoother than Tomas, but both men are saying the same thing, and if I'm honest, I prefer Tomas's blunt, no-bull-shit approach. "You guys did nothing wrong, and it's Simon I should sue."

Tomas frowns.

"Exactly," Daniel says, jumping in before his friend gets a chance to snipe about something else. "However, given that you and Tomas will be working together, we'd like to make it up to you. In the interests of maintaining a peaceful and collaborative partnership—"

"A bit late for that," I mutter under my breath.

Daniel pretends not to hear me. "We thought it best to compensate you for the inconvenience involved in this transition."

"You're going to buy me off. How much?" I fold my

arms over my chest. This has the unintended effect of pushing my breasts up. Tomas's eyes snap to my ample cleavage before he drags his gaze away.

Ha. Made you look.

My bluntness seems to disconcert the lawyer. "I beg your pardon?"

"How much are you prepared to offer?" Whatever the initial amount, I'm going to haggle hard and get him to double it. As much as I would like to pretend that I can't be bought, the gym needs repairs, and money would solve most of my problems. Twenty thousand euros would pay for some of the most urgent items. Fifty would be even nicer. "And before you tell me what that number is, let's not forget that the contract I signed with Simon specified that each partner would be at the gym for thirty-five hours a week and teach half of the classes. Signor Aguilar isn't going to be able to adhere to those terms." I give my new partner a slow and dismissive once-over. "He's obviously not a fighter."

The intended insult rolls off Tomas's back. "Obvious-ly," he agrees, looking down his long nose at me like I'm a speck of dirt on his sleeve. "Fighting is a waste of time, and besides, my schedule doesn't allow me to be here thirty-five hours a week. Even if I wanted to, *which I don't.*"

"Too manly for you?" I ask snidely. This guy is bringing out the worst in me because I'm now evidently an advocate for toxic masculinity. *Ugh.*

The corners of his mouth twitch. "It's impossible to dry-clean the smell of testosterone out of a woolen suit," he agrees.

Daniel clears his throat again pointedly. "If the two of you are finished, some of us have places to go and things to do." He sets a folder on the counter. "This is a new contract proposal with revised terms. Tomas recognizes he doesn't bring the same skills to the table as Mr. Groff did—"

"I don't, for example, molest every woman in sight," Tomas says.

I wince. That's a direct hit. Simon made the women in the gym extremely uncomfortable, but as much as I hated it, there wasn't a damn thing I could do to stop him. God knows I've tried.

"Like I was saying," Daniel says, giving Tomas an irritated glance, "he doesn't bring the same skills, and so he's proposing a different profit distribution. If you're willing to hire instructors to teach classes, he'll take twenty percent of the profit instead of the fifty that Groff took."

"Twenty?" That definitely sounds too good to be true. "What's the catch?"

"There isn't one," Tomas says with irritation. "I invest in businesses for the long-term. Without a change in your profit distribution, you won't stay open for another six months."

Daniel sighs with exaggerated patience. "I believe what Tomas meant to say is that you should do your own due diligence. This folder has a copy of the revised contract proposal. I recommend running it by your lawyer before you sign it. And to answer your earlier question about the goodwill amount—"

"Ah, yes, the bribe." I'm not sure if there's enough money in the world to buy a peaceful working relationship with Signor Jerk-in-a-Suit, but I wisely keep that thought to myself. "How much?"

"Two hundred thousand euros," Tomas answers. My

mouth falls open, and he smirks at my surprise. "That's the offer. Shall we shake on it?"

He holds out his hand again. In a daze, I reach out to take it. The moment I touch him, a zing of electricity goes through me.

Oh, no. *No, no, no, no, no.* The zing is that mysterious thing that I can't explain, the chemistry that makes me lose my mind and make stupid, *stupid* decisions like going into business with Simon. And now I'm feeling tingles from shaking hands with the man who bought out his share.

No. Not again. The Queen of Bad Decisions isn't going to make the same mistake twice. Tomas Aguilar is the last person I should get involved with—no matter what the butterflies in my stomach suggest. No, I refuse to be attracted to my new partner, the one who was foisted on me without my consent. *I refuse.*

I drop his hand like it scalds me.

The sooner I buy out his share, the better. Two hundred thousand euros or not, I'm going to be a royal pain in his ass. I'm going to be snide and snarky every opportunity I get. There will be no truce. Tomas Aguilar is going to discover that it's a really bad idea to go into business with me.

"I'll take your proposal to my lawyer," I say grudgingly. "We'll see what he has to say." I'm not going to go on the attack immediately; I need time to plan my strategy. "If that's all, I have a class to teach." I give him my most innocent smile. "I'd invite you to join, but..." I shrug my shoulders and let my voice trail off suggestively.

He's not fooled by my sweet tone, not even a little.

"But you're afraid I might be hurt," he finishes. "That's smart. After all, if I get a hangnail, I might sue."

Daniel shakes his head and shuts his suitcase. "I can see this is going to be an eventful partnership. Come on, Tomas. I'll buy you a drink. There's a restaurant next door, Il Doge, that I've been meaning to try."

It takes superhuman effort to keep from laughing out loud at the look on Tomas's face. "I've heard the food is truly exceptional," I say helpfully.

"Of course you have," Tomas says, his voice bone dry. Then he drops his next bombshell. "As your new partner, I'll need to be consulted about the improvements you'll be making. Let's do a walkthrough on Monday."

Ugh. I should have known the money came with strings. Damn it all to hell. Tomas Aguilar might have injected very necessary funds into the gym, but it's going to come with him micromanaging my every decision.

This is going to be lovely.

My grip tightens on my pencil, and I stab it hard enough into the pad to tear the paper. Baring my teeth at him in a terrible imitation of a smile, I say, "I'm looking forward to it."

I can't kill him—I can't afford bail or a lawyer. But one way or the other, this guy needs to go.

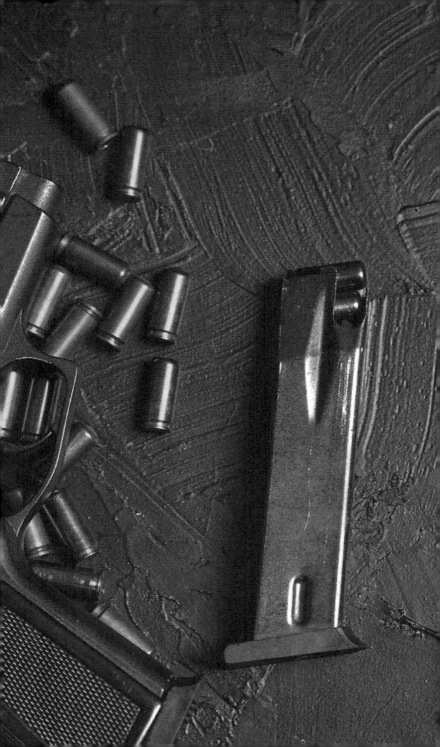

3

TOMAS

"Two hundred thousand euros?" Daniel says the moment we step outside. "That's not the number we discussed."

I should have realized he'd remember. Daniel is the Venice Mafia's go-to lawyer for a reason; the man has a mind like a steel trap.

I shrug uncomfortably. "Well, you saw the place. It needs work."

"It does," Daniel agrees, his voice amused. "That's why you're taking a reduced share of the profits. Remember?" His grin turns sly. "Did I sense some tension between you and the lovely Alina Zuccaro?"

"If by tension you mean she doesn't like me, then I'd say that's rather obvious." Alina hissed and spit at me like an angry kitten. She reminds me of Freccia when I first got her. The line between play and prey was so fine it was invisible. She'd be playing with a ball of wool, and in the blink of an eye, she'd transform into a feral creature that only wanted to attack.

Alina was like that. The two of us were starting a perfectly pleasant conversation, but the moment I mentioned that I owned part of her gym, her claws came out.

"But the feeling's not mutual, is it?" Daniel gives me a sidelong look. "She's very pretty. I wonder if she's seeing anyone? I should ask her out."

Daniel's clearly baiting me. "Signorina Zuccaro seems like an interesting woman, and under different circumstances, I might be interested," I say calmly, tamping down my annoyance. But I am going to own a business with her, and there's no need for that kind of complication." I pull out my phone. "She mentioned a contractor, which suggests she's hired somebody who's not doing his job. I need to remind him that's a terrible idea."

"You're going to call the contractor? I thought you were planning to be a silent investor, not take an active role in the day-to-day operations." He chuckles. "Time to revive the office betting pool."

Oh, for fuck's sake. First, the padrino gets married, followed quickly by Dante, and then Leo gets engaged to the woman he's been pretending he's not interested in, and now everyone is looking at the world through rose-tinted glasses. Even people like Daniel, who, as a practicing lawyer, has seen the worst of people and should know better.

I fell in love once, five years ago. It cost me my home, my job, and my family. I'm not interested in repeating that disaster.

"I'm just protecting my investment, Daniel. That's all there is to it. The gym is in an excellent location. Despite its current state of disrepair, and despite Groff harassing every woman there, membership has not taken a precipitous drop. People keep showing up because Alina is extremely good at what she does. Last week, she won an industry award for innovation in teaching. With a little effort, I'll be recovering my money in no time."

"Hmm. You paid a million. You think you can get a one point three in a year? That's a thirty percent rate of return."

"I've put an additional two hundred, so it's really a twenty-five percent return," I correct. "And if that's the best I can do, Antonio should fire me."

"You're really planning to sell in a year? To whom? Alina?"

"Alina, someone else, I don't care. I bought the gym to get Simon Groff out of Venice. This isn't the kind of business I typically invest in. My goal is to improve it enough so I can sell at an acceptable profit."

He gives me a sharp look. "You're going to let Alina do all the hard work, and you're going to profit from it? And then, just when she's in the black again, you're going to sell it from under her feet?"

When he puts it that way...

"It's just business, Daniel. It's not personal. If Alina can afford to buy me out, she's welcome to make an offer. Once the contract is signed, I doubt I'll be seeing her again."

Daniel smirks. "Au contraire, my friend. You're going to see her on Monday for a walkthrough, remember? You want to be consulted on how she spends your money." His smile turns positively gleeful. "Or maybe you just want to see her again."

I give him a withering glance, but he's undeterred. "I

also noticed you didn't contradict her when she thought you weren't a fighter."

My lips curl into a grin. "No, I didn't."

"She's going to feel pretty foolish when she finds out."

Yes, she will. I can picture her fury. Maybe she'll come at me, spitting fire out of her eyes, and shove me hard against the wall. Then I'll pull her down on top of me and roll over, trapping her underneath my body. "Tap out," I'll whisper, licking the shell of her ear. "Tap out, and I'll let you go."

But she won't give up that easily. She'll fight back, her body moving under me, her rage turning into hot passion...

I hastily shut off that train of thought. Alina Zuccaro is the last person I should be physically attracted to, and there's no reason I should be fantasizing about her. It's obvious what's going on. I've been busy at work, and it's been a while since I've had sweaty, mindless sex. It's an itch, and I need to get it scratched. That's all.

That's the *only* reason I'm picturing Alina naked.

4

ALINA

I'm exhausted once I finish teaching my classes. I drag myself upstairs to my studio apartment, shower and put on pajamas, and survey the contents of my refrigerator. For a change, it isn't empty—there's a glass container of couscous salad I made on Thursday. I spoon some into a bowl, head to my couch, and turn on the TV, looking for something mindless to watch.

The salad was my mother's recipe. It was her way of getting rid of the stray vegetables in the crisper. Half a cucumber? Toss it into the bowl. Strips of red pepper left over from the stir-fry she made earlier in the week? One solitary chicken breast? It all went into the bowl on Friday nights, then liberally garnished with raisins and unified by her herb-lemon dressing.

God, I miss her. It's been two years, and I'm no longer walking around with a hole in my heart, but every now and then, a wave of sadness hits me so hard that it almost knocks me off my feet.

It was always just my mother and me. I never met my father; I don't even know who he is. Every time I asked her about him, she'd refuse to discuss it. I asked her about my grandparents once—her parents—and her reply was terse. "They're dead," she said shortly. "And before you ask, I don't have any brothers or sisters, polpetta."

I was desperately curious about my mother's childhood. I used to snoop when she wasn't at home, looking in her closet and under her bed for hidden family photos, but I never found anything. I stopped asking about her family when I realized my questions were bringing her pain, but I never stopped being curious. After she died, I even took one of those online DNA tests to see if I had any long-lost family, but there was nothing. No aunts, no uncles, no cousins.

It's a lonely way to live.

Enough self-pity. I shake my head violently as if that'll get rid of my feelings and warily eye the red folder containing the new contract.

It's still on the coffee table where I dropped it when I walked in, doing its best to look harmless. But I know better. Tomas Aguilar might roll his smoky gray eyes and state that there's no hidden catch, but bitter experience has taught me otherwise. Even if the contract is airtight, what's going to make my new partner adhere to its terms? Simon certainly didn't, and there wasn't a damn thing I could do about it. I didn't have enough money to sue him into compliance.

And things will be even worse with Tomas. The guy drips money from every pore, from his expensive watch to his handmade shoes. If I try to take him to court, his shark lawyer would crush me to smithereens. Probably while Tomas watches, a smirk playing about his lips.

I'm going to buy him out, I promise myself. I don't know how, and I don't know when, but I'm going to reclaim my dreams. I'm going to tear my gym away from the hands of careless men, and I'm going to finally make it my own.

First thing Monday morning, I'm going to take this contract to Jonathan Burke, my contact at the legal aid office. Jon's a retired corporate lawyer who volunteers there three days a week. "Penance for my sins," he likes to say. I'm going to make him go over this document with a fine-toothed comb. If there's a catch, Jon will spot it. If there's a loophole, he'll find it.

Tomas Aguilar had better watch his back.

I'M FLIPPING BETWEEN SHOWS, trying to decide what I'm in the mood for, when my phone rings, Marcelo Laguna's name popping up on the display.

That's a shock. The contractor has been avoiding my calls for *months*, ever since he 'renovated' the gym. He's left the changing rooms in worse shape than when they started—leaky taps, uneven tiles on the floor, and so much more.

"Signorina Zuccaro," he says when I answer the call. "I'm sorry for calling you this late, but I was very anxious to reach you. You left a message about your changing rooms."

"I've left *multiple* messages," I retort, too tired to be diplomatic.

"Yes, yes." He sounds nervous. "My sincerest apologies. My office girl didn't understand the urgency. You're not happy with our work, and we want you to be. When is a good time for me to come over so we can discuss what needs to be done?"

I stare at my phone in disbelief. Did I fall asleep on the couch, and is this all a dream? "You're offering to fix the mess you made?" I ask dubiously. "How much is this going to cost me?"

"Nothing," he replies instantly. "We'll work until you're satisfied."

Huh. I don't know what inspired Marcelo's about-face, but I'm not about to waste this miracle. "I'm teaching all day tomorrow, so how about Monday? Ten?" Ten in the morning will give me enough time to talk to Jon first and maybe even get a run in. I don't know what time Tomas was planning to grace the gym with his presence, but I refuse to move things around to accommodate him. "But if that's too early—"

"Ten is fine. I'll see you on Monday."

So weird. I rub my eyes once I hang up, but I don't wake up, so it can't be a dream. Marcelo really did call, and even better, he said he'd fix his mess for free. It's not the most astonishing thing that's ever happened to me, but it's definitely in the top three.

Tomas says he's putting two hundred thousand euros into the business. What can I use it for? Remote classes? Other instructors? Advertising to bring in new customers? The possibilities are endless.

I find a notebook and start jotting down ideas. For about five minutes, I'm hopeful in a way I haven't been in two years. It's only when I'm halfway down the page that reality rears its head, and my enthusiasm dims.

First, there's no guarantee that the two hundred grand will even show up. After all, Simon made promise after promise, only to break them almost immediately. He was going to put money into the business, he said, but then his father wouldn't release his trust, so could he work for his share instead? We should name the gym Groff because of his large following on Insta, but then the bots shut down his account. And so on and so forth.

I wouldn't put it past Tomas to come up with some excuse on Monday about why he can't actually contribute two hundred thousand euros, and oh, by the way, can we look at the contract again, because giving me eighty percent of the profits is just too much?

When I first saw Tomas, I thought he was hot. I flirted. Had he asked me out, I would have accepted.

Thank heavens I found out why he was at my gym before that happened. Even if the money were to somehow materialize, I still have a new partner, one who doesn't know anything about MMA but still expects me to run all my decisions by him.

This partnership is going to be a *joy*.

5

TOMAS

On Monday, we have our weekly meeting with Antonio Moretti. The padrino arrives exactly at nine and listens attentively as Dante, Valentina, Leo, Joao, and I give updates about our respective areas.

I go last. "Our finances have recovered from the hit we took last year." I give them a quick update about the various investments we're holding and how they've been performing for us.

My presentations used to be longer and more detailed. My last boss, Alonzo d'Este, got a real kick when I didn't know something, so to counter, I would spend hours preparing for one of his meetings. But unlike the senior d'Este, Antonio Moretti isn't interested in playing stupid games. Still, it's taken me almost four years to let the habit go. It's only in the last year or so that I've finally let myself believe that Antonio trusts me to handle his finances.

"If things remain stable, we're on track to have our most profitable year," I finish.

Antonio nods. "Excellent work, Tomas," he says. "Thank you. I'm hoping for a stable year as well. The Bergamo integration is going well. Gafur OPS, the Russian bratva that wanted to smuggle guns through Venice, has also given up on that venture."

"How did you manage that?" Joao asks curiously. "I thought they had a ton of money already committed to the project. I could have sworn we weren't done with them."

Antonio smiles like a shark. "I might have let it slip to Andrei Sidorov that Gafur was overextended," he says. "And of course, the Sidorov bratva didn't become the juggernaut it is by passing up on the opportunity to prey on an injured opponent."

Joao laughs out loud. "Nicely done," he says appreciatively. "Sounds like I should cancel my Moscow hotel reservation. Pity. There's a Mongolian restaurant on the outskirts of the city that's rumored to serve an amazing noodle bowl."

The padrino nods. "Cancel it for the moment," he says. "I'll let you know if things change."

Officially, Joao is in charge of our smuggling operation. Unofficially, he's Antonio's assassin. He laughs often and spoils his cat. He's a passionate foodie who spent a year in Japan learning how to make the perfect soy sauce or some such thing, and he's never met a slice of cake he didn't want to eat. But underneath that amiable mask, he's a stone-cold killer.

Dante looks at his phone. "Are you concerned about

this VDL thing?" He slides the device over to Antonio. "Sabrina Laurenti was killed yesterday while she was on holiday in Tunis. A car crash. The Tunisian authorities are calling it an accident." The second-in-command takes in our mystified expressions. I'm not the only one who's lost; judging from their blank faces, neither Leo nor Joao have any idea who Sabrina Laurenti is. "Sabrina is Vidone Laurenti's daughter, his only child. And Vidone Laurenti is, of course, Il velo delle lacrime's underboss."

Ah. Il velo delle lacrime, or VDL, is a new-ish mafia organization in Sicily. They're practically in Cosa Nostra's backyard, but despite that, they've managed to thrive. Made up of former Cosa Nostra members, the outfit is growing rapidly, and so far, they've resisted every effort to crush them.

"Of course," Joao says dryly. "How could I forget? Oh wait, I know why. Because a man can go crazy trying to keep track of what's going on in Southern Italy."

Antonio grins before his expression turns serious. "Interesting timing," he says. "Sabrina Laurenti was engaged to the son of the pakhan of the Kutuzovo OPG. They're a Russian outfit that operates out of St. Petersburg. It was a union that would have also made Vidone a shoo-in for the head role. Now, though—" He shrugs his shoulders. "It's yet another internal power struggle in Palermo. I'm surprised Kutuzovo has time to flirt with Italy; I thought they needed all their resources to keep the Sidorov Bratva at bay. Keep an eye on it, Dante, just in case, but I'm not concerned. It's got nothing to do with us."

Once the meeting is done, I swing by Leo's office. "Did you have to break both his hands?" I complain, sitting down and frowning at our enforcer. Granted, Leo had cause. Simon Groff, Alina's former partner, touched Leo's fiancée Rosa without her consent—but still. You try getting a man with two broken wrists to sign a contract.

"Yes," Leo replies. "I absolutely did. How did you find out about that?"

"I went to see him on Saturday."

He leans forward. "What did you do, Tomas?"

"What I always do," I say with a shrug. "I offered a stick and a carrot. I told him if he set foot in Venice again, I would have him killed, and then I bought out his share in the gym."

Leo shakes his head. "You paid his asking price? A million euros for a half-share in a small gym? Why?"

"A million two," I correct. Two hundred thousand euros to fix the interior, and I have a sneaking suspicion it's going to need more. "I don't like rapists." Simon Groff has a deeply unsavory history. It irritates me to leave a man like that alive, but unfortunately, Groff's father is a politician in London, and killing Simon would bring more trouble than it's worth. The best I could was get him out of town.

"Interesting woman," I add.

"Who is?"

"Alina Zuccaro." I take a sip of my coffee. "You're looking a little shell-shocked, by the way."

"Rosa and I have set a wedding date," he responds. "October sixth. Clear your schedule."

Leo looks remarkably content for a man who insists his marriage is just a business arrangement. But I've seen the way he looks at Rosa when he thinks no one is watching. There's so much yearning there. So much want.

It reminds me of the way I used to look at my girlfriend. When Leo bought Rosa an expensive engagement ring, it felt like a kick from the past. I bought Estela Villegas a ring once, a yellow diamond surrounded by smaller white ones. When I got down on one knee, I was confident I knew what she was going to say.

She turned me down.

"You didn't think this was serious, did you?" she asked me, her voice harsh and her eyes mocking. "I'm a mafia princess, Tomas, and you're Alonzo's favorite whipping boy. You didn't really believe that I was serious about you?"

It's taken me a long time to realize that I hadn't been deluding myself. Estela had led me on. Deliberately, cruelly. Maybe she did it because her ego needed every man around her to fall in love with her, or maybe she enjoyed the chase. Either way, it doesn't matter. She taught me a valuable lesson, and for that, I'll always be grateful. Love clouds your thinking and affects your judgment.

Leo's waiting for me to respond. "Congratulations." I jot down the date in my calendar and then, as quickly as I can manage, leave. I head to the coffee machine to top up my mug, and Dante and Valentina are there, kissing like a couple of newlyweds, which, to be fair, they are. I look around and see Antonio on the phone, his expression tender, which means he's talking to his wife, Lucia.

Married couples are everywhere. It's an epidemic.

It's a good thing I've sworn off relationships. Because my friends look really happy, and if I wasn't determined to avoid love, I might start wanting it in my life again.

6

ALINA

I should have done an Internet search the moment Tomas Aguilar left my gym on Saturday, but in my defense, I was pretty flustered. But the moment my alarm goes off at six on Monday morning, I jump out of bed, make myself some coffee, and sit down in front of my laptop to google him.

I doubt I'll find anything useful; Tomas doesn't strike me as the sort that spills his heart on social media. But Google comes through. The first result is from the Università Ca' Foscari. Tomas Aguilar is an Adjunct Professor there, and he teaches an Introduction to Accounting class twice a week on Tuesday and Thursday evenings.

I stare at his picture on the screen and try to reconcile it with the man I met. On the screen, Tomas is smiling, a wide, affable grin that makes him look like the friendliest accounting professor you'd ever meet. The short bio tells me that before moving to Venice five years ago, he taught accounting at the Universitat de València. He has a bachelor's degree in economics and a master's degree in accounting from the same school.

He's Spanish? That explains his faint accent.

I reread his bio, a frown turning my lips down. This doesn't add up. Adjuncts are not well paid, and Tomas only seems to teach that one class. He's good at it, though, judging from his flattering reviews, but even so, there's no way he can afford to buy Simon's share of my gym on his salary.

Where does the money come from? What's paying for the fancy suit, the handmade shoes, the expensive watch? Am I being scammed somehow? Is this all an elaborate con?

That's not the only thing that doesn't make any sense. Let's say Tomas is really a lecturer. Where would Simon meet someone like him? It couldn't have been at the university. I can't picture my former partner spending time in a place of higher education, not unless it was to chase after pretty, barely legal undergrads.

I've never seen Tomas Aguilar before; I'm sure of it. I would remember him. Simon's never mentioned his name either, which suggests he's not a friend. Yet he was in the right place at the right time when Simon decided to sell?

Something's going on here, something fishy.

SHORTLY AFTER EIGHT, I take the contract to the Legal Aid society. Jon Burke reads it from start to finish, and when he's done, he leans back in his chair and steeples his fingers. "So, Simon finally quit. Who is the buyer, this Tomas Aguilar? Someone you know?"

"No, he's a perfect stranger. What do you think of the contract?"

"It looks legit."

"No hidden catch? Are you sure? Because I googled Aguilar this morning. He's an Adjunct Professor at the Ca' Foscari. How does someone like that have more than a million euros to invest in a gym that's barely breaking even?"

"Family money?" Jon suggests.

"Or I'm being scammed."

"How?" my lawyer asks practically. "And for what? Like you said, you're barely breaking even."

"But I own the building outright. That's in my name, not in the gym's." Simon hated it, but I stuck to my guns. "Maybe he's targeting that somehow?"

"Hmm. Well, to answer your question, if there's a scam here, it's not in the contract. Everything in here lines up with what they told you. Well, with one exception—the money Signor Aguilar is injecting into the business. In the contract here, it says he's putting in seventy-five thousand euros, not two-hundred-thousand."

There it is. "I knew it," I say grimly. "I knew there was something fishy."

"It's marked as provisional," Jon points out. "It might just be an honest mistake."

"Since when do you believe that lawyers make honest mistakes?"

"I don't, but this might be the exception to the rule. This is the clearest legal document I've ever read. The lawyer who drafted it is extremely good at their job. If Aguilar is planning on cheating you, this is too obvious."

I'm unconvinced. "That's one explanation. The other is that Tomas Aguilar thinks I'm an idiot who will sign a contract without reading it."

"I'm sensing some hostility, Alina."

"I'm sick of being jerked around," I burst out. "First, Simon barely does any work, ignores our contract terms with impunity, and gets away with it every single time. Then he sells to this random guy, completely ignoring the part where he needs to come to me first, and once again, I'm supposed to go along with it. This is my gym, Jon. My sweat and blood. I'm the one who's there at the crack of dawn every single day. I'm the one teaching all the classes. And somehow, my wishes never seem to matter."

And Tomas called it a dump.

Jon regards me levelly. "You're frustrated, and I'm sympathetic," he says. "But you're not blameless here. You *chose* not to take Groff to court to make him live up to his contractual obligations. It would be a mistake to bring those emotions into this new partnership."

As much as I hate to admit it, he's got a point. "Fair enough," I mutter sullenly. "Though you could really work on your delivery. There are other lawyers here, by the way. *Nicer* lawyers."

Jon chuckles. "You should consult them," he advises. "See how far *niceness* gets you in court."

My phone beeps. I glance at it. "I just got an email from Daniel Rossi," I tell Jon. "Tomas Aguilar's lawyer. He says he made a mistake and has attached a revised contract." I open the attachment and scroll to the relevant section, and sure enough, the seventy-five-thousand-euro amount has been replaced by two hundred thousand.

"In that case, I'm going to recommend you sign the contract. It's more than fair, Alina. You need a partner who will invest in your gym in a way Groff never did. Judging from this document, I'd say that Tomas Aguilar is your man."

"Let's see if the money materializes," I say grudgingly. "I still think there's a scam here somewhere. Maybe I should hire a private investigator to investigate this guy." Okay, fine. I may have read my mother's entire collection of Perry Mason novels as a child and developed a huge crush on Paul Drake. "How does one go about doing that, anyway?"

"I can give you a name if you'd like." Jon regards me with a frown on his face. "Or you could just ask Aguilar about his background before you waste your money."

"Fine," I grumble. "You're right again. I'll ask him, and I'll even sign the damn document. But Jon, this is a temporary truce. I'm done with partners who don't pull their own weight." Tomas *is* pulling his own weight by putting two hundred thousand euros into the business and taking a significantly reduced share of the profits, but I'm too annoyed to admit it. "How do I get out of this contract? Is there a way to buy Aguilar out?"

"If you can afford it, yes. You can buy his share anytime in the next two weeks for the same price he paid Groff. After that, the cost rises depending on how long he's been involved. If you wait a year, you'll have to pay him one-point-three million, a thirty percent return. Section 2.3.2 has the details."

That's insane. The man bought a share in an MMA

gym, not a tech stock. This is not a business that makes three hundred thousand euros in a year in profit. Not even close. Even if I have a record year, I'm not going to make enough money to buy him out, not unless a miracle happens.

I thank Jon for his time and get to my feet. I need to buy a lottery ticket tonight. The way things are right now, that's the only way I'm going to get rid of the insufferable and mysterious Tomas Aguilar.

7

ALINA

I half-expect my contractor to ghost me, but when I get to the gym five minutes before ten, hot and sweaty from my quick run, Marcelo's already there, standing outside the front door with a cup of coffee in his hand. "I'm sorry it's taken me so long to get to you," he apologizes again. "Like I said, my office girl didn't realize how urgent the problem was."

"That's okay." It's not, not even a little, but I'm still shocked that Marcelo's actually here, and I'm half-waiting for the other shoe to drop. "Let me show you what's wrong."

I pull up the list I made on my phone about the things that need addressing and walk the contractor through them, one at a time. We finish in the women's changing room. "All the bathroom taps are leaking," I tell him. "And there's a musty smell in the showers. I don't think the water barrier was properly installed. If there's mold, then the tiles will need to be ripped out."

"Mmm." He removes a chisel from his tool belt and

pries one of the tiles loose. What he sees there makes him look acutely unhappy. "Yes, this will need to be redone."

Crap. It took six weeks for Marcelo's guy to install the tiles the first time. It was a disaster. They ordered the wrong tile, and then the man doing the tiling looked like he'd never done it before. The second day he was here, he installed six tiles. Yes, *six*. A blindfolded toddler could have worked faster.

"How long will that take?" I ask warily. "I can't afford to shut down the gym while this is being fixed."

He scratches his chin. "You're closed Tuesdays, yes? I can get a team in here as soon as you close tonight. They'll work around the clock to fix the tiles and will be done by Wednesday morning when you're ready to open."

My mouth falls open. "I'm sorry, what? Are you telling me you can redo the work in thirty-six hours? Because it took six weeks to do it the first time around."

He has the grace to look discomfited. "I didn't understand the situation," he says, shifting his weight from foot to foot. "But given the circumstances..."

"What circumstances?"

He scratches his chin. "Well, you know," he mumbles. "When Signor Aguilar called..."

I stiffen. "What does Tomas Aguilar have to do with this?"

Marcelo looks at me as if I'm an idiot. "I'm not going to get on his bad side, am I? I'm not a fool."

I'm missing something here. "I've tried to get you to fix your mess for months, and you've been ignoring every single one of my calls. But when Tomas Aguilar, a guy who looks like a paper cut would ruin his entire day, makes a phone call, you come running. Why? Do you owe him money?"

My contractor crosses himself. "Dios no," he says fervently. "And I'm going to do my best to keep it that way. Only the desperate borrow from the mafia."

"The mafia?" I repeat in disbelief. *Oh shit.* Simon, the gift that keeps on giving, has gotten me involved with *the mafia.* "Are you telling me that Tomas Aguilar works for the mafia?"

"I'm their bookkeeper," a man's voice replies. Tomas. Damn it, I didn't hear him walk in. He's wearing another expensive suit today, and he's carrying a brown cardboard box that he sets down on the counter before nodding to Marcelo. "You have a plan to fix this mess?"

Marcelo bobs his head like a puppet on a string. "I'll put my best people on it, Signor," he promises.

Tomas straightens his shoulders. "That's not good enough," he replies. He towers over Marcelo, and though his voice stays mild, the threat is clear. "You're responsible for this job. You're the person I'll be calling if Signorina Zuccaro isn't satisfied. Is that understood?"

The contractor swallows nervously. "I'll be here myself," he blurts out. "We won't leave until you're happy."

"Not me," Tomas corrects. "Signorina Zuccaro." He gives Marcelo a nod of dismissal, and the contractor falls over his feet as he rushes out. Tomas waits until he's gone and turns to me. "How was your weekend?"

No, we're not going to pretend as if that bombshell revelation didn't happen. "You're part of the mafia?" I demand through clenched teeth, taking care to keep my voice as low as possible. It's almost eleven, a slow hour at the gym, but there are still a dozen people here, lifting weights and sparring in the ring. A couple of my regulars, Sara and River, who don't normally waste their time ogling the guys in the gym, keep shooting Tomas interested glances. So does Sergio Diaz, who's been a member since the day I opened the doors. "What about the teaching gig at the university?"

The corners of Tomas's lips tilt up. "You looked me up? I'm flattered, Alina."

It's the first time he's called me by my name, and I hate that I like the way it sounds, all slow and stretched out and growly. "Of course I looked you up," I snap. "It's called doing your homework. Is it all fake? The university job and the glowing reviews from your groupies, all talking about how hot you are and how delighted they'd be to get some private coaching from you?"

His smile widens to a smirk. "You've been very thorough," he says. "Interesting how you focused on that one review from four years ago. There's due diligence, Alina, but this seems a little excessive. And no, it's not all fake; I really do teach. It's part of my cover. Drop by anytime you want to see me in action."

Oh God. Mafia bookkeeper. I can't believe this is actually happening. Somebody wake me up from this nightmare. "My new partner works for the mob. *Fantastic.* That's all I need."

Tomas tilts his head to the side. "This bothers you. Why?"

He's got to be joking. "Let me count the ways," I hiss. I head behind the counter to put some distance between us. Tomas is gorgeous, and you'd think that him being part of the mafia would dim his appeal. Unfortunately, *it does not.* I'm very aware of him. I want to ogle him just as much as Sara and River. I want to touch him again, shake his hand and see if that spark is still there, and I want to do sweaty, *carnal* things with his body.

He's watching me as if he can read my thoughts, and damn it, I feel my cheeks heat. *Stop this, Ali. You're not going to blush and simper at the asshole who now owns half your business. The asshole who is a member of the* mafia. *Cut it out now.*

"I'm waiting," Tomas prompts, glancing down at his expensive watch, an exaggerated look of patience on his face. "You were saying...?"

I imagine wrapping my hands around his neck and squeezing. That image restores my inner calm. "How many people do you think will join a gym that's owned by the mafia? Zero. And what are you going to do if the profits are down? Break bones in my body until I give you what you need?"

"Antonio Moretti owns half the businesses in this city, and they all seem to be doing just fine." He has the nerve to roll his eyes at me. "It's not like we put a sign on the door advertising our involvement. As for your non-existent profits..."

I hate him.

For as long as I've fought, I have one rule. You don't step into the ring with anger; those turbulent emotions only get in the way. You step in with a cool head. You watch your opponent carefully, and you wait for them to reveal their weakness. And then you strike.

I'm willing to make an exception for Tomas Aguilar.

"What is this box on my counter?" I snarl. I start to move it, but it's heavier than its size would indicate. *Huh.*

Tomas held it like it weighed nothing. There must be some muscle under that finely tailored summer-weight woolen suit. "What's in it, the heart of the last person you did business with?"

"Regrettably, Simon Groff is still alive," he replies. "Your smoothie machine isn't working, so I brought you a new one."

My mouth is open, ready to hurl another insult. Then his words sink in. "A smoothie machine?" A drink counter is one of the most profitable parts of a gym. Smoothies, protein drinks, and supplements have an insanely high markup, even after you factor in the cost of hiring someone to make them.

I've been telling Simon for months that our machine needed to be fixed, but like with everything else, he kept procrastinating on the task.

"Yes," he says. "I would have bought the same model as yours, but according to hundreds of reviews, the motor tends to burn out. This one is a heavy-duty industrial model."

That's... pretty thoughtful, actually. "Thank you," I say, impressed but still determined to hate him. "How much is this machine going to cost me? I'm assuming you'll deduct it out of the two hundred grand?"

"It's a gift." He looks puzzled as he lifts the box off my counter and moves it to the smoothie nook. "Have you checked your bank account this morning? Maybe you should pay better attention to your finances. The money should already be there."

Oh. I grab my phone and navigate to my banking app, and sure enough, my checking account's balance is two hundred thousand, seven hundred and thirty-five euros and forty-three cents.

I can't decide if I want to scream for joy or just yell in pure aggravation. I haven't even signed the new contract yet. I'm going to; it's not like I have another choice, but still. "Thank you," I say grudgingly. "I didn't expect you to follow through this quickly."

He grins, clearly enjoying my mortification. "You're welcome. Now, let's do the walk-through and talk about your plans for improvement, and then I'm going to need to look at your books."

I'm still annoyed at Tomas's presence in my gym and at the way he unilaterally bought Simon's share of Groff's.

But so far, I have nothing to complain about. There are clearly some advantages to being in the mafia. Tomas has only been involved with my gym for two days, and already, my contractor has promised to fix his mess, my checking account is two hundred thousand euros richer, and I have a new smoothie maker.

Sketchy employer aside, Tomas Aguilar is competence personified. And unfortunately for my libido, there's nothing I find more attractive in a man than competence.

Gah. I'm still determined to hate him, but he's making it really, *really* hard.

No. Hell no. Not again. The only reason I'm in my current predicament is because I mixed business with pleasure. No matter how good-looking or how *capable* Tomas is, I refuse to have the hots for him. I don't even like the man.

8

TOMAS

We start heading toward the office, but before we can get there, Alina gets waylaid by a member with a billing question.

Estela, my ex, never had a hair out of place. Her makeup was always impeccable, and her wavy brown hair was always styled in soft waves around her heart-shaped face. Even during sex, she never looked anything less than perfect. Never sweaty, never mussed.

Alina Zuccaro could not be more different. Her face is flushed from exertion, and strands of damp hair cling to her forehead. She's wearing yoga pants, a faded oversized T-shirt, and scuffed running shoes.

And I can't take my eyes off her.

Maybe it's the way her muscles flex as she moves. Maybe it's the angry glint in her eyes, the way her chest heaves and falls as she tries not to react when I bait her. She looks strong and confident, and fuck me, I want to see her naked. I want to see all that passion channeled into sex, those full breasts bouncing as she rides my cock, that sassy mouth sucking my fingers, taking them deep because, underneath that spit and that fire, she's a good girl, my good girl...

What. The. Fuck.

I need to get my head out of my ass. *Now.* Otherwise, I'm going to be sporting an erection every time I see Alina, and that's just creepy. We're in business together, and I need to keep it professional. Even if she were willing to indulge in some no-strings-attached sex, it's still a bad idea. As I told Daniel, I'm going to sell my share of this gym in a year. *Sell it from under her feet,* as he put it, although I have no idea why my lawyer is having an attack of conscience. Compared to some of the shit he pulls, my plans are positively angelic.

But Alina might feel betrayed when I sell, and she will *hate* me, even more than she does already. Since I'm not a complete asshole, I'm not going to sleep with her before I bail.

Alina looks up from the computer screen and says something soothing to the man with the billing problem. She's good at customer service, I realize as I watch her in action. She's calm, patient, and honest. The guy starts out irritated but is soon nodding his understanding at the mix-up and agreeing that there's nothing to worry about. "I trust you," he says. "You'll take care of it."

And that's why her partner couldn't wreck this place, no matter how hard he tried.

"Sorry about that," she says, jerking my attention back to the present. The member is gone. "Simon was changing billing systems, and somehow, Edward ended up getting billed twice. With any luck, it's an isolated issue. Otherwise, I'm going to be dealing with irritated customers all week long."

"Knowing what I do of Groff, I wouldn't hold out too much hope."

She gives me a sharp look. "I've been wondering about that. How did you and Simon even meet? Did he borrow money from the mafia?"

"Not exactly." I tear my eyes off her ass as I follow her to the office. "He did something even more stupid. He made a pass at the enforcer's fiancée." She's already leery at the mention of the mafia, so I don't mention that the enforcer is Leo, and the fiancée in question is Alina's good friend Rosa. She'll find out soon enough on her own.

Alina shakes her head without breaking stride. "Sounds like Simon."

We have a file on Simon Groff. Alina met him in Tenerife two years ago, only a few days after her mother's death. The two of them had a short vacation fling, and for some inexplicable reason, Alina decided to go into business with Groff.

Was she in love with him?

Is she still in love with him?

If she is, she's a good actress. There's nothing in her voice that betrays that she's upset by my revelation. So far, every time the topic of Groff has come up, she's sounded exasperated, not crushed. She doesn't look broken up by the fact that she's never going to see the man again.

Are you sure you can trust your instincts? After all, you thought Estela loved you as much as you loved her.

That stray thought jolts me back to reality. Alina's feelings about Groff don't matter, and neither does her motive for going into business with him. I meant what I told Daniel; I don't have time to run a gym. I'm going to take a quick look at the books, make sure everything is fine, and then I'm out of here. I'm a silent investor and nothing more. I don't need to be here in person. If Alina and I need to make decisions together, we can communicate via email. There's no reason to see her again.

THE OFFICE IS a tiny room the size of a closet, wedged between the men's and women's changing rooms. It's barely big enough for one person, let alone two. "Cozy," I comment, keeping my tone even with effort. I don't know why I'm annoyed by the thought of Alina and Groff squeezed into this space.

"That's one word for it." She waves me to one of the chairs. "The bookkeeper uses that computer. There's accounting software on it, I think, but I don't know which one. Numbers aren't exactly my thing."

She looks embarrassed by her admission, and I jump in to reassure her. "That's okay, I'm familiar with most of them." I nudge the mouse, and the monitor wakes up. "That's how you had it set up? Groff handled the finances while you taught the classes?"

There's a Post-It note stuck on the edge of the monitor with passwords on it. If Valentina saw it, she would flay us alive at the lax security. Our hacker takes her job extremely seriously. In one memorable instance last year, she was squabbling with Dante about how vulnerable our computer systems were, so to prove a point, she hacked into all our accounts. It was mortifying how easy she made it look.

I enter the password, the computer lets me in, and I navigate to the accounting app. That's when I find my first surprise. "There are two sets of books here." The fucker. There's only one real reason someone has two sets of books, and that's because they're doing something fraudulent.

"What does that mean? Is that bad?"

Icy rage goes through me. Who was stealing from Alina? Her no-good partner, Simon Groff, who I just rewarded with a million euro payout or the bookkeeper he hired? Which one of them do I need to hurt?

"It's not good," I confirm. "You saw one set of books." I navigate to the fake entries. "According to this statement, you lost fifteen thousand euros in the last three months."

"It's the renovation," she explains. "It was expensive. Marcelo initially quoted ten thousand euros for the job, but it's cost us twenty-five so far. I asked Simon about it. There was an issue with the septic runoff, and the city got involved because they thought our waste was running into the canals. It wasn't, but Marcelo needed to hire a specialist to sort it out. The permits alone cost hundreds of euros."

"Groff said that to you?" I'm clicking through the real numbers. "None of that happened. There was no septic runoff. The city wasn't involved, and Marcelo has only been paid two thousand euros for the project so far." No wonder the contractor's slow-walking the job.

There's a slowly dawning look of awareness in Alina's eyes. "Simon was siphoning off money from the business?"

"Yes. And the bookkeeper was in on it."

She looks like she wants to murder someone. "The fucker," she swears. "That's why he dumped all those classes on me. If I was overwhelmed with my teaching load, I wouldn't have time to figure out why we were losing money. I couldn't investigate his bullshit stories when I was working over a hundred hours a week." She clenches her jaw. "What are the real numbers?" she asks through gritted teeth. "How much money did the asshole steal?"

It takes me a minute to find the answer. "Sixty-three thousand euros, give or take."

"Sixty-three thousand." She squeezes a stress ball in her fist. "I was seriously thinking of getting rid of the cleaners and scrubbing toilets myself until things got better." Her gaze snaps to me. "You work for the mafia. Can you find him for me? Because I would like to wrap my hands around his neck and squeeze."

The angrier she is, the harder my cock gets, damn it. "Don't waste your energy on him," I advise. If anyone is going to hurt Groff, it'll be me. "You're too pretty for prison. What's the bookkeeper's name?"

"Why?" she asks suspiciously. "You're not going to beat her up, are you?"

Damn it, it's a woman. I don't like hurting women, even when they're obviously asking for it. "You already know my thoughts on fighting."

Her lips twitch. "You hate it because you faint at the sight of blood." She tilts her head to the side. "No, wait, I have a better theory. It'll crumple your jacket, and you can't have that."

"Do you have any idea how difficult it is to find a good

tailor these days?" She's fighting back a smile; trading insults with me has cheered her up. She has a nice smile, Alina. It lights up her entire face. I click through more files in an effort to stop staring at her. This is a mess, and it's going to take weeks to clean up. I know someone who can do the work, but Luigi never met a woman he didn't flirt with, and from what I hear, they all seem to like it. The thought of the two of them crammed together in this office...

"Her name is Felicity Fletcher."

"She's American?"

"English. She was one of Simon's expat friends. She didn't speak any Italian, so he dealt with her mostly, and I was happy to let him." She makes a face. "I don't think she liked me very much."

"Considering she was robbing you blind, her approval is meaningless. Do you have an address for her? A bank account number? Her codice fiscale?"

"No." She looks uncomfortable. "She wasn't legal because of Brexit, so Simon paid her in cash." She slumps in her chair. "I'm not being very helpful, I know."

"Don't worry about it. I'll find her." Valentina, our hacker, is a bloodhound. Felicity Fletcher doesn't stand a chance.

"I need to find a new bookkeeper, don't I? Not just a bookkeeper, but someone capable of fixing this mess." She stares despondently at the wall. "Great. Just great. I can't believe I let Simon dupe me so badly. What a fool I've been."

Her smile is gone again. And maybe that's why the stupidest words I've ever spoken come out of my mouth. "No need," I say. "I'll fix your books in my spare time."

9

ALINA

You're too pretty for prison.

Men have called me pretty before, but it's always been because they're making a move on me. That wasn't what Tomas was doing. No, his voice had been matter-of-fact. Almost offhand. Tomas called me pretty with as much energy as if he'd said the sun rose in the east.

It's been four hours since he left, and every time I think about those words, a shiver goes down my spine.

The last time I had sex was two years ago with Simon, and that ended as soon as we went into business together. I'd insisted on it. "It'll complicate things if we're sleeping together," I said. He agreed without protest. At that time, I admired his professionalism, but it quickly became apparent that the only reason he didn't grumble about it was because it left him free to hit on anyone who walked into our gym. His latest obsession was my friend Rosa, one of our regulars. She's repeatedly told him she's not interested, but Simon doesn't know how to take no for an answer. She's taken to texting me to ask if he's around before she shows up. *I hate it.*

Simon's gone—Tomas bought him out. You'll never have to deal with him again.

That thought brings a smile to my face.

Before Simon, there had been another long drought. Being a caregiver to my mother left little energy for anything else. I had a vibrator to take the edge off, and that's all I needed.

That same vibrator got a lot of use this weekend. I closed my eyes and pictured Tomas's tattooed hands on my body, squeezing my breasts and asking me if I was going to be good for him, and that was all it took to bring me to several shuddering orgasms.

Gah. It's never been more obvious to me that humans are animals in the grip of powerful and primal urges. It makes no sense that I'm attracted to Tomas Aguilar—he's not my type. He's too polished. Too put together. But yet, for whatever insane reason, I'm drawn to him, and I cannot seem to resist. Crammed together with him in that tiny office, I was powerfully aware of him. Of his every breath, the leather and spice aroma of his soap, his cool steel-gray eyes that saw too much...

And he's going to fix my books, which means I'll be seeing him every single day this week.

I hate it.

My only hope is that overexposure is going to quench my lust. Because I cannot—*will not*—jump into bed with my annoying partner.

THERE ARE a handful of MMA gyms in Venice, and most of them are closed on Mondays. Not Groff's. It was a strategic decision I made when we first opened, and I've never regretted it. As exhausting as it is to open the gym after a full weekend of teaching, it's worth it. Most new members join at the start of the week. They eat badly over the weekend, or they drink too much, and then they resolve to be better come Monday.

Sure enough, at five in the evening, a woman walks into my gym.

She's obviously never been here before. She looks around at the space with wide eyes. Sara and River are in the nearest ring, jabbing at each other. In another, two guys whose names I can't remember are working on their Brazilian jiu-jitsu grapples. The free weights benches are busy tonight, and so are the cardio machines. I make a mental note to buy more ellipticals before greeting her with a friendly smile. "Hi, can I help you?"

"You're Alina Zuccaro, aren't you?"

"Yes, I am. Do I know you?" I'm pretty sure I've never seen her before. She's in her late twenties or early thirties; I can't tell. Her dark blonde hair is drawn back in a sensible bun at her nape, and her clothes are similarly conservative—a high-necked blouse, a narrow skirt, and low black pumps.

Her face breaks out in a smile. "Not exactly. My name is Gemma. I'm a fan."

I blink in confusion. "A fan?"

"I used to work out at MMA Roma," she says, naming the gym I taught at before I moved to Venice and struck out on my own. "My instructor, Camilla Bottino, still uses your techniques."

My expression clears. Camilla used to be one of the junior instructors there. We were work acquaintances, not friends. "Ah, okay. How is she doing? I haven't talked to her in two years."

"She's doing well," she replies. "She just got engaged to an extremely rich doctor who is at least twenty years older than her. I think she's going to quit the gym."

Yeah, that sounds like Camilla.

"Anyway, I'm moving to Venice for three months on a work assignment," Gemma continues. "I was looking for a gym to work out in, and when I discovered you'd won an award for innovative teaching methods at the Leone d'Oro, I knew where I had to go."

Umm, okay, weird. Yes, I won an industry award, but it's not a big deal. The annual Leone d'Oro ceremony is just an excuse for the MMA people in Italy to get together, gossip, drink, and hook up. I didn't even get to do the last thing because Simon showed up unexpectedly and told everyone at our table that he had come up with the teaching method that won me the award. By the time the evening was done, I was too irritated for casual sex. Not even my vibrator got a workout that night.

Gemma has to be one hell of an MMA groupie to even know about the existence of the Leone d'Oro, let alone track the winners.

"Umm, thank you." I take one last sip of the smoothie I made in place of lunch. "Would you like a tour?"

"Yes, please."

I show the woman around my space. "When are you moving?" I ask when I'm done, not from any real desire to know, but because she's staring at me in a way that's making me mildly uncomfortable.

"Next month, if my transfer comes through." She gives me a wry smile. "To be perfectly honest, I'm not sure if I want it to happen. Venice is a little chaotic. There are a lot more tourists than I expected, and finding an apartment has been insanely difficult."

"Chaotic is about right," I agree. It's September, and the peak rush is technically over, but Venice is still swarming with tourists. It feels like there are more Airbnbs than homes on the island these days. The mayor is even proposing an entry fee to combat the increasing numbers of day trippers who throng the city but don't spend any money. "If I didn't need to be here every day, I'd flee during high season."

She gives me a curious look. "Do you like living in Venice? Have you lived here long?"

"Two years. And yes, I love it. My mother used to bring me here for a week every year, and I've wanted to live in Venice for as long as I can remember."

Gemma smiles a little wistfully. "For me, it was Paris. My mom grew up on the outskirts of the city, and she'd take me back there every year. She died four years ago, and I haven't been able to make myself visit Paris ever since."

Losing a mother is so hard. Especially if they're the only parent you've ever had. I give Gemma a sympathetic look. "You should go to Paris," I say softly. "My mom died two years ago, and yes, when I came back to Venice the first time, it hurt. The first year was awful, and if I hadn't already bought property here, I would have fled back to Rome. But I'm glad I didn't. When I eat a pastry at our favorite bakery, or when I haggle with vendors at the Sunday antique market, my mother is right next to me." I take a deep breath and push back the wave of grief that overtakes me. "That got really heavy really quickly. Back to the gym. We'd love to have you once you're here. Our latest class schedules are always online."

"Perfect." She slings her tote over her shoulder and nods at my paper cup. "You want me to toss that in the trash for you?"

She looks like she's trying not to cry. I shouldn't have talked about my mother; I think it's brought back memories for Gemma that she'd rather not have. I remember too well the embarrassment of breaking down in public places. I have a trash can under the reception desk, but if she needs my smoothie cup as an excuse, she can take it. "Thank you. I'll see you in a few weeks?"

"You will." She grabs the cup and turns around to leave. I watch through the glass window as she hurries away, her head bent with grief. She's not looking where she's going and almost collides with Samuel, one of our regulars, and then rounds the corner and disappears from sight.

SARA AND RIVER swing by the front desk a few minutes later. "Who's the guy, Ali?" River demands without preamble. "The hot one you were chatting with this morning."

Biting back a smile, I pretend I have no idea who they're talking about. "Marcelo, the contractor?" I ask, switching to English. Sara and River are American. Their Italian is good for getting around Venice but not for anything deeper than that.

"Not unless your contractor rocks a suit like nobody's business," River replies. "God, I've never wanted to tear a jacket off someone faster. If he's going to be teaching here, put me down for that class." Her expression turns dreamy. "I'd like to grapple with Mr. Sex-on-a-Stick. I can picture it already. He'll be all hot and bothered as we wrestle, and then, oops, his crotch ends up in my face. Don't know how that happened, but hey, it's right there..."

Her voice trails off suggestively, and I laugh out loud. There's not a single coy bone in River's body, and I love it. Sara rolls her eyes at her friend. "You're married," she points out. "And I'm not. If anyone's going to be grappling with the mysterious hottie, it's me."

"The mysterious hottie is my new partner, ladies. And, I hate to break it to you, but he thinks fighting is a waste of time." Tomas isn't Sara's usual type *at all*. "He probably runs for a Band-Aid when he gets a paper cut."

Sara grins. "I can handle that; I nursed my ex through many man colds. When's he going to be in again?"

"Wednesday morning," I say shortly. Sara's persistence has never annoyed me before, so I don't know why I'm in a snit now. Whatever. If she wants to throw herself at Tomas, it's none of my concern. She's almost as tall as he is and beautiful enough to be a supermodel. The two of them would look good together. "He'll be here at ten."

10

ALINA

True to his word, Marcelo shows up at closing time with two of his guys. I feel guilty about them working through the night, so the next morning, I bring them a giant thermos of coffee.

I'm more than a little grouchy about being here. I don't normally work on Tuesdays—it's my only day off, and I guard it with ferocity. But Tomas wanted to get started on the books right away, and I'll be damned if I'm going to let him prowl around my gym unsupervised.

"Thank you, Signorina," Marcelo says gratefully, pouring himself a cup of coffee. "It's very kind of you."

"It's the least I can do," I reply, meaning every word. Marcelo's helpers are hanging back, so I take it upon myself to pour the coffee into paper cups. "I also brought some pastries, so help yourself, please."

The three guys have made a ton of progress in just one night. The old tiles have been removed, as have the old rotten subfloor and drywall, and it looks like they're almost done installing a new subfloor. And that's only the visible changes. "This looks really good."

"It's coming along," Marcelo says, looking around with satisfaction. "Everything's on schedule. We're going to break for a couple of hours while things dry, and then we'll be back at noon to start laying tile."

"Okay."

Tomas walks into the gym just then. I glance at my phone. Ten exactly. Gah. "There you are," I say without enthusiasm.

His lips quirk. "Good morning to you too, Alina," he says, sounding as if he's trying not to laugh. He greets Marcelo and his men with a polite nod before turning back to me. "Don't stop what you're doing; I can get started without you."

"No, you can't," I retort. "I always leave the office door locked, and only Simon and I have keys. Unless he gave you his copy?" I don't know why I'm being bitchy. Maybe because he's a little too good-looking. He's wearing another bespoke suit today. His face is cleanly shaved, his hair is perfectly ruffled, and his eyes dance with laughter, and the combined effect makes my stomach do a flip. River's voice sounds in my ears. *I'd like to grapple with Mr. Sex-on-a-Stick. I can picture it already. He'll be all hot and bothered as we wrestle, and then, oops, his crotch ends up in my face. Don't know how that happened, but hey, it's right there...*

"Unfortunately, he didn't," Tomas replies calmly. "He wasn't exactly thinking about the details when I went to see him."

No, he was probably freaking out about the danger he was in. Richly deserved danger.

"Until I get a copy made, I'm at your mercy," he continues with a disarming smile. "But you don't have to stay once you let me in." He lifts the now-empty thermos. "No coffee for me? I'm crushed."

That smile should be illegal. When he smiles, he looks cocky, charming and impossibly sexy. He looks like the bad boy your mother warned you away from, one that would charm you into bed and give you the best sex of your life.

Except Tomas isn't a boy. He's a man. And judging from his choice of employers and the fear Marcelo seems to display around him, he's a man with seriously dubious morals. That stuff is only sexy on TV.

"Don't worry," I reply. "I can always make a *special* cup for you."

He laughs out loud. "Poison *does* tend to be the weapon of choice for women. I thought you'd be more creative, though."

Marcelo's team decides now would be a great time to get the hell out of the gym. Smart. They gulp down their coffees and flee. I wait until they're gone before replying. "Sorry to disappoint you," I say sweetly. "But don't worry, Signor Aguilar. Before I increase the dosage to lethal amounts, I need to do some research on partnership laws. It would be a shame to kill you if your share of the business didn't come to me."

"It's always important to pay attention to the details," he agrees solemnly. His eyes are still laughing as he gestures for me to go ahead of him. "Signor Aguilar sounds so formal. Please, call me Tomas."

TOMAS and I work in silence for an hour. It's excruciating. The two desks in the tiny office are arranged in the shape of an L, and the backs of our chairs touch each other. I go through my emails as best as I can, but I'm intensely aware of his every movement, and it's difficult to focus. At some point, I lean back to stretch, and my hands hit his shoulders. The accidental contact sends a frisson through me. I make a week of social media content, pulling up photos of myself from my phone, and even though he doesn't stop typing, I imagine I feel his eyes on my screen.

Finally, I need a break. I jump up and collide with the back of his chair again. "I'm going to get another cup of coffee. You want one?"

He's frowning at the screen. "No, thank you."

Huh. No quips about attempting to poison him. Something must be wrong. "How's it going?"

"Your ex is a criminal, and your bookkeeper is so bad at her job that it's offensive. This is the worst record-keeping I've seen in a while."

"I wouldn't call Simon an ex." My brain catches up with my mouth. "Wait a second, how do you know Simon and I dated?"

"I do my research."

"And this research involves looking into a vacation fling that happened two years ago?"

"I'm very thorough."

"Thorough? I believe the word you're looking for is nosy. What else do you know about me?"

"Very little, unfortunately," he replies. "My usual source is busy with other, more pressing projects. I've had to do my own research."

My traitorous brain conjures up an image of a naked Tomas settling himself between my legs, ready to do his own research. *I'm very thorough,* he says, and then brings me to several screaming orgasms.

He's your partner, you idiot, I tell myself sternly, making myself quell the stab of desire that runs through me. *Stop picturing him naked.*

"Well, Simon wasn't my ex. Ex suggests... feelings." I don't know why I'm even telling Tomas this. "My mother died a few days before Christmas a couple of years ago. I needed something to take my mind off things, and Simon was there." I shrug. "I don't hate myself for sleeping with him, but I do hate myself for going into business with him."

I look up to find him surveying me with those maddening gray eyes. "Your mother died," he says softly. "You were grieving, and Groff took advantage of you. Don't hate yourself, Alina. Save that emotion for him."

All the air seems to have left the room. I stare at Tomas for a long moment. Have his lips always been this full? This inviting? There's a tiny scar just under his lower lip—one I've never noticed before. I wonder how he got it. My fingers itch to touch it, and I clench my hand into a fist.

This is madness. I need to snap out of this insanity. *Now,* before I do something I'll regret forever.

"I'm happy to hate Simon," I agree, taking a step back to widen the distance between us. Of course, the room is so small that my ass hits my chair. I stumble and nearly

69

fall face-first into Tomas's lap. "After all, he saddled me with you." I smile to rob the words of their sting. "Still, the money seems real, and Marcelo is finally fixing the showers, so maybe it isn't all bad. As long as you don't blatantly come onto every woman in the gym, you'll be an improvement."

"You just paid me a compliment." His lips curl up at the corners. "It was grudging, yes, but it was still a compliment. I'll treasure this moment forever."

Competent as hell, *plus* a sense of humor?

I'm in so much trouble.

11

ALINA

On Wednesday, Tomas loses the suit jacket and the tie and comes into the gym with his shirt sleeves casually rolled up to his forearms. Sara and River are not the only two members to stare as he strides into the foyer as if he owns the space.

"Here." I hand him a cup of coffee. I'm in a fantastic mood this morning. True to his word, Marcelo was done by the time I opened. The new showers look *amazing*. They painted the foyer and even brought in heavy-duty fans to ventilate the space so the smell of new paint wouldn't be overwhelming. I'm so happy that I'm even feeling civil toward Tomas. The paint fumes must be going to my head. "I didn't know how you take it, so I got it black. Like your soul, probably."

"Good morning to you too, Alina," he says with a grin. "I hate to disappoint you, but I drink my coffee disgustingly sweet. Not just sugar but sweetened condensed milk levels of sweet."

"Sweetened condensed milk?"

"It's a Valencian thing," he says. "It's called café bombon. Sadly, I can't find a single coffee shop in Venice that makes it."

"Because it sounds awful," I tell him with a shudder. "Still, that much sugar will make it easier to hide the taste of rat poison. Valencia is home then?"

"Google didn't satisfy your curiosity? Yes, I grew up there. I moved to Venice five years ago."

"Your Italian is very good." *I'm not being nosy,* I tell myself. *I'm just learning about my new partner.*

His lips twitch. "You make it sound like an accusation, Alina. My mother is Italian, my father Spanish. I speak both languages. What else do you want to know?"

Too much. I want to know everything about Tomas Aguilar, and that's a big problem. "This is the first time I've seen you in shirtsleeves. What happened to your suit today?" Another stray thought strikes me. "Doesn't your boss care that you've been here instead of at work every day this week, by the way?"

"Do you think that working for the mafia is a nine-to-five job?" He's laughing at me again; I know it. What I don't understand is why I like it. "That I dutifully show up every morning, clock in, and then leave at the stroke of five?" He shakes his head. "The padrino doesn't care as long as the work's getting done."

I notice he ducked the question about his suit. "And the jacket?" I prompt. "Casual day at the office?"

For the first time, he looks faintly discomfited, and my curiosity only deepens. Tomas didn't even blink when I mentioned lacing his coffee with rat poison, but I ask him about his suit and he's avoiding answering? *I have to know.*

"Would you rather I guessed?" I fold my arms across my chest, and his gaze locks onto my breasts. For a moment, a hot, male expression fills his face before he blinks it away. Despite all my good intentions, a thrill shoots through me. "Let me see. You slept with your dry cleaner and never called her again, so she slashed all your jackets in revenge."

"Not a terrible theory, all things considered." He takes a sip of coffee. "But no, I didn't sleep with Signora Milici. For one, she's sixty-seven and happily married. Also, I don't mix business with pleasure. Try again."

Tomas is my partner, so it should relieve me that he doesn't plan on sleeping with me, even if I was interested. Which I'm definitely *not* because he's not my type. There's no reason I should feel... disappointed. *No reason at all.*

"I don't know," I say, turning away from him and opening my laptop. "Just tell me. Or not, I don't care."

"I forgot to hang up my jacket, and my cat decided it would make a perfect bed. Freccia sheds like the devil." He makes a face. "By the time I rescued it, it was covered with her hair."

Whatever I thought he was going to say, it's not this. "You have a pet?" I pivot around and stare at him in disbelief. "No way, it's got to be the dry cleaner thing. You're too much of a control freak for a cat. What's next? You're going to tell me you have a wife and three children?" Fine, I admit it. I'm snooping. Tomas doesn't wear a ring, but a lot of men don't. The Internet hasn't revealed anything about his personal life, and yes, it's none of my business, but I'm dying to know.

Besides, it'll be a lot easier for me to keep my thoughts about him professional if I know he's married.

He gives me an amused look. "If you want to know if I'm single, Alina, you could just ask."

Are you? "I don't care about your relationship status," I reply. "You're not my type."

He tilts his head. "No wife, no children, not seeing anyone. What *is* your type?"

My face feels too warm. He's too close. He's staring at me with an intense look, like my answer *matters* to him, and I need to shut this down. I've fought for my gym. I've worked my ass off for the last two years to make it successful. I've already jeopardized it once by going into business with someone I was sleeping with. I will not make the same mistake again.

"Someone who can handle themselves in a brawl. Someone who doesn't think that fighting is a waste of time."

He chuckles. "I stand by my opinion. I guess we won't be having dirty, sweaty sex anytime soon, then."

He doesn't lower his voice. He's not trying to be seductive. He doesn't purr the words; his tone is matter-of-fact.

And yet, when he talks about dirty, sweaty sex, I'm imagining it. I'm imagining Tomas braced over me, naked, hard, his strong arms on either side of my shoulders, his hips weighing me down, and his thick cock grinding into me.

Ugh.

WEDNESDAY NIGHT, I press my vibrator down on my clit and pretend it's Tomas's fingers and mouth instead. I bring myself to a wrenching orgasm, but my subconscious isn't done, not even close, because when I fall asleep, I dream of Tomas.

We're in a room with a high vaulted ceiling. Sunlight pours in through the many tall, arched windows. There's no furniture except for a bed that is smack dab in the middle of the expansive space.

A massive four-poster bed with hooks on the posts.

Perfect for tying someone up.

Someone like me.

I'm standing in front of one of the windows, wearing a silk V-neck dress that hugs my body, giving me more curves than I possess. Tomas leans against the door, dressed in a bespoke suit as usual, smiling that maddening half-smile of his. A pair of fur-lined hand-cuffs dangle from his fingers. "Want to play, Alina?"

A thrill goes through my body. Goosebumps erupt on my skin, and my nipples harden into bullets. "Control freak," I accuse, keeping my voice steady with effort.

His lips curl up in a smile. "Guilty." He takes a step into the room and crooks two fingers at me. "Come here."

A thousand responses hover on the tip of my tongue. Go to hell. Make me. Fuck you, you don't get to order me around. Instead, I look at him through my eyelashes and take an unwitting step closer. "Why?"

"I'll make it worth your while," he says. "If you're a

good girl, I'll spread you open, tie you up, and let you come."

"And if I'm a bad girl?" I ask, taking another step forward.

"I'll spread you open and tie you up. The orgasm, however?" He shakes his head, another smile ghosting across his face. "Only good girls get to come."

"If you put it that way..." I move so I'm standing in front of him.

He laughs. "It's all about the right incentive, isn't it?" He turns me around and cuffs my hands behind my back. It's only after he secures my wrists that he seems to realize I'm still fully clothed.

"Ha," I gloat. "Should have planned ahead, Mr. Attention-to-Detail. What are you going to do now?"

He kisses me hard and spanks my ass, *and I like it*. "Every time you sass off," he says, "I'm going to punish you." He spanks me again, and warmth blooms at the spot of impact. "Just like that." He grips the vee of the neck and stares me in the eyes. "As for your dress..." His forearms flex, and in one fluid motion, the fabric rips. Metal buttons go flying everywhere, each one hitting the concrete floor with a little ping.

I'm naked under the dress. His gaze turns predatory and intensely male. "No bra, Alina?" he says, squeezing my breast. "No panties either. Admit it. You wanted me to do that."

I wake up at that moment, hot and sweaty, my entire body poised on the brink of an orgasm.

Damn it. It's irrational, yes, but I'm angry at Tomas for invading my dreams and furious with myself for letting him. He's spent a couple of hours a day all week at the gym. By this time, the initial shine should be off. I shouldn't still be fantasizing about him.

But I am.

I don't even bother reaching for my vibrator—my fingers will do. I bring myself to a shuddering climax that rips through me with the force of a tsunami, yet barely takes the edge off. I'm just wondering if I have time to come again when there's a knock on my door.

Weird. My apartment is above the gym, and the only way to access my stairwell is through the door tucked just inside the foyer. It's a quarter to six, and the gym isn't open yet. Simon has a key to the front entrance, but he's hiding in the UK. The only other person with a key is—

I jump out of bed and grab my dressing gown off its hook. Tying the belt firmly, I wrench open my door.

It's Tomas.

12

TOMAS

Alina stands in the doorway, her hair tousled, her dressing gown slipping off her shoulder. For a long moment, I can only stare. At her, at those sleep-kissed brown eyes, at her swollen lips, and at the vibrator that's clearly visible on the bedside table behind her.

A vibrator.

Her sheets are tangled in a bunch as if she had a restless night, and her skin glistens with a sheen of sweat. My mind conjures a fantasy of Alina lying naked on the bed, spread-eagled for me, begging me to use the vibrator on her, and my cock instantly hardens. I do my best to rip my gaze away from her vibrator, but my imagination won't let it go. If I tug off her dressing gown and lift her T-shirt, will I find her cunt slick and swollen and ready?

Get yourself under control, for fuck's sake.

I swallow a lump in my throat and wrench my thoughts out of the gutter. "Good morning."

"It's five in the morning." She sounds outraged. "What the hell, Tomas?"

"Sorry." Her question reminds me of the reason I'm really here. "The door to your stairwell was ajar, and I wanted to make sure you were okay." I had a moment of pure panic when I saw the open door. If someone managed to break in... If someone hurt Alina... My heart is still racing, and my body is flooded with adrenaline.

Her expression turns sheepish. "Oh, right. I went out last night to get takeout. I must have forgotten to lock it when I came back. Sorry to give you a scare." She stifles a yawn. "What are you doing here so early? I thought we were meeting at ten."

"We were." My fingers itch to stroke her silky shoulder. Kiss her nape, push her backward until the back of her knees hit her bed. I need to get the hell out of here before I do something I regret. "But something's come up, and I'm going to be busy all day."

Her eyebrows rise. "Taking Freccia to the spa?"

I bite back my laugh. God, that mouth of hers. "My cat loves a good pampering, but sadly, today is not her lucky day. I'll be doing some financial analysis for Antonio. I came in to set up remote access, since I won't be back until tomorrow night."

"Okay. I'll be here."

I frown. She's opened the gym every single day, and she's usually there until closing. Six days a week, sixteen hours a day, and when she's not teaching classes, she's staffing the front desk. She's got to be exhausted. "You're working too hard. I don't like it."

Alina's shoulders stiffen in outrage, but she ruins the effect by yawning again. She doesn't let it stop her. "I know this is going to come as a shock, Tomas, but I don't care. The hours I work are none of your business."

"They are, actually. If you read the details of the contract, you'll find that in exchange for a reduced profit share, I require you to be able to run the gym *effectively*. You're useless to me if you collapse from overwork."

Her eyes ignite with fire. "If you think you get to order me around because of that stupid contract—"

She's picturing wrapping her hands around my neck and squeezing, and I'm picturing her naked. God, I'd love to order her around. Spank that tight ass of hers every time she sasses me, shove my fingers inside her soaking wet cunt, and bring her to the edge, over and over. Sex with Alina would be *amazing*. All that fire, all that passion, all that burning intensity...

"Then I'd be right," I finish her sentence. "We had a deal, one that requires both of us to honor our commitments. There are two hundred thousand euros in the bank account. You haven't spent any of it. Why not?"

"I can't spend it. I intend to buy you out."

Maddening woman. "You're working sixteen-hour days. You haven't had time off in over two weeks. Hire someone to manage the front desk and bring on a couple of instructors."

"And if I don't obey your orders? What then?"

My cock is painfully hard. "I don't make threats, dolcezza." The term of endearment slips out before I can catch it. "I make promises. Hire some help before you drive yourself into an early grave."

13

ALINA

I slam the door shut on Tomas, furious about his ultimatum. Then I turn around and see it.

My vibrator.

Sitting there in all its penis-shaped glory, right on the nightstand, in full view of the front door.

Where Tomas undoubtedly saw it.

Kill me.

Kill me now.

Because I can never look at my annoying, aggravating, irritating-as-all-hell partner's face again.

IN THE SHOWER, I plot my next move. The moment I'm dressed, I call my friend Lidya in Milan. "I need to make money, fast," I tell her. Lidya Kaleb is, like me, a fellow MMA gym owner, but that's where the similarities end. idya has four times as many members as I do, and she owns her business outright. No infuriating partners to deal with. "Give me some ideas."

"How much money?"

"A million euros."

"A million euros?" she repeats, her voice rising in disbelief. "Are you in trouble?"

"No, it's to buy out my partner."

"Oh, good, you're finally getting rid of Simon. I almost punched him in the face at the awards dinner. He did not teach you everything you know, my God."

"It's not Simon I need to get rid of. He's gone."

"What do you mean, gone?"

"He ran afoul of someone in the mafia, so he upped and left in a hurry. But because this is Simon, and he couldn't pass up the opportunity to fuck me over one last time, he sold his share of the gym to some random guy who *also* works for the mafia." Also, I masturbated thinking of that random guy, had a sex dream about him, woke up, made myself come again, and then he knocked on the door.

"What? Ali, it's six in the morning, and I haven't even had my second cup of coffee. You can't spring this on me without warning. Go back to the start, slow down, and tell me everything."

I fill her in as I drink my own coffee, leaving nothing out. Tomas and his lawyer walking into the gym last week, Jon's opinion of the contract, Marcelo's sudden willingness to finish the job he's been neglecting. The two hundred thousand euros in my bank account—money that gives me the freedom to hire instructors and upgrade the facilities. I finish with my inconvenient attraction.

"I'm in serious lust," I admit reluctantly. "I need him out. He has to go."

"He sounds like a perfect partner," Lidya points out. "He can deal with the numbers while you focus on teaching. If you have the hots for him, why don't you just bang it out?"

"No," I say at once.

"Why not?" my friend demands. "Is he married?"

"No, he's single."

"Are you opposed to casual sex?"

I exhale in a long breath. "I'm opposed to sex with a business partner, Lidya. That's how I got stuck with Simon, remember?" Yes, annoying bossiness and mafia connections aside, Tomas seems perfect. But the moment I start to believe that, everything will go to hell. The only person I can trust is myself. "So, any money-making ideas?"

"Hmm. According to this romance I'm reading, you could auction off your virginity to the highest bidder."

And people think I go off on conversational tangents. "First, that ship has sailed. Second, what the hell are you reading? Virginity auction, really? The very concept of virginity is a tool of the patriarchy, a way to repress women's sexual desires."

"I agree," Lidya replies. "But that's not what romance novels are doing. They're tapping into the underlying fantasy of your first time being amazing. How was yours?"

"Adequate." I didn't have an orgasm—I don't think Dino even knew what a clitoris was, let alone how to locate it. Mostly, I remember wishing he'd hurry up already and finish.

"Mine was... underwhelming. Romance novels offer you a chance to remake that experience into one that's better. I wrote an entire PhD thesis about it. But back to the point. It's not anything close to a million euros, but there's a fight this weekend in Milan."

"A fight?"

"Underground cage fighting."

I make a face. "Don't those pay next to nothing? A guy from my gym in Rome used to do them, and he said the money didn't even cover the doctor's bill."

"Not this one. Ciro Del Barba runs it. According to the rumors, he controls Milan's underworld. There'll be illegal gambling, but the fighting itself is legit. Five hundred euros to show, twenty thousand if you win. Four rounds, one right after another, and it'll be live-streamed."

"Are you doing it?"

"Not this weekend. I have to go to Addis for my grand-mother's birthday next week, and my mother will lose her mind if I show up at the party with a black eye. But I've done it before, and I can get you in."

"What's the competition like? Do I have a shot at winning?"

"You better win; I'm planning to place a hundred euro wager on you."

Five hundred isn't much. Twenty thousand doesn't seem like a lot either, not when I'm trying to raise *a million euros.*

But it's a start.

"Okay, I'll do it."

Later that morning, I'm still thinking of Alina when Dante swings by my office. "I haven't seen you much all week. Where have you been?"

"I bought a gym."

He chuckles. "Yes, Daniel mentioned your impulse purchase. How's it going?"

The people who think women gossip too much have never met my co-workers. "It's a mess. I've been fixing the books all week."

He raises an eyebrow. "You, personally? That's rather like buying a Ferrari and only using it to run errands. Couldn't you find someone else to do the grunt work?"

Joao walks by just then and catches Dante's comment. "He likes the girl," he says with a grin. "Isn't it obvious? That's why he's been there every single day this week."

Oh, for fuck's sake. "I've been there every single day this week," I bite out, "because there are two sets of books, one real and one fake, and it takes a certain amount of skill to reconcile them."

"Luigi couldn't do it?" Dante asks, referring to the bookkeeper we sometimes use. "He's good at that kind of work, isn't he?"

"He was busy," I lie shamelessly.

Joao's grin widens. "If you say so," he says. "Looks like the work agrees with you. You've been in a good mood all week."

I give him an exasperated look. "I'm always in a good mood."

"No," he says. "You're always even-tempered. But this week, you've been smiling throughout the day." He shudders exaggeratedly. "It's freaking me out. Tell us about her, Tomas. What color are her eyes?"

Dante laughs out loud at my expression. "Alina Zuccaro is my business partner," I bite out. She has big brown eyes that mirror everything she's thinking. When she's angry, the color of her eyes reminds me of an aged cognac—fiery, lush, and irresistible. When she's laughing, they deepen to a dark chocolate, addictive and sinfully tempting.

And I've just missed what Dante said because I was daydreaming about her eyes.

"Yeah, she's totally hot," Joao answers. "Even better, she can handle herself. I went into her gym when she first opened, and she was sparring with a partner, her face all flushed and pretty. Huh. Now that I think about it, I can't remember why I never went back. I really should work out more often. What do you think, Tomas? Is there a friends and family discount?"

"Yes," I reply pointedly. "For *friends*. Don't you have anything to do? According to the calendar, you're supposed to meet the padrino at..." I glance pointedly at my watch. "Five minutes ago."

"Fuck," he swears. "How did I miss that?"

He takes off running. Dante pulls out his phone and navigates to the shared calendar. "That wasn't nice, Tomas," he chides, though he's laughing as he says it. "Joao looked like he was going to have a heart attack. He's going to run all the way to Antonio's house before he realizes there's no meeting."

"How do you know there isn't one?"

"Because you're giving the padrino your analysis of Spina Sacra's holdings in five minutes. Antonio asked me to sit in on it. Ah, speaking of the devil, here he is."

Antonio Moretti walks up to us. "The devil?" he asks. "I'm not sure if I should be flattered or offended." He enters my office and sits down. "What do you have for us, Tomas?"

Dante shuts the door behind him and takes a seat. I flip my screen toward them. "Spina Sacra's investment strategy has changed in the last six months," I begin, forcing myself to drag my thoughts away from my maddening partner.

My maddeningly *attractive* partner. Who makes me smile with her sassy mouth and smart-ass remarks. Who sleeps in a T-shirt that's been washed so many times it's translucent, with a vibrator within arm's reach. Who I can't stop fantasizing about.

She won't be smiling when you sell your share of Groff's to the highest bidder. No. There's only one way she'll take that—as a betrayal.

I have to keep my distance from Alina. I can't start letting myself care. The last time I did that, it almost wrecked me, and I will never put myself in that position again.

BY THE TIME I'm done with teaching Thursday evening, I'm cranky and restless. Of course, Joao notices and gives me grief about it. "Didn't get your daily fix?" he says. "You could still drop by, Tomas. Doesn't she teach a beginner class tonight?" He has a big shit-eating grin on his face. "Maybe you could take it. She'll show you some moves, and then the two of you could wrestle."

"Very funny," I retort. "Don't you have someone else to harass? Leo, for example?"

"Why would I harass Leo?" Joao asks. "He's obviously head-over-heels in love with Rosa. They've even set a wedding date. You're much more interesting, Tomas. Are you planning on asking her out?"

"Asking who out?" I say, pretending ignorance.

"Ah, that's the way we're playing it. If I wandered down to Dorsoduro and took Signorina Zuccaro's class, you'd be okay with that, would you?"

I imagine Joao and Alina on a mat and see red. I slam the lid of my laptop shut and get to my feet. "Do whatever you want," I say coolly. "As for me, I'm getting out of here."

I don't have any plans for the evening. Nowhere I want to be and no one I want to be with. In any case, I'd be terrible company. Right now, all I want to do is punch someone.

Then I remember that Ciro Del Barba always runs a fight at midnight.

I can be in Milan in time.

Two hours of beating the shit out of my opponents is *exactly* what I need to get my head on straight.

THE FIGHTS TAKE place in a nondescript warehouse on the outskirts of Milan. Del Barba isn't usually there on a Thursday night. But when I'm done with my fight, Renzo Gallinari, Ciro's second-in-command, shows up and tells me his boss would like a word.

I wipe the blood off my face—split upper lip, a lucky hit—and follow him up a flight of stairs to a balcony that overlooks the ring and provides a great view of the action. Ciro Del Barba is there, ensconced in a black leather chair, contemplating a cigar with expressionless eyes, looking for all practical purposes like a king surveying his kingdom. He's not alone. A dozen other people crowd around him. Eight women dressed in skimpy gowns and four men in tuxedos. They all burst into applause when they see me.

Oh, for fuck's sake.

"Ladies and gentlemen," Ciro says with a flourish. "I give you tonight's champion. Tomas Aguilar, or, to use his ring name, The Asset." He waits until the applause dies down and waves me to a seat. "Cigar?"

"No, thank you." I look around. "Quite a party. I'm glad to be the entertainment."

"They're a bunch of idiots titillated at the sight of

blood," he says sourly. "I hope you're in the mood for groupies. Maria was drooling during your last bout. I'm surprised she didn't toss her panties into the ring."

"Is that why you invited me up?" I ask dryly. "I didn't realize you were in the pimping business."

He chuckles. "I'm in the business of doing favors, Aguilar, you know that. You're an adult. If you don't want Maria's attention, turn her down. She's the one in the red dress." He holds up a bottle. "Wine? It's a Barolo from one of my vineyards. You'll find it's much more complex than any of Moretti's offerings."

I don't know if he thinks he's doing me a favor or if it's Maria who's going to incur the debt. Knowing del Barba, the answer is both. "It's wasted on me," I say bluntly. It's hard to believe, given that they're constantly sniping at each other, but Antonio Moretti and Ciro Del Barba are good friends. Well, as good friends as you can be in our world. "I don't know anything about wine."

He pours me a glass anyway and watches me expectantly as I take a sip. "Pretty good," I say truthfully. "Do you want me to tell you it tastes like rose and chocolate or some such pretentious nonsense?"

"Your palate is better than you think," he responds. "It *does* have a chocolate undertone." He leans back in his chair. "So, what brings the Asset to Milan? You don't need to fight your way through the ranks."

The Asset. Gabriel d'Este coined the nickname back when I worked for Alonzo, and he meant it as a compliment. He's cut from a very different cloth than his father. When I started fighting competitively, I decided to co-opt it as my ring name. "I could use the exercise."

"Hmm."

He wants something. I could hang around here for another hour and watch Ciro smoke his cigar and drink his pretentious wine, or I could cut to the chase. "Why did you really invite me up here, del Barba?"

He's about to answer, but before he can, Maria walks over. "Hello there," she purrs. "Ciro, aren't you going to introduce me to the champion?"

His eyes fill with frustration for a brief second before his expression turns neutral. "Of course," he says, waving a languid hand. "Maria Isgro, meet Tomas Aguilar."

"The Asset," she purrs. There's an empty chair next to us, but Maria ignores it and plants herself on my lap. Not a fan of subtlety, I see. Then again, I've spent the last two hours pounding my fists into my opponents' faces, so who am I to talk? Maybe Maria figures that she's better off getting directly to the point. "Your fight was sooo hot," she says breathlessly. "I love a man who can take care of himself."

She's a beautiful woman, Maria. She reminds me of a young Sophia Loren, big breasts, tiny waist, round ass, and curves in all the right places. But when she bends forward, giving me an extended look at her bountiful cleavage, it's not the obviously willing woman on my lap I'm thinking about.

It's Alina.

I exhale in frustration and ease Maria off my lap. "Thank you," I say, trying to turn her down as gently as possible. Any other night, I'd have taken her up on her offer. Fighting leads to fucking—the adrenaline and the testosterone needs some place to go, and there's never been a shortage of women who are happy to oblige. It's not Maria's fault I can't get Alina off my mind. "As much as I'd like to get to know you better,"—*lie*—"I'm seeing someone." *Another lie.*

Ciro comes to life like a shark sensing blood in the water. "You are? I didn't know. Who is she?"

"No one you know," I say flatly. "And that's just the way I'd like to keep it."

Maria folds her hands over her chest with a pout. This has the effect of lifting her breasts up so they're practically tumbling out of her dress, an effect she fully intends. "But she's not here, is she?" she asks, biting her lower lip suggestively. "I won't tell if you won't."

"No, thank you," I say again, this time with considerably less patience. I abhor cheating. I glance around and spot Rufo Crivello, my opponent in the last bout, coming up the stairs. *Perfect.* I drain the rest of my wine and beckon him over. "Rufo, meet Maria Isgro." I lift my empty glass. "I'll be right back. I need a refill."

It's not easy to escape. Del Barba corners me again, this time to introduce me to a Mexican couple. "Stick around, Aguilar," he insists. "Or do you have plans with your girlfriend tonight? Who is she, by the way?"

It's driving him insane that he doesn't know the identity of my imaginary girlfriend. "No, I don't have plans," I respond tersely and turn to his guests. The woman is an archaeologist, and her husband is a deep-sea explorer, and they're currently living in Valencia. We fall into conversation, and I reluctantly admit that it's my hometown. "I love it there," Felipa gushes. "Everyone is so friendly. And the paella is so good…"

A sharp pang of homesickness goes through me. I haven't been back since I moved to Venice. At first, it was heartache keeping me away. Every time I called home, the conversation invariably returned to the Villegas wedding. Estela was marrying Lucián Navarro, a scion of the Buitres cartel. The wedding was taking place in the Iglesia San Juan del Hospital, Valencia's oldest church, and the lavish details were the foremost topic of conversation in the city. Between that and a desire never to run into Alonzo d'Este again, it was not a difficult decision to stay away.

But it's been five years. Time passes in the blink of an eye, and standing there in a warehouse in Milan, I've never felt its passage more.

Below us, the ring is being dismantled, and the floors are swabbed. A makeshift bar appears in one corner of the warehouse, and a DJ sets up her equipment against the back wall. "Astri Kilen," one of the partygoers tells me, her voice awed. "Her sets are epic."

Epically loud, too. Norse metal isn't my thing in general, but especially not tonight. I retreat to a corner and pull out my phone. The gym bank account still shows a balance of two hundred thousand euros. Stubborn woman.

> Spend the money, damn it.

It's only after I text her that I realize it's well past midnight, and Alina's probably asleep. But her reply comes almost immediately.

> Why are you texting me in the middle of the night?

> Why are you still awake?

95

She starts to respond. I watch the dots appear on the screen, but her next text doesn't materialize.

> Why?

> Okay, fine. I'm mopping up the gym. The cleaners didn't show up tonight.
> Evidently Simon hasn't paid them for the last three months. I took care of it, but they can't put us back on their schedule until next week.

> Did you not hear what I said this morning about overwork? Why didn't you ask for help?

> You want to mop the floor in your Armani suit and handmade loafers? No? Didn't think so. Don't worry, I can handle it.

I bite back a curse and call Paulina, our cleaner. "Sorry to bother you so late, but I need you to clean a gym."

"How many bodies?" she asks crisply.

"Not that kind of job." I explain the situation. "Triple your usual rate," I add to sweeten the pot. "Please, Paulina. It's an emergency."

"Fine," she sighs. "And Tomas, it's on the house. I took your investment advice and bought shares in that biotech company. I've already tripled my money. I owe you one. I'll be there in ten minutes."

"Thank you. Alina will be expecting you. Do not let her help you, no matter what she says. She needs to sleep."

Paulina laughs into the phone. "Ah, I see, it all makes

sense. Don't worry, Tomas, I'll take good care of your girlfriend."

"She's not my girlfriend," I respond, but our cleaner's already hung up. Great. Joao is going to have a field day with this. With a shrug, I switch back to my texts.

> You are teaching a class tomorrow morning at seven. It's one right now, and you need rest. I've arranged for cleaners. Paulina and her crew will be there in ten minutes. Let them in and go to bed.

> That sounds suspiciously like an order. You're not my boss, Tomas.

> Go to bed, or I'll have to come back and put you there myself.

And then, neither of us will get any sleep. I push that image out of my mind and down another glass of Del Barba's precious Barolo. There are dozens of women here, beautiful, available, and willing, and instead, I'm hiding and texting my business partner, the one I can't stop fantasizing about. What a fucking mess this is.

15

ALINA

It takes a lot of coffee the next morning to get me going. *A lot.* I can't even peel my eyes open until the second cup.

As promised, I'd just put away my phone last night when there was a knock on the door. I opened it to see two women there, their arms filled with cleaning supplies. "Hello, I'm Paulina," one of them said, giving me a speculative look. "And you must be Alina."

Paulina refused to let me help. "Tomas told me to make sure you went straight to bed," Paulina said with a twinkle in her eyes. "Don't worry; we'll handle it."

So, I did. I even managed four hours of sleep. That's not enough to face the day ahead, but it'll have to do. Thankfully, my seven a.m. class doesn't have any beginners in it. Even better, there are only five people signed up.

I shower, drink another cup of coffee, and head downstairs at a quarter to seven to unlock the front do

Sergio Diaz is already there. "Sorry, Sergio," I apologize. "Have you been waiting long?"

"I just got here," he says. "And you're not late." He gives me a wide smile. "Congratulations, Ali. What a coup. The moment word gets around, you're going to be flooded with new members."

The four cups of coffee haven't been enough to jump-start my brain because I have no idea what Sergio is talking about. It's not my award; Sergio has already congratulated me for that. "What are you talking about?"

"Signing the Asset." He says it like it's a title. "I thought the smoothie machine was great, but getting him on board? I saw him fight last night. He went through the other competitors like a machine. Watching him was a masterclass."

"Sergio, I have no idea what you're talking about."

"The Asset," he repeats. "I saw him here on Monday. I knew he looked familiar, but it wasn't until I saw him in the ring last night that I realized who he was."

"Hang on. You're talking about Tomas? No, he's not a fighter. He's an *accountant.* He teaches at the university."

"He's definitely a fighter." Sergio pulls out his phone. "Look."

A video starts to play. I see the familiar shape of an octagonal ring, and then two fighters step in. They're both lean. Cut. One guy in a pair of green shorts has his back to me. Then he moves, and the camera zooms in on his face.

It's Tomas.

My ears ring with all the things he's said to me. *Fighting is a waste of time. It's impossible to dry-clean the smell of testosterone out of a woolen suit.* All the insults I've thrown at him and about him. *You faint at the sight of blood. You'll get a hangnail. He'd probably run for a Band-Aid when he got a paper cut.*

He deliberately misled me when we first met, and all week, he's let me make a fool of myself.

What's your type?

Someone who can handle themselves in a brawl. Someone who doesn't think that fighting is a waste of time.

I guess we won't be having dirty, sweaty sex anytime soon.

Blood pounds in my ears, and I see red. All week long, Tomas Aguilar has been having a laugh at my expense. Very funny. Very funny indeed.

"Can you send me a copy of that video, Sergio?"

My voice must betray some of what I'm feeling. He gives me a curious look. "Is everything okay, Ali?"

"Everything is fine."

Tomas is going to be here tonight late, after the gym closes. That's good. Because when I get my hands on him, I'm going to show my smug new partner exactly how funny I think he is.

16

TOMAS

It's after ten at night when I finally make it to the gym, thirty minutes after closing. I hadn't intended on being this late, but some days spiral out of control almost from the get-go, and this was one of those. Antonio wanted more analysis about Spina Sacra, and then, when I was shutting my laptop, Dante swung by and asked if I could look into a company for him. I texted Alina to let her know I was running late, and she responded with a one-word answer. *Okay.* No snide comment about whether I'm late because I'm getting my nails manicured or because I'm getting fitted for another overpriced suit—both things she's said to me this week. No insults, nothing. Just 'Okay.'

Not going to lie. I missed the snark.

Arriving at Groff's, I look up at the sign in displeasure. We really need to change it. Alina does all the work around here—the gym should bear her name. It's a travesty that it doesn't.

The door is locked, and the exterior lights are out. I

fish out my key and let myself in. The interior lights are turned off as well, all except one over the main octagon. I'm about to flip them on when I notice the woman in the ring.

Alina.

She's wearing a sports bra and gym shorts, her hair tied back in a ponytail. Her feet are bare, and as I draw closer, I notice her toenails are painted pink.

My cock hardens, and my throat goes dry. A deadly fighting machine with pretty toenails. God, she's beautiful, and the contradictions just make her more irresistible.

"The Asset makes an appearance," she says, her voice low and lethal. "You've been lying to me, Tomas."

The Asset. Ah. She's discovered the truth, *and she is pissed.* I hear it in her voice and see it in her eyes, which radiate fury. If looks could kill, I'd be a shriveled husk of a man.

I should be apologetic for my deception, but I'm not.

Right now, the only thing I'm feeling is desire.

"I usually wait a couple weeks before I start spilling my secrets," I reply, shedding my jacket. "And, as a point of clarification, I didn't lie. You made some assumptions about me, and I let you run with them."

"You're splitting hairs." She beckons me forward with two fingers. "You've spent all week laughing at me, Tomas, and I don't like it. Get in the ring. I looked up the Asset. You've built up quite a reputation. Show me what you can do."

I toe off my loafers and start to unbutton my shirt. She is fire, and I'm a moth drawn right to the flame, diving into the inferno, *reveling* in it as it burns me alive. "This is a terrible idea," I say as I slide a cufflink through a buttonhole. "I have at least fifty pounds on you." I give her lean, taut body a slow once-over. "Make that sixty. You're not going to win this fight."

"That's a lot of words to say that you're scared."

"Have it your way." I shrug off the shirt and remove my socks. Tug my belt free from the loops. My trousers are a lightweight summer linen, and I leave them on. They don't give me a lot of moving ease, but I won't need much. I step into the ring. "Here I am. Do your worst."

We circle each other. She's looking for an opening, and I'm trying to think of something—anything—other than how beautiful she looks. I'm doing my best to breathe through the wall of heat in my chest, to ignore the desire tightening my groin. I notice everything: the way her bra pushes her breasts together and up, her curvy ass hugged tight by her gym shorts, and those pretty pink toenails.

My cock *aches* for Alina.

I've watched her all week. When she's teaching classes, I sometimes come out of the office and watch her fight. She's quick on her feet, agile and lightning fast, as good a street fighter as any I've seen.

She uses that speed now. She launches a flurry of strikes, quick, fast jabs at my torso. I sidestep, avoiding the blows, and pull her close in a tight clinch. "Nice try," I murmur into her ear.

Her eyes flash. "Shut up and fight," she hisses. I let her go, and she follows her jab with a round kick that I block. She doesn't back down. She continues to attack with the grace of a ballerina, lunging forward and dancing back, her fists and feet slicing through the air.

She aims another kick at my midsection, and this time, I'm not quick enough to avoid it.

She grins victoriously at my grunt. "How's that for a nice try?"

"Did you connect?" I block her next kick with a lazy grin. "I couldn't tell."

"Bite me," she snarls.

"Was that an invitation, dolcezza?"

She launches herself at me in response. As angry as she is, she isn't rash. I haven't gone on the offense yet, but she doesn't leave herself open. She kicks and punches, her attacks coming faster and fiercer. But I wasn't boasting when I said she wasn't going to win the fight. If I were untrained, she'd absolutely take me down, but I'm not. As good as she is, there's nothing she can bring to counter the weight advantage I have.

She's breathing hard, her chest rising and falling with each breath. I can feel the heat of her body as she presses closer. "Give up."

"Fuck you."

Anytime, dolcezza.

I use her momentum against her, deflecting her strikes and controlling the pace of the fight. She knows what I'm doing, and it infuriates her. She tries a single-leg takedown. Dropping to one knee, she grabs my right leg.

Oh fuck.

The single-leg takedown is a basic beginner wrestling move, one I've done thousands of times.

But this is Alina. She's on one knee, her right arm locked around my thigh and her left at my ankle, and the move puts her lips mere inches from my crotch.

My cock is rock hard, the bulge clearly visible beneath my lightweight trousers.

She notices. Freezes. Sucks in a breath. For an instant, neither of us moves. The air crackles with tension. She tears her gaze away from my cock, and our eyes meet. "Tomas," she whispers.

Her dark hair shines under the overhead light. Her skin glistens with sweat. She is raging fire and glittering ice, a multi-faceted diamond that sparkles brighter the more you look at it.

And I want to do a whole lot more than *look*.

I want to get close enough to *burn*.

All thought has fled my brain, and all my rules are out of the window. The voice of caution that has kept me away from her all week is temporarily mute. I stare into her eyes, and I want to sip that lush cognac—drink it with abandon—until my head is dizzy and spinning.

"Alina." My voice is quiet in that dark room. This is a mistake, yes, but it's the sweetest one.

Then the spell shatters. Awareness returns to Alina's eyes, and she realizes the position we're both in.

A victorious smile tugs at her lips. She thinks she has me exactly where she wants me. "One tug," she says, her tongue swiping her lower lip. "One tug, and I'll take you to the mat."

"I don't think so, dolcezza." She's good, but my body is in a wide, defensive stance, and I have sixty pounds on her. I put some pressure on her back, drop to the floor, and take her down with me. I roll over so she's under me, my hips pressing down on hers, my forearms caging her in. "Ready to submit?"

17

ALINA

eady to submit?

No. What I am is ready to combust.

When Tomas took his shirt off, my mouth fell open. Underneath those suits of his, underneath the neatly knotted ties and the crisp cotton shirts, my new partner is *cut*. His body is sleek, muscled perfection. His deltoids are defined; his biceps are a thing of beauty. As for his sculpted abs... I want to lick each and every ridge. I want to tongue his navel and follow the trail down to his waistband, rip off his trousers, pull his cock out of his pants, and take it into my mouth. I want him to hold my head and thrust deep, making me gag.

There's an invitation in his eyes, and I've been staring at him for too long to pretend.

The pulse on my neck races, and my breath comes in small gasps. Tomas is everywhere. He smells like sweat and soap, and his aroma is catnip to me. A shiver goes through my body as he pins me down, his intimidatingly large cock pressing into my hip, his lips a whisper away from mine. My breasts are crushed against his hard chest, my nipples erect.

This might have started out as a fight, a way to work off some of the mortification I felt when I learned the truth about his underground MMA chops, but it's not a fight any longer.

This is a sweaty, no-holds-barred prelude to sex.

My insides *ache*, a sensation that feels like both pleasure and pain. "What are we doing?" I manage through dry lips. I swipe my tongue through my lower lip, and his gaze locks onto it. "I don't even *like* you."

A smile ghosts across his face. "I know." He bends his head and licks the fluttering pulse at my neck. "Does it matter?"

Oh God. A shock of need jolts through me. That was... A shiver of arousal runs through me as he licks me again, slowly, *leisurely,* as if I'm a feast laid out for his pleasure. His tongue feels like fire, and I'm burning up. Heat pools in my core, and I squirm underneath his body, restless for more. I want him to hold me down and fuck me with that massive cock so hard that it hurts. When I touch myself in the shower tonight, *I want to ache.*

In vain, I reach for some common sense. "It should." Tomas is my partner. We have a tenuous working relationship. Sleeping with him would complicate *everything.*

But I'm not thinking with my brain. I'm in the grip of something raw and primal. Call it lust; call it chemistry. This is animal attraction hard-coded into my DNA, and I can no more resist Tomas than I can walk past a piece of dark chocolate.

I'm playing with matches. *And I'm going to get burned.*

"It should," I say again. Perhaps if I keep repeating it, I

can convince myself to tap out of this dangerously tempting situation. "But it doesn't seem to." I press my thighs together, my skin prickling with anticipation. His eyes aren't cool any longer. They blaze with the same fire that's incinerating me. "I'm going to regret the hell out of this tomorrow, but my bedroom is upstairs." I wrap my leg around him, pulling him even closer, and rock my hips against him. "Want to get out of here?"

He stares at me for an eternity. His eyes drop to my mouth, and I know—*I'm absolutely sure*—he's going to kiss me.

Then he exhales in a long breath and shakes his head. "When you invite me to your bedroom, Alina, you're not going to regret it. But until that happens—" He rolls off my body and jumps to his feet in one fluid movement. "I'll work on your files remotely for the next week."

He vaults over the ring, grabs his shirt and jacket, and puts on his shoes. I watch in silence as he leaves, his hands clenched.

What the hell just happened here?

I CAN'T FALL ASLEEP. I lie awake in bed for hours, tossing and turning, Tomas's words running through my head.

When you invite me to your bedroom, you're not going to regret it.

What did he mean by that? Was it a boast? Was he being cocky? Judging by the girth of his cock, he's more than capable of backing it up. Certainly, he was able to back up his trash talk in the ring. The fight was more than a little embarrassing. Tomas defended against my attacks with laughable ease. And it's not because he's in a different weight class—I've fought men his size and won, using my greater speed to my advantage. No, it's because he's good. Really, really good. I've never been beaten quite that comprehensively before.

I should hate it.

I don't.

Or did he mean that he wanted me to sleep with him without regrets? If so, he's going to have to wait a long time. No matter how much I want Tomas to fuck me, the underlying reality hasn't changed. He is still my business partner, and this is still a terrible idea. It will always be a terrible idea.

My body is on fire. The adrenaline of the fight hasn't worn off. I can still feel the weight of his body on mine. His thick cock grinding into me. I've already had one cold shower, and it's done *nothing* to calm me down. I need to take the edge off, and quickly, otherwise I'm never going to fall asleep. Lidya has arranged for me to fight tomorrow night, and if I'm hoping to win, I need all the rest I can get.

I roll over, grab my vibrator from my nightstand, and turn it on. I hitch up my T-shirt and tug the gusset of my panties aside. Some days, I like to press the head against my clit, light at first and then harder as I get more aroused, but tonight, that's not what I'm looking for.

Tonight, I need a hard cock inside my aching pussy.

I close my eyes and push the thick cock into me. I barely wait for my muscles to adjust to its girth before pulling it out and slamming it in again. My eyes flutter shut, and the moment I do, *Tomas is there.*

I imagine him knocking on my door. I don't answer right away; I'm far too busy masturbating to deal with interruptions. He knocks again, insistently, and when I fail to materialize, he kicks the door in with a loud crash.

Then, he takes in the scene in front of him. Me. Naked, my legs spread wide, holding a penis-shaped vibrator in my hand.

He leans against my doorway. His shirt is unbuttoned, and his sleeves rolled up to the elbow. "Is that toy satisfying you?" he asks. His tone is polite, almost disinterested, but his gray eyes bore into me like bullets. "Or do you want the real thing?"

He steps into the room. Gets naked. All of his glorious muscles come into view, but I don't have eyes for them. My gaze locks on his cock, and he is *huge*.

I fantasize about him tying my wrists to the headboard so I can't move, and I shudder my way to my first orgasm. I picture him fisting his cock, raising one eyebrow, and asking me if I'm sure I can handle his length, and I come a second time.

I imagine him yanking the dildo out of my sopping wet cunt. "You're going to scream when I fuck you," he says calmly. "And we can't have you waking up the entire neighborhood, can we?" Then he pushes the dildo into my mouth and thrusts into me in one hard, brutal stroke.

And I scream and shiver my way into a third orgasm.

But though my cunt is puffy and swollen, and my clit is too sensitive to touch, I don't feel sated. Tonight, my trusty vibrator cannot give me the release I need. Tonight, only the real thing will do.

It's not the worst thing in the world if I sleep with him.

Is it?

Enough. I toss the vibrator aside and give myself a stern talking-to. Of course it's a terrible idea to sleep with Tomas. I want to buy him out, and I'm assuming he wants to get the gym back on its feet as quickly as possible so he can sell his stake to the highest bidder and move on.

He doesn't care about me; he just doesn't want me to burn out because if I do, that'll interfere with his ability to make a profit on his purchase. Bringing me a smoothie maker, getting Marcelo to finish the job, arranging for a cleaning crew in the middle of the night—these are things a partner *should* do. If I'm impressed, it's only because Simon set the bar so low.

It's a good thing Tomas is going to work remotely for a while. Some time away from him is exactly what I need to get my head screwed on straight.

SERGIO ISN'T the first member to arrive at the gym on Saturday morning; Luke Barnes beats him to it. Luke is Canadian, a big, strong guy in his forties. He's not chatty and almost never volunteers information about himself. But I like him a lot. There's something about his presence —he just exudes zen. It's calming to be around him.

"Good morning, Ali," he says, holding out a plain unmarked envelope. "Someone left this for you."

"That sounds very mysterious."

He laughs. "It's probably another petition to limit tourists on the island. Hey, can I talk to you about something?"

"Sure." I set the envelope on the counter and turn to Luke. "What is it?"

"I'd like to work here," he says. "Are you looking for instructors?"

Tomas pretty much ordered me to bring on a couple of instructors. I want to turn Luke down just to spite my bossy partner, but I need help. Rather desperately. I haven't taken a vacation in the last two years. I can't remember when I had two days off in a row.

"Have you ever taught before?"

He has. He lists his qualifications, and they are impressive. When he's done, I just stare at him, my mouth open. "You've been a member of the gym practically since we opened. Why have you never said anything?"

He shrugs. "I didn't want to work here when Simon was involved," he says matter-of-factly. "It was all I could do to keep from punching him in the face. But now that he's gone..." His voice trails off. "I don't know if you're looking...?"

"I am. Definitely." I smile at him, feeling a weight lift off my shoulders. "Let's talk salary. Also, how soon can you start?"

THE GYM IS BUSIER than usual, and it isn't until almost noon that I remember the envelope Luke handed me. I sit down at the front desk with a smoothie and tear it open. If it's a petition to ban Airbnb rentals, then I'm all for it. The building to the right of me has five apartments in it that are always listed on the platform. It's also one of the few places that allows pets. Which isn't bad in itself—I like animals. But pet owners who don't clean up after their animals are the *worst,* and all of them seem to rent from Ricardo.

But when I unfold the piece of paper, a photo falls out. I pick it up and freeze. It's of a young couple, both dressed in ripped jeans and plaid shirts. The man, I don't recognize.

But the woman?

It's my mother.

With shaking fingers, I pick up the paper and read the letter.

My dearest Alina,

I've started writing this letter a hundred times, but I never know what to say, how to introduce myself, and how to tell you that I'm your father.

My name is Vidone Laurenti. Twenty-eight years ago, I met your mother, Teresa, on the beach in San Vito Lo Capo, and I fell in love.

Your mother was the best thing that ever happened to me. We were together for two years, two of the happiest years of my life. But then, one day, she disappeared.

I searched everywhere for Teresa. I went to the police; I tried to find her family—nothing worked. I raged and mourned, and eventually, I made my peace with her disappearance. I had no other choice.

A week ago, I did an online DNA test. Imagine my shock when it said I had a match.

You. The daughter I never knew I had.

I don't know why Teresa hid you from me. Chances are, I will never know. I have spent the last week wrestling with the knowledge of your existence, and I find myself angry—furious— that I never got a chance to watch you grow up. To be your father in more than blood.

This letter will probably come as a shock, and I don't want to pressure you for a relationship. But I'd love to meet you. Show you the beach where your mother and I met, take you to the apartment where we lived together. I'd love to get to know my daughter.

I've included my address and phone number. I'll be waiting for your call.

Your loving father,

Vidone

I stare at the letter in shock. Picking up the photo and studying it, my heart races. It's a photo of my parents. They look so young. My dad has dark hair and a bump on his nose. Just like me. I can't make out the color of his eyes, but he's smiling into the camera, and there's a dimple in his chin. *Just like mine.*

Sudden tears fill my eyes.

All my life, I've wanted to know my father.

And now he's only a phone call away.

18

TOMAS

I like sex as much as the next man. When a woman I'm wildly attracted to invites me to bed, you know what I should say?

Yes.

Instead, I turned her down. What the hell was that about? Two hours later, I'm still cursing myself for that boneheaded move. She was available and willing, and so was I. It was too late to want to keep things professional between us. The moment I entered the ring, I knew it. There was no way to fight Alina and keep the sexual attraction at bay. None at all.

So why the hell did I turn her down?

Because I'm an idiot. *That's why.*

But when she said she was going to regret inviting me to her bed in the morning, something inside me had balked. A sour taste filled my mouth when I imagined waking up next to Alina and watching the sleep in her eyes be replaced by awareness and horror.

That's not what I want. *Not at all.*

Spend the night? Waking up next to her? What the fuck? Since when do you do those things?

Maybe it's a good thing that I turned her down and got the hell out of the gym.

Working remotely on Alina's books is a smart thing.

It would be an even better idea to hire Luigi to fix the books and wash my hands off the gym completely.

But as much as I *should* make that call, I find that I can't do it. *I don't want to.*

I wasn't planning on heading to Milan again. But the restlessness is back and stronger than ever. At ten at night on Saturday, I find myself pulling into the same warehouse on the outskirts of the city.

It's significantly more crowded tonight than it was on Thursday. "What's going on?" I ask Renzo when I make it inside.

"The women fight tonight," he replies. "You forgot? Those repeated blows to the head taking its toll?" He grins. "That'll make the boss happy. He's still bitter about some investment opportunity you stole from him."

I roll my eyes. "I didn't steal it—del Barba could have invested too. He chose not to."

Renzo laughs and holds up his hands. "I'm not getting involved in this pissing match." He gestures to the staircase. "Don't bother making your way through the crowds —just go on up. The first fight is going to start any minute now."

I didn't come here to attend another of Ciro del

Barba's parties. I came for a fight, and it looks like I'm not getting one. And I don't want to watch the women in the ring. It'll remind me too much of Alina.

I'm about to turn around and head out when the bell rings. The first two contestants enter the ring to shouts and applause. Zarina Simonini bounds out onto the octagon, as does her opponent.

Alina.

The woman who's taken up center stage in my fantasies. The woman I've been trying to get out of my mind for the last twenty-four hours. No, longer. From the moment I first set eyes on her, I haven't been able to stop thinking about Alina. Her face haunts my dreams, and her touch lingers on my skin like a brand.

She's cast a spell on me.

I drove three hours to escape her, and here she is. In a country of fifty-eight million people, I'm drawn to Alina like a magnet.

It's as if fate is willing us together, and there's not a damn thing I can do about it.

Shrugging my shoulders, I head up the stairs to find a vantage point to watch Alina Zuccaro fight.

19

ALINA

After the tumultuous day I've had, fighting feels amazing. There is no room for ghosts in the octagon. No space to wonder why my mother left my father, no room to question why she kept my existence a secret from him.

I found jiujitsu when I was seven. A kid in my class taunted me about not having a father, so I punched her in the mouth. My mother made me apologize, and then she took me to a nearby gym to see if they could redirect some of my aggression.

The first time I stepped out on the mat, I felt like I'd come home.

Before she got sick, I used to fight all the time. Once she started forgetting, I made myself stop. She didn't always remember why I was coming back hurt from the gym, and the bruises distressed her.

It's not until I pin my opponent down on the mat, my forearm wrapped around her neck until she taps out, that it sinks in how much I've missed this. There's something clean about a fight. Something cathartic. When you're in the middle of it, there's no room for thought. Muscle memory takes over, and it's all about instinct and action.

The ref holds up my hand. The crowd hoots and hollers. I fully expect them to scream out ribald suggestions about other things I can do with my body, but to my surprise, there's none of that. The over-whelming majority of the crowd are men, and they're definitely here to ogle the fighters, but they're not crossing a line.

Maybe that's Ciro del Barba's influence. His stone-faced people are everywhere, and nobody looks anxious to cross them.

I have thirty minutes until my next fight. I grab a towel and wipe off the sweat. One of the other fighters brings me a bottle of water. "You're new, aren't you? I haven't seen you here before. Are you from Milan?"

"Venice. What about you?" I drain the contents of the bottle down. I need to stay hydrated. The evening's only just beginning; I still have three more rounds to go.

"Bergamo."

Her name is Samia Kouri. She sits next to me and tells me her life story. She's eighteen years old, and her parents are from Egypt. Her mother isn't happy about this fight, but her father used to be a wrestler and is in the audience tonight, cheering his daughter on. "What about you?" she asks. "You tore through Zarina. It was *textbook*. Anyone here to watch you fight?"

A pang goes through my heart. All day, I've stared at the photo of my parents. Memorized every word of my father's letter. I craved a family so badly as a child. I wanted uncles and aunts and cousins, grandparents who would fuss over me and buy me presents. I dreamed of a father who would teach me how to ride a cycle. He would pick me up when I fell and kiss my skinned knee better.

Maybe some of my childhood dreams can actually come true.

A thousand times during the day, I reached for my phone. But I never called the number. I went so far as to program it into my contacts, but I couldn't follow through.

"Ali?" Samia prompts, her expression concerned. "Did I say something wrong?"

I shake free of my thoughts and smile at the young woman. "No, of course not. Looks like you're up. Good luck."

She leaves. I pull out my phone and stare at the screen again. Should I call my father now? But it's too late; he might already be in bed. There's so much I don't know. After my mother disappeared, did he ever get married? Does he have other children?

My finger hovers over the call button when I receive an incoming text. It's from Tomas.

> I'm planning to spend ten thousand euros of the gym's money on an investment opportunity.

I didn't hear from him all day. After the way he left, I fully expected not to hear from him anytime soon, which is, as far as I'm concerned, *a good thing.*

It doesn't explain why I'm so happy to hear from him.

I bite back my smile and text him back.

> And you're telling me about this why?

> If you read the contract, Alina, you'd discover we both need to approve any expenditures over five thousand euros.

> It's eleven. You're starting to make a habit of texting me in the middle of the night. Do you know that? Sounds like an insomnia problem. Maybe a glass of warm milk will help.

> Duly noted. You should review that contract, by the way, before hiring any pretty boy teachers.

My smile widens. Pretty boy teacher? Is he jealous? And how did Tomas even find out about my new hire? I gave Luke an advance earlier today. My partner must be keeping *very* close tabs on the gym's bank balance.

A devilish urge fills me.

> Who, Luke? He is very pretty, isn't he? All those yummy muscles.

Tomas takes three long minutes to reply. When he finally writes back, he completely ignores my attempt to make him jealous.

> Is that a yes to the investment?

Umm, Ali, why are *you trying to make him jealous?*

One of the organizers comes up. "Start warming up again," she says. "You go on in ten."

Okay. As much as it's fun to tease Tomas, I need to focus on the next fight. Twenty thousand euros are at stake, and Lidya has already warned me she placed a bet on me and will be extremely annoyed if I lose.

> Sure thing. As long as you don't lose.

> I doubt I will. But if I do, I'll cover the loss.

Setting my phone aside, I stand up and do my stretches. I wonder what Tomas is planning.

20

TOMAS

Alina is new to Ciro's ring. The oddsmaker doesn't know anything about her except that she teaches MMA classes in a struggling gym in Venice. Davide is a retired fighter, old-school in his thinking. In his opinion, those who can't do, teach.

He sets the odds of Alina winning the tournament at twelve to one. *And I take advantage.*

Ciro Del Barba is not happy when Alina hoists the belt up at the end of the night. He glares at me as I collect my winnings. "Damn you, Aguilar," he says. "Ten thousand euros. A gym instructor. How the hell did you know? You can't possibly be familiar with every fighter in Venice."

Del Barba will make it his mission to find out *everything* about Alina. By this time tomorrow, he'll know as much about her as humanly possible. "Not every fighter, no," I say with a grin. I just won one hundred and twenty thousand euros of Ciro Del Barba's money. Dante is going to get one hell of a laugh out of this. So is Antonio. "But

Alina and I co-own the gym she teaches at, and I've seen her fight."

"That's insider information," he accuses.

"Groff's is open to the public," I reply. "Nothing is stopping Davide, or you, or anyone else from walking in there and taking a class."

Del Barba is richer than God, but he didn't get that way by losing money on sports bets. If Alina fights again, the odds won't be anywhere as lopsided. But he also isn't a sore loser. "Fair enough," he concedes with a shrug. "Enjoy your windfall." He turns to one of his guards, hovering unobtrusively in the shadows. "Lara, would you invite Signorina Zuccaro up, please, as well as the other fighters?" He waits for her to leave before giving me a sly smile. "Is she the woman you're dating?"

"What?" I ask before remembering that's the line I used on Maria, Ciro's handsy friend in the red dress. "No, I'm not dating anyone; I just said that to get rid of your friend. Alina and I are business partners, nothing more."

"Are you sure?" He quirks an eyebrow. "I was watching you during that last fight. You looked very *involved*. Concerned, even."

He's fishing, and I'm definitely *not* going to take the bait. "Alina is the face of the gym, and she teaches the majority of the classes. If she's hurt, I'll have to scramble to find a replacement."

His eyes dance with laughter. "I thought you only invested in the stock market, Tomas. Buying a gym—that's new. Why'd you do it?"

"It's important to diversify," I lie through my teeth.

"If you say so." He looks unconvinced. "And here she is." He makes a sweeping gesture toward the top of the stairs. "Ladies and gentlemen, I give you tonight's champion. Please put your hands together for the beautiful and *lethal* Alina Zuccaro."

The room bursts into applause, and Alina freezes in her tracks. She scans the room, taking in the dozens of beautiful people dressed as if they were at a charity gala, not at an MMA ring in an abandoned warehouse on the outskirts of Milan. She sees the linen-covered tables against the wall, overflowing with champagne, caviar, and much more, the carnival that Ciro Del Barba surrounds himself with.

She takes a step forward and comes into the light. She's had time to take a quick shower and change into her street clothes. She's wearing a pair of black leggings that hug the curve of her ass and an oversize Groff's T-shirt with a wide neckline that slides off her shoulder. Her hair is pulled back in a high ponytail, her face freshly scrubbed. No makeup except for a slick of lip gloss across her soft, full lips.

There's a cut on her right cheek. Another cut on her arm. Bruises and injuries are part of fighting, and I'm used to them.

But when I see Alina hurt, everything inside me rebels.

Then, in that overcrowded room, her eyes find mine. For an instant, they're wide and surprised, and then she moves.

Toward me.

"Tomas," she says, crashing to a halt in front of me. Her words tell me she's pissed; her eyes tell a very different story. "You're here. In Milan. Why am I not surprised?"

21

ALINA

ownstairs, when the invitation to join Ciro Del Barba's party came through, I asked Zarina, my opponent in my first fight, what it entailed. Mix obnoxiously rich people and copious amounts of alcohol, and they start believing they're entitled to sex with the fighters. "Are we being pimped out?"

She immediately shook her head. "No," she said. "Don't get me wrong, sex can be on the table. Fight, then fuck, right? But only if you're interested. Signor Del Barba doesn't tolerate sexual assault of any kind. I've seen him personally snap the wrist of a man who got too handsy." She splashed some water on her face and applied a coat of mascara. "You don't have to attend. It's an invitation, not a requirement. It's usually pretty fun, though, and the food is always excellent. And Signor Del Barba only stocks the best prosecco."

Fight, then fuck. *I wish.* Adrenaline-fueled sex sounds good, but the only man I want to fuck is three hundred kilometers away. I'm only here for the prosecco.

TARA CRESCENT

Then I climb the stairs, and...

Tomas is here.

Our eyes connect. The noise of the room fades into the background. I walk up to him, my heart beating so fast that I think it's going to explode. "Tomas," I say through dry lips. "You're here. In Milan." I'm not dreaming. He's definitely here, dressed more casually than I've ever seen in a black T-shirt and dark-wash jeans, and he looks hot enough to devour. "Why am I not surprised?"

His lips quirk into a smile. "Hello, Alina. Nice fight."

Last night, there had been a fresh cut on his upper lip. Today, it's started to heal, and the puffiness has died down. My fingers itch to stroke it. *Stroke him.* It's late, well past midnight, and the night feels strangely magical. Anything could happen tonight, and I wouldn't be surprised.

Maybe I'm not here for just the food and wine after all.

Maybe I do want to fight, then fuck.

His compliment warms me from the inside out. "Well, I'm no Asset." A waiter wanders by with a tray of prosecco, and I snag a glass. I'm parched. "What are you doing here?"

His fingers close around the stem of my glass. "Drink some water first."

I narrow my eyes. "Are you telling me what to do, Tomas?"

"Risking life and limb in the process." He takes two pills out of his pocket. "Ibuprofen. You're going to need it. Take them, otherwise you're not getting out of bed tomorrow. And I don't think your new pretty boy teacher is ready to handle a full class load yet." I glare at him, and he adds, "I have some experience with this."

He does. As he so convincingly demonstrated last night. "So do I."

"When was the last time you fought five rounds in a row?" he asks pointedly. "Yeah, that's what I thought."

Damn him; he's right. "Smugness isn't attractive," I grumble. He hands me a bottle of water, and I swallow my pills. "And his name is Luke."

His eyes search my face. He's looking at me like I'm the center of his universe, and it's an addictive feeling. I want to grab it in my hands and never let go. "I don't give a damn about Luke," he murmurs. His fingers trace the cut on my cheek, his touch a soft whisper on my skin. "Does it hurt?"

It feels like it's burning up. Heat radiates from the point of his touch and fills my body. My heart is racing, my breath feels like it's coming in small gasps. I want to run away; I never want him to stop touching me. "You never told me why you're here."

He drops his hand. "I fight here from time to time. Why are *you* here?"

"Same reason as you." What's happening? My insides feel molten. Achy. I want to grab his hand and put it back on my face, feel his callused fingers on every inch of my body. Last night, I told him I'd regret sleeping with him in the morning. I was wrong. Staring at Tomas, the two of us tucked away in a corner of Ciro Del Barba's warehouse, the only thing I regret is stopping. "I'm here for the twenty thousand euro cash prize."

"Why?"

"Isn't it obvious? I'm going to make enough money to

buy you out. At twenty grand a week, it'll take me…" My voice trails off. My brain isn't capable of math right now.

"Fifty weeks." A line etches between his brows. "That's insane." He blows out a breath. "You can't fight every week for a year. You'll get hurt." He touches my cut again, and my knees turn to water. "You're already hurt."

"It's nothing."

"You need rest and relaxation. Stop adding things to your plate."

"You're being nice to me. Why is that suspicious?"

A smile tugs at the corners of his mouth. "I'm always nice to you. You just don't notice."

"Really? You're not planning to turn the gym around and then sell your stake to the highest bidder?"

Surprise flashes on his face. Ha. This is a first— Tomas Aguilar is at a loss for words. It takes him a few seconds to formulate a response. "You don't seem shocked."

"Why would I be shocked? You've always made it obvious that this is an investment." He's still touching me, his fingers warm on my face, and I feel cared for. Safe. *Seen.* I should pull away, but instead, I stay exactly where I am. "Still, unlike Simon, you've kept up your end of the contract."

"I'm nothing like Groff," Tomas growls.

A thrill shoots through me at his tone. Suddenly, I'm picturing him backing me into a corner, pushing my arms over my head, holding my wrists prisoner as he cages me in with his body. His fingers on my lip before he lowers his mouth to mine. His hands tugging my pants down, pushing between my legs to stroke my aching pussy…

I drain my glass of prosecco in one gulp, but the cold

liquid does nothing to quench the fire raging inside me. "I have no complaints," I concede. "So far."

He exhales a laugh. "So far," he repeats. "You sound so skeptical. Why are you so ready to hate me, dolcezza?"

I have to hate you. Because if I don't, I might start falling for you. And you've had one step out the door from the moment I met you.

But when he calls me dolcezza, every thought flies out of my brain. Dolcezza. Sweetness. He called me that during our fight last night, and I simultaneously wanted to strangle him and launch myself into his arms. Tonight, it's definitely Option Two.

I feel the weight of several pairs of eyes on me. I look around to realize more than one person is watching us. Some discreetly, some openly staring. Every single one of Del Barba's guests is dressed to the nines, and I'm in my gym clothes. "I feel very out of place," I whisper to Tomas. "Had I known I was going to get invited to a fancy party, I would have borrowed something to wear from Rosa."

"It doesn't matter what you wear," he says as if the words are being torn out of him. "Everyone is looking at you because you light up the room. In a roomful of peacocks, you are a hawk."

I try to throttle the dizzying current racing through me. "Is that a compliment?"

He starts to reply, but then his expression turns alarmed. "Pretend you're my girlfriend," he says urgently, taking a step closer and putting his hand on my chin.

"What?"

"Just go with it. Please."

"Why? What are you going to give me for my coop-eration?"

"Anything," he says. "Anything you want." His hands cradle my face. His gray eyes search mine. "Yes?"

"Yes," I whisper. There's a tingling in the pit of my stomach. The very air around us seems electrified. Every-thing about Tomas is making my head spin. Making me dizzy with anticipation.

And then Tomas kisses me.

Have I imagined this? Yes. A thousand times. From the first moment we met, Tomas Aguilar has taken center stage in my fantasies. But the reality? The reality tran-scends my imagination. His lips are soft and warm. He nibbles my lower lip, his hands roaming over my body as if he owns it. One arm wraps around my back, tugging me even closer until I'm pressed right up against him, my breasts mashed into his chest.

A shiver of pure need runs through me as I kiss him back. I slide my tongue over the cut I wanted to touch, and he growls into my mouth, his grip tightening.

He kisses me as if I'm a dish worth savoring, one morsel at a time, slowly, leisurely, until I am a creature of need and want and desire. He kisses me as if he can't get enough, as if he's ready to tear the clothes off my body, lower me to the concrete floor, and thrust into my heat, and I want that.

I want everything he's offering *and more.*

He fists my ponytail and sucks my lower lip through his teeth. Desire punches me in the gut, and I moan into his mouth.

"Oh wow," a woman's voice says, cutting through my fog of lust. "What a beautiful couple you two make."

Tomas pulls back, slowly, reluctantly, his eyes dark with heat. He runs a shaky hand through his hair. "Alina, meet Maria Isgro."

22

ALINA

Maria Isgro could be a supermodel. Okay, maybe she's not tall enough to walk the runway, but she's beautiful. Lush dark hair that spills over her big breasts, a tiny waist, and a round butt.

I hate her.

"So you're the girlfriend," she says to me, her eyes sparkling. "No wonder Tomas likes you. You were amazing out there." She runs her hand down his back before taking my hand to shake it.

No, not shake.

Caress.

"All that barely leashed aggression," she murmurs. "So hot."

Hang on, is she flirting with me?

Her next words all but confirm it. "If you're looking for a play partner," she purrs, still holding onto my hand, "let me know. I would love to have a three-way." She takes in my expression, and a wicked smile curls her lips. "Tell me, Alina, aren't you at least a little bi-curious?"

I've honestly never given it any thought.

Tomas spins me around so my back is resting against his chest. His arm wraps around my waist, holding me against his body. "That's a very tempting offer, Maria," he says, far more calmly than I'd be able to manage. "But I'm going to have to decline." He bends his head and kisses the side of my neck, his lips pressed to my fluttering pulse. "I would be far too jealous to share Alina."

The other woman tucks a small business card into my back pocket. I half-expect her to pinch my butt in the process, but to her credit, she doesn't. "If you change your mind, call me," she says. "That goes for both of you. Separately, or together."

She winks at me and strolls away. I wait until she's out of earshot before I pull away from Tomas's hold and spin around to face him. "Did that really happen?"

"Ciro's parties," he says with a shrug. "They tend to attract a certain type."

I shake my head, resisting the urge to touch my swollen lip. I still feel the touch of his mouth on mine. The pressure of his tongue in my core. "I thought Maria was an ex."

"Nope. Just someone who was rather obviously interested." He laughs. "In both of us, evidently."

And in response, he said he would be far too jealous to share me.

It's a line, Ali. Just pretend. It's not real.

But the thrill that shot through me when he wrapped his arm possessively around my waist—that wasn't pretend at all. That felt all too real.

Tomas plucks the empty glass of prosecco from my hand. "How did you get to Milan?"

I have to stop thinking about his kiss. The way his tongue slid into my mouth, sure and unhurried, the way his breathing quickened, the way he growled as I deepened the kiss...

"I took the train."

He frowns. "It's one in the morning. How were you planning on getting back? There's no train until the—"

"Morning. Yes, I know. I was going to wait at the station. It's only a few hours before the first train."

His look of displeasure deepens. "No, you're not," he says. "I'll give you a ride back home."

"Was that in the contract, too?" I ask sweetly, grabbing another glass of prosecco from a waiter. For a brief second, I contemplate turning down his offer, and then sanity wins. I'm already exhausted, and the idea of sitting around the station for hours waiting for the first train home sounds truly awful. There's no point cutting off my nose to spite my face. "Thank you, a ride would be wonderful."

TOMAS DRIVES A BMW SEDAN. It's a nice car, comfortable and spacious. I sink into the leather seat with a sigh. "I'm exhausted," I confess. I pull out my phone and realize my battery is completely dead. "You wouldn't happen to have a phone charger, would you?"

"In the glove box." He gives me a sideways look. "You

were going to wait for five hours in a train station without a working phone?"

"When you put it that way..." I find the cord and plug it into the USB port in the console. It takes a few minutes for my device to power up. When it finally does, I see that I have multiple messages from my bank. After the two-sets-of-books disaster, Tomas took Simon's name off the bank account and signed me up for a fancy service that alerts me every time there's a withdrawal. "Why is the bank texting me in the middle of the night?" I open the most recent one. "There's been a one hundred and nineteen thousand euro deposit into the gym's bank account? That's not right. It's got to be some kind of mistake."

"One hundred and nineteen thousand, nine hundred and eighty-eight euros," Tomas says, not taking his eyes off the road. "It's from the investment, the one I called you about."

What kind of investment converts ten thousand euros into a hundred and twenty in less than six hours? I turn in my seat and stare at him. "Tomas, where did this money come from?"

"I bet on your fight."

My mouth falls open. Did I hear him right? "You did what?"

"I bet you'd win," he repeats. "They set the odds at twelve to one, the idiots." A smile plays about his lips. "I had to walk a fine line with that bet. Del Barba gets notified anytime someone bets over ten thousand, so I bet nine thousand, nine hundred, and ninety-nine."

"You bet ten thousand euros?" Yes, I sound a little shrill, but can you blame me? "What would have happened if I lost?"

"I guess I would have been out ten grand," he replies, accelerating around a slow-moving transport truck. "But I wasn't worried, and I'm not reckless; I only bet on a sure thing. I knew you were going to win."

He says it with complete confidence, and for a moment, I can't breathe. A lump wells up in my throat. The last person who had this much faith in me was my mother, but even before she died, the Alzheimer's took her mind. It's been a long, long time since someone believed in me.

I think I'm going to cry.

And I can't do that in front of Tomas. I just can't. I can't expose myself that way.

"You bet on my fight with the gym's money," I make myself say, my tone snarky. "How confident could you have been?"

"Look at what time the text came in."

I pull up the details. The text from the bank alerting me to the money deposited into my account came in only a minute or two after Tomas called me. Which means... "You put the winnings into the gym's account before the fight even happened? I don't understand..."

"Like I said, I knew you were going to win." He glances at me, a long, lingering look that sets butterflies fluttering through my stomach. "I owe you for the kiss. What do you want?"

You.

I take a deep breath. "I want first right of refusal when you sell your share of the gym. I want you to offer it to me first and give me enough notice so I can raise the money."

"How much notice?"

"A month," I reply, reaching for the stars. My

previous contract with Simon specified a week. That contract wasn't even worth the paper it was printed on, but I know enough about Tomas now to know that if he agrees to do something, it'll get done. His word means something.

"Done," he says. "I'll have Daniel draft up the changes tomorrow." He takes his attention off the road once again. "You could have asked for anything you wanted," he says. "I didn't put any conditions on it. You could have asked me for my share of the gym."

Anything I wanted. My heart starts to beat faster. "You paid a million euros for that share," I say lightly. "That seems excessive for one kiss."

His gaze rests on me, an invitation in the smoky depths of his eyes. If we weren't speeding on the E70, I'd be tempted to take him up on it, consequences be damned. "You're selling yourself short, Alina," he murmurs. "Never underestimate your worth. Any man with a pulse would pay that and more for a chance with you."

Any man with a pulse would pay that and more for a chance with you.

He drops that bombshell as if it were nothing and turns his attention back to the road. I hug his compliment to myself for the rest of the way home, and it warms me from the inside out.

TOMAS PARKS his car in Tronchetto. The trains aren't running yet—it's too early—and in any case, I feel like walking. The two of us stroll in silence toward Dorso-duro. "Where do you live?" I ask him.

"Giudecca."

"Like Antonio Moretti." The mafia boss of Venice famously lives in Giudecca. His wife, Lucia, just opened an art gallery there. I saw a fawning article about her in one of the magazines in the gym's lobby.

"The padrino prefers we live close. It's easier that way."

Easier for what, I wonder, though I don't ask. "Is he a good boss?"

"Yes," Tomas says. "Very much so. It makes for a very pleasant change."

"A change from what?"

I don't think he's going to respond, but to my surprise, he answers my question. "Back in Valencia, I used to work for a man called Alonzo d'Este. He was... not a good boss. On my first day, I wanted to impress him, so I prepared a presentation about how he could improve his investment strategy and triple his returns. Alonzo flew into a rage. He took my critique as a personal affront." He exhales in a long breath. "It was not the best working environment."

"Why didn't you leave?"

"I should have. But I thought I was in love with Alonzo's assistant, Estela. It wasn't until that blew up in my face that I quit."

He said he moved to Venice five years ago. Estela—I even hate her name—should be firmly in the past. There's no need for my stomach to sink the way it does when he mentions another woman.

"What happened?"

He shrugs. "I asked her to marry me, and she turned me down. I thought we were in love with each other, but she told me in not so many words that she was slumming with the help. Her father was an enforcer for one of the Colombian cartels, and she was only working for Alonzo to learn the business. She intended on marrying cartel royalty, and I was too much of a nobody. After that, the idea of working alongside her didn't appeal, so I looked around for another job, and Antonio offered me one."

I stare at him, my heart aching. Tomas is gorgeous and smart, witty and capable. He's someone you can count on in a fight, someone whose word is his bond. I can't think of why any woman would turn him down. "Estela clearly has the brains of a pea."

The look in his eyes is affectionate. "That almost sounds like another compliment, Ali."

"Don't hold your breath for the next," I respond automatically. Barbs and insults and sharp banter—that's been the nature of our relationship so far. Why do I feel like I'm standing on the precipice of something new?

"Do you ever miss Valencia? How often do you go back?"

His shoulders tense. "I haven't," he says, his voice clipped. "Not since I left."

He's been away from his home for five years. He misses it—I know he does, even if he doesn't admit it to himself. I can see it in his eyes and hear it in his voice.

But he's stayed away because he's still in love with Estela.

My heart feels like it's been tossed into the smoothie machine. I take a deep, steadying breath. "It didn't bother you that you'd be working for the mafia in Venice? Or did you already work for the mafia in Valencia?"

He chuckles. "Officially, there's no mafia in Valencia."

"And unofficially?"

"Unofficially, Spain is where the mafia, the bratva, and the cartels hang out and learn from each other. Mallorca is filled with villas belonging to the Russians, the Colombians, and the Italians. Alonzo d'Este wasn't connected to any one organization; he profited from them all."

We've reached our destination. I come to a halt outside the gym and fumble in my purse for the key. I'm not ready to say goodbye. Not yet. Almost four hours after it happened, I can still feel his kiss on my lips. "How will you get home? The vaporetto won't start running for another hour."

"I have a boat." He looks up at the lightening sky. "What time does the gym open on Sunday?"

"Eight."

"Tell me you arranged for someone to open." He glances at my face, and he shakes his head. "No, of course you didn't." He follows me into the lobby and waits for me to open the door to my stairwell. "Sleep in, Ali. I'll open the gym for you."

It's the first time he's called me Ali, in a tone that is exasperated and affectionate all at once. My heart does a funny little flip when I hear it. "You should make that offer only if you mean it," I warn him. "Because I'm going to take you up on it."

"I mean it." He brushes his finger over the cut on my cheek. "Put something on this."

His touch sends a surge of desire through my bloodstream. "You keep telling me what to do," I whisper. "I don't like it."

A smile ghosts across his face. "I think you like it more than you're willing to admit." He strokes my cut again, his touch as light as a feather. Need rises sharply in me, an aching need that demands the weight of his body on mine.

I swallow again. "I don't like it," I repeat stubbornly.

"Okay." He doesn't pull away, and neither do I. We stand in the doorway, staring at each other. *Make a move,* I think urgently. *Ask me to invite you inside. Because if you do, I'm going to say yes.*

He lets his hand drop.

"Goodnight, Ali," he says, taking a step back. "Lock this door behind you and get some rest."

I watch him turn around and walk away. "Tomas," I call out just as he's at the front door. "Last night, I might have lied."

He freezes in his tracks. "About what?"

"About inviting you upstairs. I wouldn't have regretted it the morning after."

He doesn't move. Doesn't react. If it wasn't for a muscle ticking in his jaw, I'd be wondering if he even heard me.

For one brief, hopeful moment, I wonder if he's going to turn around and come back to me. Kiss me hard and hurry me up the stairs.

Finally, he breaks the quiet. "Sleep well, dolcezza," he says.

And then he leaves.

23

TOMAS

I didn't like the people I worked with in Valencia. Nobody stood up for me when Alonzo d'Este decided to make me his punching bag; they were all happy his attention was redirected away from them.

That's not the case in Venice. I've been here for five years, and I genuinely like the people I work with. Antonio is a really good boss, always calm and in control of his emotions. Dante, the second-in-command, is cut from the same cloth. Leo, the mafia enforcer, is loyal to a fault. He would give you the shirt off his back if he thought you needed it. Joao, our assassin, is always quick with a joke. Daniel, who is a shark of a lawyer, is impossible to ruffle. Valentina used to keep to herself and was only brought in on special projects, but she's been playing a larger role in the organization since she married Dante.

I care about my team. I would take a bullet for any of them, and they would do the same for me.

And yet, I've never told them about Estela. The

wound cut too deep. The only person who knows is Leo, and that mostly happened by accident. Shortly after I joined Antonio's organization, the two of us found ourselves in a bar after a messy day of work. Long story short: we both got very drunk and spilled our secrets. Leo confessed that he felt responsible for the death of his wife, and to distract him from the excruciating guilt he felt, I told him the real reason I left Spain and moved to Italy.

But today, I bared my soul to Alina without a thought. I told her about the most painful, shameful thing that happened to me, and funnily enough, the memory of Estela didn't hurt. Not even a little. That episode is firmly in the past.

And in the present, there's Alina.

I wouldn't have regretted it the morning after.

She wanted me. I could see the invitation in her eyes and hear it in her voice, and fuck, I was tempted. So tempted. It hurt me to walk away. Every nerve in my body strained toward Alina. Every atom wanted to take a step toward her, hurry her up the stairs, rip off her clothes, and kiss my way down her body. It took superhuman control to walk away.

But she needs rest.

Alina has my emotions all tangled up. I'm torn between wanting to fuck her hard and wanting to put ointment on her cut. I want to smack her ass, and I want to hunt down the person responsible for the bruise on her face.

For the last five years, my relationships with women have been about sex. About getting my physical needs met and nothing else. I don't date; I break things off before anyone can get involved. I hook up at Casanova and don't bring them home, so there's no room for misunderstandings. I don't buy flowers, and I don't bring presents. I'm not the nurturing kind.

But when it comes to Alina Zuccaro, I'm tearing up all the rules.

"HI THERE." The American woman who comes up to the membership desk is one of the gym's regulars. She's in here every day, sparring with her friend. "I have a problem I'm hoping you can help me with."

Her Italian is hesitant, so I switch to English. "Of course." It's noon, and there's still no sign of Alina. I don't care; it's Sunday, and I don't have anything to do with my day except grade a stack of accounting quizzes for my cover job. "What's the problem?"

She gives me a relieved smile. "It's my membership," she says in English. "I think I've been billed twice a month for the last three months?"

I look into it, and yes, it's more of Simon Groff's fuckery. This reminds me that I still have to track down his crooked bookkeeper. "Give me a few minutes to straighten this out. If you want, I can take care of it while you're working out."

She gives me a flirtatious smile. "That's okay, I'm in no hurry. My name is Sara. You look really familiar, by the way. Have I seen you before?"

"Tomas. I'm Alina's new partner. I was here all of last week, so maybe that's why?"

"No, not at the gym. Have we met somewhere else?" Her forehead furrows, and then her expression clears. "I've seen you at Casanova."

Now that she mentions it, I *have* seen her at the club. "Are you allowed to talk about it?" I quip. "You know the rules. What happens in Casanova stays in Casanova."

She looks around with exaggerated fear. "But the terrifying Liam Callahan isn't here," she says, referring to the club manager. "And what Liam doesn't know can't hurt him. So, what made you buy Simon out? Are you an MMA fighter?"

"From time to time."

"Really? That's not the impression I got from Alina."

"Did she tell you I faint at the sight of blood?"

Sara laughs. "Something like that. She said you're the type who'd run for a Band-Aid when you got a paper cut."

I laugh. "Of course she did. Do you want your Visa charges refunded or the American Express?"

"The Amex, please."

"Okay." I finish cleaning the mess up and make sure the refund goes through. "Sorry about that."

"It's no problem." She gives me an arch glance. "I was looking for an excuse to talk to you anyway."

Sara is more subtle than Maria, but once again, I'm not interested. I'm about to open my mouth and tell her that when Alina comes up to us, a travel mug of coffee in her hand. She's wearing a black crop top and a pair of pink shorts, and her hair is in its usual high ponytail. "Tomas," she says, her voice bright and cheerful, setting the mug down on the counter and lacing her arm in mine. "You're here already. How *energetic*. I thought I kept you up really late last night."

Well, well, what do you know. *Alina's jealous.*

A devilish urge seizes me. "You did, dolcezza," I say with a wink. "But, as you already know, I recover quickly."

Her cheeks turn red. Sara's eyes are wide as she looks at Alina and then at me. "Umm, I had no idea the two of you were together," she says awkwardly, transferring her weight from one foot to another. "Tomas was just helping me with a double-billing issue."

"Of course," Alina says sweetly. "Tomas, can I see you in my office when you're done?"

"We're done," Sara says hastily. "And look, River's here. I better go."

She darts off. I follow Alina to the small office. When we're there, I shut the door behind me and turn to her with a wicked smile. "I've never been fought over by two women. It's very... *enjoyable.*"

She glares at me. "Don't flatter yourself," she snaps. "I wasn't fighting over you. I was just helping you keep the interactions with our members professional."

I push her against the door and press my body into hers. "Is that what you were doing?" I murmur into her ear, nibbling her earlobe.

"What are you doing?" she gasps.

"Isn't it obvious? I'm showing you how energetic I can be."

And then I claim her mouth in a searing kiss.

I kissed Alina last night in Ciro Del Barba's warehouse, but I had to remember that I was surrounded by a roomful of watching eyes. Today, nothing is holding me back. I wrap my fingers around her ponytail and tilt her head up, pressing kiss after drugging kiss on her soft lips.

I've wanted to do this from the moment I first laid eyes on her. She tastes like coffee and toothpaste and a sweetness that's all Alina. I dive into that heady sweetness over and over, my heart hammering in my chest, my cock so hard for her that it hurts.

After a brief surprised gasp, she parts her lips and kisses me back, her arms wrapping around me, her tongue slipping into my mouth with a hint of shyness that melts my heart and makes me pause.

With the greatest difficulty, I pull back. "Tell me to stop," I rasp. "Tell me to stop, and I will."

Her cognac-tinted eyes are liquid pools of desire, and a man could drown in their depths. "No," she whispers, her grip tightening on my waist, tugging me closer. "Kiss me again."

Fuck, yes. My self-control snaps. I capture her lips again, grabbing her left hand and holding it above her head. I squeeze her breast through her sexy crop top and push my knee between her legs, and like a good girl, she spreads them wider for me. "I wanted to do this last night." I stroke my thumb over her nipple. "I wanted to tear that stupid Groff's T-shirt off your body. Push down your leggings. I wanted to pin you down and fuck you hard."

I pinch her nipple, and she writhes against me in response, moaning loudly into my mouth. My cock goes even harder at the sound. If she keeps this up, I'm going to come in my pants like an out-of-control teenager. "No, no," I chide sternly. "This won't do, dolcezza, this won't do at all. We can't disturb the members, can we?" I give her a wicked grin. "You need to keep quiet."

She glares at me. "Your sudden concern for the members is touching," she says. "I'm sure Sara will appreciate it. What were the two of you talking about?"

I pinch her nipple harder. "Sara again," I tease, trailing kisses over the side of her neck. "I didn't think you were the jealous type, Alina. This is *very* illuminating." I tug that crop top up, pull down the cups of her sports bra, and feast my gaze on her lush breasts and swollen dark-rose nipples.

Fuck, she's irresistible. I capture an engorged tip between my teeth, and she sucks in a breath. "Tell me more."

"Your imagination is working overtime," she pants. "I'm not jealous of Sara."

"Liar." I squeeze her firm breast again and bite down on her nipple, just a little, and she whimpers in her throat. "Too loud, dolcezza. It looks like I need to gag you. Open your mouth."

Her eyes flash fire at me, but her lips obediently fall open. *Fuck me, this is every fantasy of mine come to life.* Alina is all fight and ferocity, and underneath, she's as eager to play these games as I am.

And it's taking every bit of willpower I possess not to shove her down on the floor and take her hard.

"Such a good girl," I breathe into her ear. "Keep your hand where it is; that's my good girl." I push two fingers into her mouth, pressing them against her tongue. "You're going to keep quiet for me, aren't you?"

A small smile curls her lips, and she sucks my fingers

deep. *Oh, fuck, yes.* Her tongue slides delicately over me, her head bobbing over my fingers as if she were imagining that it was my cock instead, and it's the sweetest torture. I groan out loud, and her smile widens into a smirk. "Shh," she mumbles around her makeshift gag. "Someone might hear."

"Brat," I accuse. I pull my wet fingers from her mouth and pinch her tightly beaded nipples again. They seem to swell even more as the cold from the air-conditioner hits her sensitized, wet nubs. "I should spank you for that." I search her expression to see how she reacts to that suggestion, and *fuck me, she's on board.* "You want to get spanked, dolcezza?" My cock is going to explode. "Such a naughty girl. If I push my fingers into your pretty little cunt, will I find you wet?"

She doesn't answer, but her face tells me everything I need to know. My pulse pounds like I'm in a fight. Adrenaline shoots through me, and my entire body feels like it's buzzing with arousal. I slip my hand between the waistband of her shorts and slide two fingers into her. She's so wet, so ready. Her muscles grip me tight, and she's so fucking hot that I can't breathe. "Oh, fuck, yes," I growl. "I like this reaction."

"Stop gloating," she replies, pushing her hips forward. Her gaze locks on my crotch, where the outline of my erection is clearly visible underneath my pants. "I'm not the only one enjoying this, am I?"

I need *more.* I tug her shorts down impatiently past her hips. Her panties follow a moment later. She kicks them off, and my throat goes dry. I wrap my fingers around her right ankle and lift her foot on the closest office chair. She's so beautiful. Her ponytail is coming undone, and her lips are swollen from my kisses. In this position, her back braced against the door, one leg on the floor, and another propped on the chair, she's spread open for me, her nipples hard and her cunt swollen, wet, and ready.

She's a meal laid out for my pleasure, *and I intend to feast.*

I kneel in front of her. "Don't make a noise," I remind her sternly.

"Or what?"

"Or I'll punish you." I glide my hand up her legs and spank her soft inner thigh. She sucks in a sharp breath and clenches her eyes shut, but she doesn't pull away. My little hurricane likes being punished. "I'll spank you until your ass is red, and then I'll tie you up, find the vibrator on your nightstand, and use it on you until you can't come anymore. Until you're begging me to stop."

Her cheeks turn pink. "You saw my vibrator that day, didn't you?"

I laugh softly. "I saw your vibrator," I confirm. "I pictured you using it. I jerked off in the shower to that image."

I spank her again, and an expression of intense pleasure washes over her face. God, she's glorious. I can't wait another second. I move closer to her, so close I can feel every breath she takes. I run my fingertips through her folds, and she jerks, a shiver running through her body. "Keep your legs spread for me, dolcezza." I *have* to taste her. I bend my head and lick her, swiping my tongue through her folds, and she gasps, her thighs trembling, and pulls my head closer for more. "Hold still, and I'll tell you what Sara and I were talking about."

"Fuck you," she replies heatedly, but she doesn't move away.

I chuckle and circle my tongue over her engorged clit. She sucks in a breath. "Tomas," she whimpers. "Please…"

"Please what, dolcezza?" I tease. I kiss her pussy lips, more teasing than contact, and she whimpers in protest. "Sara and I were talking about Casanova. She recognized me from there."

She stiffens and starts to close her legs. "Casanova, the sex club?"

"You've heard of it? Have you been?" I'm more curious than I'm prepared to acknowledge. And when I picture her flirting with someone there, kissing them, scening with them… There's a hot ball of something in my gut that feels a lot like possessiveness.

I put my hands on her thighs to keep her spread for me. "Did I tell you that you could move?"

"If you think I'm going to stand here and listen to you gush about Sara—"

What the fuck? "Look at me," I growl. "I'm on my knees in the middle of your office, feasting on your beautiful cunt, my cock so hard I think I'm going to come in my pants like a teenager. Do I look like I'm interested in Sara?" I push a finger into her, and her muscles grip me tight. "The only woman I'm interested in is you."

"Oh." The tension in her shoulders drains away. "Okay then."

I increase my pressure on her clit, and she bites her lip to keep from crying out loud. My gut clenches. I can't think straight around her. All the blood in my body has pooled to my cock. I feel light-headed, and it's not from the lack of sleep. I'm dizzy with anticipation.

I attack her like I'm starving.

And only she can satiate this bone-deep hunger.

Every time my tongue flicks her clit, her entire body jerks like she's touched a live wire. "You didn't answer my question," I say, adding a second finger inside her and feeling her muscles stretch to accommodate me. "Have you been to Casanova?"

"Of course not." She sounds breathless. "Do I look like I have thousands of euros to spend on a sex club membership? I've heard people talk about it in hushed whispers."

I lift my head off her clit for just a second. "Have they made you wildly curious?" I'd love to take her to the club. Reserve a private room for just the two of us. The things I want to do with her there... My imagination throws up one carnal image after another, and it's almost too much to bear. "Because I'm a member, and I can bring guests."

She whimpers, her hand over her mouth covering the sounds. She's close to the edge, her body trembling as her orgasm nears. "Of course you're a member," she says, every muscle taut. "Tomas Aguilar, international man of mystery. By day, you're a cat-owning accounting professor, and by night, an MMA champion fighter who is a member of Venice's most exclusive sex club. Oh, and you work for the mafia. Do you ever wake up and forget which persona to adopt?"

"I contain multitudes." I add a third finger, sucking her clit between my teeth at the same time, and the dam bursts.

"Yes," she exhales, throwing her head back. "Yes, please, fuck, yes." Her body tenses, and her muscles tighten and quiver around my fingers as she comes. I keep licking through the quivers, through the after-shocks. Alina is like a drug, and I'm powerless to resist. I keep licking until she pushes me away and slumps to the floor next to me.

I pull her into my lap. My mind is churning, a dozen emotions struggling for dominance. I want Alina. I'm greedy for her. Now that I've had a taste, I can't let go.

So many words dance at the tip of my tongue. There are so many things I want to say to her. But everything is a little raw, and at least right now, Casanova seems like the safest topic of conversation. "So, do you want to go?"

She twists around and stares into my eyes. "To Casanova? That sounds like a terrible, reckless idea."

"It probably is." She hasn't pulled away. Hasn't shut me down. "Want to go anyway? See what the hype is about?"

"When?" She wets her lower lip with her tongue, and my cock throbs in response.

"Friday night."

That maddening tongue sweeps over her lush lower lip again. I wait for her answer, my hand clenched tight into a fist. I'm a hair's breadth away from losing all semblance of control. From pulling out my cock and thrusting deep into her, right here, on the floor of her office, uncaring that the gym is filled with members, and nobody is staffing the front desk.

She wriggles her round ass over my cock, teasing me, the little brat. "Okay."

I grip her hips, holding her still. "It's a date."

"Onto more important things—" she begins before a knock on the office door interrupts us. "Ali," a woman's voice calls out. "Are you there?"

24

ALINA

Damn it. Talk about terrible timing for an interruption. I jump to my feet, look around for my shorts and tug them on, pull down my T-shirt, finger comb my hair back into a ponytail, and try not to look like someone who just had the best orgasm of her life.

Then I open the door.

It's River. She looks at me, and then at Tomas, and back at me with a smirk. "I'm so sorry to disturb you," she says. "Really sorry. But I have the same billing issue Sara did. And it's not just us. Sergio has been double-billed as well, and so have Ryan and Chris."

I frown. Tomas moves to the computer. "Groff again," he says in disgust after a few minutes. "He's been double-billing some of your members." He clicks more keys. "About a quarter of them, for the last three months."

"Damn it," I swear. So much for my sex haze. "Simon strikes again." I give River an apologetic look. "I'm really sorry. I will take care of this today, I promise."

163

"No worries, Ali." River sounds remarkably uncon-cerned for someone who has been over-billed for a quarter of a year. "I trust you to handle this."

She leaves, and I turn to Tomas in frustration. It's not fair. I was making out with him. He spanked me. He caught my hand in his and held it over my head, and he kissed me as if he couldn't get enough of me. And then he licked me with his clever, talented tongue until I came.

I don't want to deal with Simon's latest disaster. I want to drag Tomas upstairs to my apartment, lock the door behind us so no one can interrupt, and I want him to fuck me.

But unfortunately, I can't do that. This isn't a trivial issue; this is financial fraud, and I could get into real trouble.

"He really is the gift that keeps on giving," I bite out. "What a fucking mess. This is *fraud*. If someone complains to the authorities—"

"They won't," Tomas says confidently. Unfazed as usual. If I hadn't heard him growl with my own ears a few minutes ago when he pushed his fingers into me and found me wet, I wouldn't have believed it possible. "You heard that woman. Groff was a piece of shit, but they trust you, Alina. You've got this."

His words make me feel better. "Let me get a cup of coffee, and I'll start drafting an email to my members apologizing for Simon's fuck-up."

"Didn't you bring coffee? I could have sworn I saw you with a travel mug. Ah, here it is." He picks it up off his desk and hands it to me. "It's still hot."

My cheeks turn pink. "That coffee isn't for me," I say sheepishly. "It's for you." I thrust the mug into his hand.

"Here. I tried to make your disgustingly sweet concoction, but don't get your hopes up. I've never made it before, and I stirred in the sweetened condensed milk before I realized the coffee and the condensed milk were supposed to be separate layers. So, it might not be very good."

His eyes turn warm. "You made me a café bombon? Why?"

I'm too embarrassed to meet his gaze. "I told you. The sugar hides the rat poison."

He takes a sip, and a bittersweet expression washes over his face. "It tastes like home," he says, so quietly that I almost don't hear him. "Thank you." Then, that vulnerable expression vanishes, and he gives me his maddening grin. "You're still trying to poison me? I'm hurt, Alina. I thought we agreed to be friends."

"I see the lack of sleep has made you delirious," I respond with a roll of my eyes. "My friends call me Ali, by the way."

But Tomas and I are not *friends*. Friends don't spread your legs, spank you, and make you come.

We're not friends. We're not enemies either, not anymore, not after today's make-out session.

So, what are we?

25

TOMAS

She made me a café bombon. I take a sip of the beverage, and the sweetness and creaminess hit my tongue. I close my eyes and feel the warmth of a Valencian sun on my face.

"It tastes like home," I whisper. "Thank you."

Then I open my eyes, and I realize it's not the remembered feel of the Valencian sun that's warming my heart.

It's Alina.

I swallow back the swell of emotion and paste a grin on my face. "You're still trying to poison me? I'm hurt, Alina. I thought we agreed to be friends."

"I see the lack of sleep has made you delirious," she responds pertly. "My friends call me Ali, by the way."

Friends. I want to laugh. The things I want to do to her are very un-friend-like.

"Ali," I repeat, slow and soft like a caress. "Thank you for the rat poison."

A smile flashes on her face. "You're welcome, Tomas."

Our eyes connect for a moment, and then she takes a step away and turns to her computer. She opens a blank document, no doubt ready to craft the email to her members apologizing for Groff's fuckup. Alina—Ali—doesn't ease into her day. No, she attacks it head-on. "Time to craft a conciliatory, apologetic email to a quarter of my members."

"I can issue refunds automatically if you're looking for a silver lining."

"That'd be great."

She's got her hair up in a ponytail again. I want to tug the strands free and run my fingers through their length. I want to kiss those soft lips again and feel her moan into my mouth. I *need* to taste her sweet cunt, pleasure her, take her to the edge over and over until she's an aching, quivering mess, sweaty and flushed and so, so beautiful.

But sex is only part of it. There's a reason I've spent more hours at the gym this last week than at work, and it's because I like being with Ali. I like working with her in the office, joking with her about rat poison, and driving with her in the moonlight. I find myself wanting to swoop in and solve all her problems. Threatening the contractor giving her the run-around, doing her books, arranging for Paulina to step in when her cleaning service didn't show up, insisting she take Ibuprofen after her fight—I would do those things all over again and *more*.

I could have fended Maria off by myself. So why did I involve Ali in the pretense? Because deep down inside, I wanted to kiss her.

I want to be with her. I'm searching for excuses to spend time in her company.

I want... *everything.*
This feels a lot like the beginning of love.
And it is *terrifying.*

26

ALINA

G oing to a sex club with Tomas is *reckless.* It's crazy, impulsive, and insane.

And I'm going to do it anyway.

This isn't the same situation as Simon, I argue, trying to justify my decision. *He's already told you that he isn't planning on sticking around. As soon as the gym is satisfactorily profitable, he's going to sell his share. Would it be the worst idea in the world if I went out with him?*

No, my body responds, held in thrall to Tomas. It's not a bad idea. It's very, *very* good. My skin tingles from his nearness, and I feel restless and very, very aware of his every movement. I stare at the screen, trying to form the words needed for this email, but my mind is too clouded by desire to focus.

Tomas drains his coffee. "I should go," he says abruptly. "I should try to get some sleep."

"Sleep." I picture our bodies entwined on a bed, and it nearly takes my breath away. "Yes, that's a good idea."

With difficulty, I push the lust down. "Are you going to be in tomorrow?"

He shakes his head. "No, Ali," he says, his voice strained. "I don't think that's a good idea. I'm going to work remotely on your books. I'm almost done with the clean-up. Once that's done, I'll send you some names for trustworthy bookkeepers."

"Right." My heart gives an odd thud at his words. He was all in until I gave him the coffee, and now he can't wait to get out of here. "That's a good idea. You probably didn't intend to sign up as the resident bookkeeper when you bought Simon's share." Tomas is sending me a message, loud and clear. Whatever is going on between us is about sex and only sex. He's not interested in intimacy or anything else.

And neither am I.

I watched six YouTube tutorials about how to make a perfect café bombon. I shouldn't have done it. It was too personal a gesture. Too intimate.

Message received, Signor Aguilar.

I exhale through the inexplicable stab of disappointment. "Now, get out of here. Text me if you need anything."

He gives me a searching look, one I return with a cheerful smile. "See you on Friday?" he asks. There's a trace of hesitation in his voice, one I'm unused to hearing.

"Sure." I can go to sex clubs and have meaningless sex with my business partner. I'm a fighter; I've been one all my life. I know how to protect my heart.

Lidya calls me later that night. "Congratulations," she says. "There's twelve hundred euros in my bank account thanks to you, and it's going to pay for my flight to Addis."

"Thanks for getting me in." I'm one hundred and forty thousand euros richer as a result of this fight. I owe Lidya many drinks. "I really appreciate it. You didn't get in trouble, did you?"

"For what?" she asks with a chuckle. "For betting on you? I thought someone might say something, but then your boyfriend bet ten grand on you, and it totally took the heat off me."

"He's not my boyfriend. It's just casual sex." That we haven't even really had yet.

"Really?" she asks skeptically. "That's not what I hear. Samia said, and I quote, 'He looked at her as if she was the only woman in the world that mattered.'"

My heart does that odd thud again. If only it were true. But it's not. We're going to a sex club on Friday. And while I do want to go to Casanova, let's be clear; this isn't exactly romantic, first-date material.

"Samia's looking at the world through rose-tinted glasses," I reply. "Trust me, it's casual. If he was looking at me at all, it's because I made him a hundred and twenty thousand euros."

But that's not true. Tomas bet with the gym's money, and he deposited the winnings into the gym's bank account.

Why?

If he thought I'd win—and he certainly seemed pretty confident about it—why did he invest the gym's money instead of his own? Why did he give me the lion's share of his winnings?

Is there a message here, and if so, what does it mean?

For fuck's sake.

One of the unexpected benefits of my mom being sick was that I didn't have time to date. I was too busy being a caregiver. I'd occasionally go out with my coworkers, and the conversation always came around to the guys they were dating. The beautiful, strong women I worked with would spend the entire evening obsessing about the men in their lives. Why they acted the way they did, why their actions always fell short of the words they uttered. They would show me the thoughtless texts these guys sent and ask me what they meant. Every word would be thoroughly and painfully dissected; every action endlessly analyzed.

Whenever I hung out with them, I used to feel like I'd dodged a bullet.

Except now I'm doing the same thing. I'm obsessing over Tomas, a man who's made it clear, by his words *and* actions, that he's not interested in getting involved.

I don't think I'm going to hear from Tomas until Friday, but to my surprise, he texts me a couple of hours after I open on Monday.

> Any complaints about the double-billing?

> Only one. I got really lucky.

Gerald, the finance influencer, spent ten minutes bitching about my incompetence, but I bit my tongue and offered him a free month, which took care of the problem.

> Would it be tactless to point out I predicted that this would be a non-issue?

> Yes.

> Hmm. Well, then pretend I didn't say it.

His next message comes an hour later.

> The couch in the lobby is disgusting. Use some of that money I won you and buy something better before someone catches an STD off it.

> You're an expert in STDs now, are you? Is that the voice of experience talking?

> If that's a roundabout way of asking me to fuck you on that gross couch, Ali, I can be talked into it. As long as you don't take it personally when I shower in bleach afterward.

I laugh out loud.

> Fine, I'll buy new furniture. Point of clarification though: I did all the fighting, so I believe it's money I won, not you.

> Sadly, that's not how betting works, dolcezza.

I GET another text at nine in the evening on Tuesday.

> You're still at work, aren't you?

> Yes, why?

> You probably started at six in the morning, and you should be done by now. Hire someone to staff the front desk before I do it for you.

I should be annoyed by the bossiness, but there's an undertone of concern there that's really sweet. Like the ibuprofen in Milan, and insisting he give me a ride home. His directives always come from a place of caring, and they warm me up from the inside.

That doesn't mean I'm going to roll over for him.

> I think you need a contract refresher. According to Section 4, neither party may make hiring decisions unilaterally.

> You're quoting my own contract at me? Seriously?

I smile smugly.

> Can dish it out but can't take it? Goodnight, Tomas.

Someone comes up to me to ask a question, and I set aside my phone. But the rest of the evening, I can't stop smiling. Our banter always leaves me feeling fiercely alive. It's only been a couple of weeks since we met for the first time, but already, I can't remember a time when Tomas wasn't part of my life. Bossing me around, checking up on me, making sure I'm taking care of myself. He doesn't ride roughshod over my wishes—no, he makes me feel supported and cared for.

And it's been a long time since anyone make me feel that way.

TOMAS ISN'T the only person in my thoughts. I've been avoiding thinking about Vidone Laurenti, the man who says he's my father, but he's always there, lurking in the background of my mind. I don't feel excited when I think about him—no, my only emotion is a cold, gnawing uncertainty. I have too many unanswered questions. Why did my mother run away? Why did she hide my existence from Vidone?

But my mother is dead, and I can't ask her why. If I want answers, only one person can give them to me.

It isn't until Wednesday that I finally summon up the courage to call Vidone. With shaking fingers, I bring up my contacts and scroll to his name. My thumb hovers over the entry, as I talk myself into moving forward. What if he doesn't answer? What if he does? What if this changes everything?

Taking a deep breath, I press the Call button.

It rings four times. No, five. I doodle ominous clouds on the notepad in front of me as I wait for him to answer. I'm almost ready to hang up when the call connects. "Hello?" a woman says.

"Hi," I say cautiously. "Could I speak to Vidone, please?"

"Vidone?" Her voice turns suspicious. "Who's this?"

Umm, what do I say? If this is his wife, I don't feel entirely comfortable introducing myself as Vidone's long-lost daughter. I don't want my existence to come as a shock. Well, any more than it already has.

"My name is Alina Zuccaro."

"Alina—" she starts before her voice is replaced by a male one. "Alina?" a man who must be my father says. "Is that you?"

My heart starts to beat faster. My grip tightens on my pencil. "Yeah." I start adding droplets of rain to the sketch. "It's me. Alina. Teresa's daughter."

"My daughter."

I bite my tongue to keep quiet. There are so many raindrops now that it's a veritable thunderstorm. For good measure, I add streaks of lightning. *Where were you when I needed you?* I want to scream. *Where were you when my mother was dying in the cruelest way possible? You don't get to call me your daughter. You haven't earned it.*

But I'm not being fair. Going by his letter, Vidone didn't know I existed until a few days ago. His story certainly has the ring of truth to it. My mother was secretive—there's no denying that. She never volunteered information about my father, and she actively discouraged me from asking questions about him. Even toward the end, when she stopped recognizing me, he never came up. It's as if she locked the memory of him into a vault and threw away the key.

"Yeah." I don't know what to say next. "I got your letter. Thank you for the photo."

"You're welcome." His voice turns warmer. "Tell me about yourself."

"Umm, you already know I live in Venice." I frown. "Wait, how did you know that? How did you know where to send the letter?"

My question must take him by surprise. There's a

split-second of hesitation, and then he says, "I looked you up on the Internet and found Groff's."

"Right. Of course." Simon spent a lot of time obsessing about search engine optimization. "I'm working on the SEO," he used to loftily declare whenever I railed at him about how he wasn't pulling his weight. "You wouldn't understand." I wasn't convinced; we never got the surge of members that Simon predicted, but it looks like it paid off in the end.

"Well, I moved to Venice two years ago." I search for something else to say about myself. It's harder than I think. I work too much, and I haven't had time for anything else for a really long time. "I've always wanted to live here. Umm—"

"Are you married?"

I try not to get annoyed. God knows I've heard that same question far too many times from well-meaning friends and acquaintances. "No."

"Seeing someone?"

An image of Tomas swims in front of me. "It's complicated."

"Complicated how?"

This is starting to feel like an inquisition, and I don't like it. "You already know about the gym," I say, pretending like I didn't hear his last question. "I've been doing martial arts since I was seven. I started with Brazilian jiujitsu and then moved to judo, and after that, Muay Thai. I've wanted to run my own gym since I was a little girl. Some days, it's a struggle, but most of the time, it feels like a dream come true."

"You sound very passionate about it."

Okay, better. He seems to have gotten the message

about laying off my personal life. "I am." I hesitate. "What about you? Are you married?"

"Yes. That was my wife you were talking to just now. Her name is Serena."

I swallow and dig my pencil into the pad. "And children? Do you have any?" I've always wanted siblings. As a kid, one of my coping strategies before my mom took me to the gym was to pretend I had an older brother who would punch anyone making fun of me. I even gave him a name—Christian.

"I had a daughter," he says. "She died."

"Oh God. I'm so sorry." What was her name? What was she like? I want to know everything about her, but I hesitate. I don't want to put my foot in it.

"Her name was Sabrina," he volunteers. "You would have liked her." He gives a little laugh. "This is a little awkward, isn't it?"

Thank heavens, it's not just me. "A little," I agree. "I guess I don't know what to say."

"Me neither. And it feels weird to do this on the phone. Why don't you visit? I'd love to have you."

I realize I know nothing about my father. "Where do you live?"

"Palermo."

That's all the way at the other end of the country. The island of Sicily, where Palermo is located, is in the south of Italy. I've never visited, though. Growing up, my mother always headed north on vacations. Never south. I'm starting to understand why. *She was avoiding Vidone.*

What happened? Why did it turn so sour that she never wanted to see him again? Why did she hide me from him?

"I can send you a plane ticket for this weekend," he continues. "Or even earlier. Why don't you stay with us for a week? I would love to get to know you better."

"This weekend?" I have to laugh. My father clearly has no idea what running a gym entails. Even if I hire someone to staff the front desk like Tomas suggested —*ordered*—it's going to take a few months for me to feel comfortable enough to leave for an entire week. Even the thought of being gone that long is giving me anxiety. "I'm afraid I can't do that." I take a deep breath and explain, not wanting him to feel rejected. "The gym is in a period of transition. We've lost a lot of members over the last year." Tomas thinks I'm being dramatic, but he's wrong. "I have a new partner, and we're turning things around, but now is not a good time for me to take time off."

He exhales in a long breath. "If it's money you want, I'm sure I can help out."

"What?" I sit up in shock. "No, that's not what I'm saying at all. I don't want your money." I just want what I've always wanted. *A family.* "It's my gym. I've poured my blood, sweat, and tears into it for the last two years. I just hired a new instructor, and I'm going to add on a few more in the next month or two." My voice softens. "I want to visit; I really do. Once things are steady here, I'll be able to take time off."

"When will that be?"

It's almost the end of September now. "November, maybe?" That seems really aggressive—November is only six weeks away. "Or December? December is always slow."

"November," he repeats, his voice flat and displeased.

"Or you could come visit me," I say in a rush.

"In Venice? That's complicated. Maybe..." His voice trails off. "Yes, maybe I'll do that. I'll call you back."

Then he hangs up.

I stare at my phone blankly. I don't know how I thought my first conversation with my father would go, but that wasn't it. It feels almost disloyal to admit it, but I'm a little disappointed.

28

TOMAS

I've taken to texting Alina every evening to make sure she stops working. If I don't nag her, I'm pretty sure she won't leave until closing, and despite what Alina thinks, other people can do it for her. Like for example, the new instructor she hired.

I'm just concerned about the business, I tell myself, though that's complete bullshit. This has nothing to do with Groff's and everything to do with the beautiful, stubborn woman running it.

And increasingly, I'm okay with it.

On Thursday, I message Alina right before I head to teach my accounting class at the Ca' Foscari.

> Go home.

> You're starting to sound like a stuck record, Tomas. How do you even know I'm at the gym?

I roll my eyes.

> It was a lucky guess. Stop changing the topic and go home.

> And if I don't, you'll quote the contract at me? As scintillating as that sounds, I'm leaving. I have no food in my apartment. I have to make it to the store before it closes.

> Good. Text me when you get back.

> That's definitely not in the contract.

> Text me anyway.

> It'll cost you. One hundred thousand.

I laugh out loud, causing several students milling about in the hallway to give me curious looks. The gym is Alina's baby, and she's going to take every opportunity to remind me she wants me out of there. And I love it. I love her relentlessness, her passion, her fire.

> Done. It's a deal.

Estela was beautiful in a fragile, ethereal way. She never saw me fight—fighting disgusted her. She would have swooned into a delicate faint at the first sign of blood. And she never made me laugh. She never saw the real me.

Ali does. I can lose myself in accounts and investment details, and she doesn't complain that I'm boring her. I can tell her I want to tie her up and her eyes sparkle with anticipation. I can suggest going to a sex club and she's all in.

With Ali, I don't have to pretend to be anyone other than who I am.

For five years, I've used the way things ended with Estela Villegas as an excuse to avoid intimacy. I've used my hurt as a shield and built a wall around my heart. The heart I thought Estela killed.

But maybe it isn't dead after all.

Maybe it's been lying dormant.

Waiting for Alina to walk into my life.

29

ALINA

I'm about to head to the small organic produce store around the corner when a familiar-looking woman walks into the gym. It takes me a moment to place her before I realize it's Gemma, the MMA groupie who used to work out in Rome. Her mother died, and she's been struggling to come to terms with the loss, the same way I did.

She gives me a wide smile. "You'll never believe what happened," she exclaims. "I found an apartment in Castello."

Oh, right. Pieces of our conversation come back to me. She was getting transferred to Venice, but she wasn't sure if she could find a place to live in time.

"That's great," I say, smiling at her obvious enthusiasm. Can't say I blame her—it's a rough rental market out there. When I first bought the gym, I intended for it to take up both levels as soon as I could afford the renovation. That was until I tried to find an apartment in Venice

It was awful. Every place I found was both crappy *and* expensive.

"Right? When the agency told me I got the apartment, I immediately threw my clothes into a suitcase and caught the next train. I went to my new home, tossed my luggage on my bed, and came straight here. I'm ready to fight. Sign me up, Alina."

I have to laugh. "Here's the membership form," I say, retrieving a clipboard from the cabinet under the desk. "As for fighting, Thursday evenings are not the best time for a sparring partner but let me see what I can find you."

"How about you? Are you too busy to fight?"

My stomach growls loudly, reminding me I haven't eaten anything since breakfast. "I'm afraid I can't today," I say regretfully. "I've been here since six in the morning, and I'm wiped. It's dinner, followed by something mindless on TV, and then bed for me. But I'll be here tomorrow morning and all day Saturday."

"I'm going to take you up on that." She tucks a strand of hair behind her ear. "Hey, if you need to eat, do you want to grab a slice of pizza with me or something?"

I'm too exhausted to be social. I'm about to turn her down when I catch a glimpse of her hopeful expression. It takes me back to my first weeks in Venice, all alone in a new city with no friends. "Sure," I say instead. "Pizza sounds great."

GEMMA INSISTS on dragging me to a small, out-of-the-way osteria in Castello. We walk there, crossing the Grand

Canal at the Ponte dell'Accademia and continuing through the narrow streets to the north of Piazza San Marco. "You know the city well," I remark as she leads the way, barely looking at her phone for directions. I've lived here for two years, and I don't think I've ever been this way. There are no tourist attractions along the route, and the streets are blissfully empty.

"I've spent hours in front of a map," she says with a laugh. "I want to blend in, look like a local."

"Good luck," I say wryly. "I've been here two years, shopping at the same stores all that time, and my grocer still treats me like an outsider. You're never truly considered a local unless you speak Venetian."

"I'm working on it. Ah, here we are."

The restaurant is small, and if I'm being honest, not that great. It's empty inside. There's only one person in the place—a sour-faced man who seems to be the proprietor, cook, and waiter all rolled into one. The pizza is lukewarm, and the wine has an odd taste. I eat everything on my plate, but it's only because I'm really, really hungry.

Gemma doesn't seem bothered by either the food or the surly proprietor. She orders a carafe of vino sfuso and keeps filling my glass every time it's half empty. By the time we're done with the food, I'm more than a little unsteady on my feet. "I'm drunk," I tell her with a giggle.

She smiles at me. "You are," she says, signaling the man for the check. "Come on, let's get you home."

My knees feel wobbly as we get up to leave. When we head outside, my head starts to spin, and I have to cling to the side of a building for a second until the wave of dizziness passes.

The sun set while we ate dinner, so it's dark outside. Castello is one of Venice's quieter neighborhoods. The Grand Canal is brightly lit no matter how late it is, but the streets here are shadowed and spooky. Fog descends over the canals, and it feels like it's going to rain. After the stiflingly hot restaurant, the fresh air feels glorious.

Home. Home would be nice. Climbing into bed, hugging the pillow, turning on something dumb on TV. It'd be nicer if I had something to hug that wasn't my pillow. Like my sarcastic yet protective new partner. But our date is tomorrow, not today, and anyway, calling him because I'm not feeling super great is veering into relationship territory, and I'm not going to do that. He's made it pretty clear that's not what he wants.

It takes my wine-addled brain a few minutes to figure out that Gemma is walking next to me, even though she lives in the opposite direction. And then a little longer to realize that she probably means to walk me home, a thirty-minute walk out of her way.

"You don't have to come with me," I protest, swaying a little. God, my head feels like it's going to detach from my body and float away. "I'm fine."

She gives me a probing look. "Are you sure?"

"I'm sure," I lie.

"Well, at least sit down for a little while." She leads me down a narrow street to the waterfront. We're a five-minute walk from the nearest vaporetto stop. Maybe I'll take a vapo home, I think as I sink down on a stone bench. It's dark here. The streetlight is out, and the air itself feels hushed. I lean my head back and close my eyes.

I must have drifted off. When I wake up, Gemma is

nowhere to be seen. I grope for my phone to see how long I've been asleep, and there's a bunch of increasingly worried messages from Tomas. I start to text him back, but my fingers feel numb, so I call him instead.

He picks up on the first ring. "Ali, thank fuck."

"That seems like a very un-Tomas thing to say. You're always so calm and collected."

"I've been trying to reach you for an hour."

"I went out to grab pizza with a friend." My mouth feels wooly. My entire body is in rebellion. I try to stand up and my legs give out. Back to the bench I go.

I'm half-expecting him to interrogate me about my friend, and I'm thinking of a snappy retort—something about him being jealous, maybe—but instead, he says, "What's wrong with your voice?"

"Have I ever told you that you're hot?" A boat is pulling up to the dock in front of me. Its lights are out, and the engine is cut. I frown. Something doesn't seem right about that picture, but I can't figure out what.

Tomas's tone sharpens. "Ali, where are you?"

I look around to give him a landmark. Two guys are climbing onto the dock. They're dressed strangely. It's still the tail end of summer, but they're wearing caps pulled down low. No, not caps. Ski masks. That's weird—it's far too warm for skiing.

"It's far too warm for skiing? What the hell does that mean? Ali, where are you?"

I have just enough time to say, "These guys are wearing them," before one of the ski-masked guys knocks my phone out of my hand and sends it flying to the canal.

He steps right up to me, a wicked-looking knife

shining in his hand. "I thought she was supposed to be unconscious," he complains to his partner. "On your feet, signorina. We're going on a trip."

30

TOMAS

The moment I finish teaching my class, I text Ali.

She doesn't respond.

Which is a little weird. I thought she'd be itching at a chance to remind me I now owe her a hundred thousand euros.

I make myself wait ten minutes and text her again.

Once again, nothing.

She was supposed to go to get groceries. She didn't go back to the gym after, did she? I'm not too far from Groff's —the university is only a short walk away—so I head in that direction, mocking myself the entire way there. *She probably just forgot to charge her phone. What are you going to say when you see her? Are you going to pretend you forgot something in the office? Idiot.*

This is starting to approach stalker territory, and I find *I don't care.*

I arrive at Groff's, and there are about a dozen or so people here, half of them lifting weights and the other half in a class being taught by Luke Barnes, Ali's new instructor. I watch for a little and grudgingly realize that he's a good hire. He's firm but patient, and he doesn't take himself too seriously. A little too good-looking, though.

Fine, I'm jealous. I admit it.

Ali isn't in the lobby, and she isn't in the postage-stamp-sized office either. I pick the lock of the door leading to her apartment with laughable ease—note to self: get her better locks—and knock at her front door loudly, insistently—but there's no reply.

My heart starts to race.

Where is she? I talked to her at seven, right before I headed into class. It's now a quarter after nine, and she's not at the gym or in her apartment. Where could she be? She didn't have plans for the evening; she was going to buy food and then head straight back home. She couldn't have forgotten to text me; one hundred thousand euros is riding on it, and Ali wouldn't pass up the chance to gloat about what a terrible deal I made. So where is she?

You're freaking out for no reason.

Maybe I am. But something about this situation feels *off*.

I call Valentina, the Venice Mafia's resident hacker. "I'm sorry to disturb you so late," I say when she answers. "But I need a favor. Could you locate someone for me from their cell phone number?"

"Sure," she replies. "Who?"

"It's Alina," I admit, feeling a little foolish. If word gets around, the guys will have a field day with it. Joao will laugh his head off. "I've been trying to reach her for the last half an hour, but she isn't answering her phone."

"She hasn't gotten in touch with you for half an hour,

and you want me to track her phone? Have you considered that maybe she's busy?"

Valentina sounds skeptical, and I don't blame her. "Please look. All my texts to her are unread. This isn't like Alina."

"Or maybe her phone died," Valentina says. "No, hang on, it's not. I'm getting a signal in Castello."

"Castello?" A sudden sense of dread fills me, and I start to move. What the hell is Alina doing in Castello? "Can you get me a precise location?"

"It's going to take me a few minutes. Hang on."

My boat is in Tronchetto, the opposite direction of Ali's location. Not enough time to get it. I hurry alongside the Grand Canal until I find a suitable speedboat moored to the side. Perfect. I cut the docking rope and jump in. It's only a moment's work to hot-wire the boat the way Joao taught me. Then I rev the motor.

Valentina's voice sounds in my ear. "Tomas, did you just steal a boat?"

"He did what?" I hear Dante say in the background.

I can't pay attention to them—not now. I speed north on the Canalasso and then turn onto one of the narrower canals that will take me to Castello. The moment I do that, I curse out loud. A gondola carrying a couple of lovestruck tourists is blocking the way, the ancient gondolier paddling at the speed of a snail.

I drum my fingers impatiently against the dash. "Well?" I bark into my phone. "Where is she?" Castello is a narrow slice of the island. "North or south?"

Valentina's reply comes after a moment. "North. Between Ospedale and Celestia."

Ospedale and Celestia are vaporetto stops. The

gondola finally turns into another narrow canal, clearing the way in front of me. Just then, my phone beeps.

Another call is coming through.

Alina.

"I'll call you back," I tell Valentina, then switch lines. "Ali, thank fuck."

She giggles. "That seems like a very un-Tomas thing to say. You're always so calm and collected."

Giggling? Alina doesn't giggle. Her voice is higher pitched than normal. Breathier. The hair at the back of my neck stands up. "I've been trying to reach you for an hour."

She giggles again. "I went out to grab pizza with a friend."

"What's wrong with your voice?"

"Have I ever told you that you're hot?" She's slurring her words as if she's had one too many glasses of wine. Is that the reason for the giggles? If she's drunk, I don't like the thought of her wandering around these streets at night. Antonio's made sure that Venice is a safe city, but even he can't control everything. This is a city with a lot of tourists, and one of them might be tempted to take advantage of her.

I've reached the open waters of the lagoon. "Ali, where are you?" I ask as I speed toward Ospedale on my stolen boat, my heart pounding. No doubt I'm being paranoid, but she's all by herself. Anything could happen.

She doesn't reply, not right away. Her answer, when it comes, doesn't make any sense. "So weird," she mumbles. "It's far too warm for skiing."

"It's far too warm for skiing? What the hell does that mean? Alina, where are you?"

My gaze snags on something that doesn't quite add up.

Venice is brightly lit at night. The city prides itself on it. On the Piazza San Marco, the ornate pink-glassed streetlamps are a famous tourist attraction. Even in quieter Castello, the docks are typically illuminated. But cruising past Ospedale toward Celestia, I see a section that is completely in the dark.

Why?

On instinct, I pull in for a closer look. Just in time to hear Ali say, "These guys are wearing them..."

The moon comes out from behind a cloud, and I see something that makes my blood run cold. Two black-clad men are on the dock, trying to get a struggling woman into their waiting boat.

It's Ali. They're *abducting* Ali.

Hot rage smothers me. Their craft is small but built for speed. I can't let them get her on the boat—it's too risky. In open water, in the dark, there's a strong chance I'll lose them. Only one thing to do then. I gun my motor, heading straight for their hull and bracing myself for the collision.

I leap forward onto the dock right as my boat tears through their escape vessel.

The impact sends a shockwave through the old, weathered wood, but I'm already moving past the wreckage, adrenaline surging through my veins. The first kidnapper doesn't even see me coming. I pull out my knife and stab his kidney, twisting the blade as I yank it back. He's dead before he hits the ground.

The other man has a knife. *A knife he threatened Alina with.* He lunges toward me, but I step out of the way and snap a high kick to his chest that sends him staggering back. He trips over a coil of rope and loses his grip on the blade. His eyes widen as he takes in his dead friend, and he scrambles backward as I advance, hoping to avoid the death that's staring at him in the face.

Then he wraps his hand around Alina's ankle.

I don't know why. I don't know if he's thinking he can use her as a shield. All I know is that the moment he does that, he signs his death warrant.

I yank the rope, pulling him toward me. "You dared to touch her?" I snarl. My reflexes are honed by years of relentless combat in the octagon. I grab his face and snap his wrist and then his elbow. He shrieks in pain, and Ali stirs. In the moonlight, I can see her face, and something clenches in my stomach. Her eyes are glazed, and her skin is pale.

Too pale.

This isn't a glass or two of wine. *She looks drugged.*

They roofied her?

One of the kidnappers, the one still alive, takes advantage of my momentary distraction. He comes for me, arm hanging limply at his side. I want to make him suffer. I want to carve him open like a turkey and watch him bleed out.

But Ali's scrambling on her feet, her body swaying unsteadily, and she needs me.

I snap his neck and fling his body into the water, rushing forward and catching her before she hits the ground. The moon shines down on her face, and she's never looked more beautiful because she's alive. She's so fucking precious, and she's alive. "Hey," I say softly. "Ali. Open your eyes, dolcezza."

She smiles at me, her eyes unfocused. "Tomas? Is that you?"

She's unharmed. "Yes," I confirm, relief shuddering through my body. "It's me. I found you."

Her forehead furrows in confusion. "Were you looking for me?"

I've been looking for you all my life.

The thought comes from nowhere and strikes me like a bolt. When the hell did this happen? And how? For five years, I've been nursing my wounds, using Estela's rejection as a shield. I don't date; I meet women at Casanova for short-term flings. For five years, I've been afraid of getting close to anyone. Afraid of being vulnerable.

But somehow, Alina's undermined my defenses. With her snark and her sass, her passion and her fire, her supposedly poisoned café bombon, *she broke through.*

And I didn't even realize it. Not until it was almost too late. She was right in front of me, and I almost lost her.

I let out a long exhale, and my heartbeat slowly returns to normal. "Come on, dolcezza. Let's get you to bed."

"Bed?" she purrs. "I *like* the sound of that. You're really hot, Tomas. I masturbate thinking of you all the time."

And before I can process that unexpected revelation, her face turns green, and she leans forward and throws up on my shoes.

31

TOMAS

She's seriously out of it. Her head is lolling back, and she looks like she's slipping into unconsciousness. I pick her up and gently set her down on the nearest bench.

My first call is to our doctor, Matteo. I quickly describe Ali's symptoms. "She's passed out on the bench," I say, resisting the urge to shout and rage. "I need you to look at her."

"Where are you?"

"Castello."

"And you said she threw up? That's a good sign. Take her home and put her to bed. Make sure she drinks plenty of fluids. I'll be there in an hour."

"Thanks, Matteo."

He doesn't sound too worried. He doesn't insist I take her to the nearest hospital. I make myself take a calming breath and look around. Shit. The dock is a mess. The collision I caused took out a support, broke the decking, and wrecked half of the railings. The structure looks like it's minutes from sinking into the water.

And then there's the dead guy lying a foot away from me. Plus, the one I threw into the canal.

In situations like this, there's a protocol to be followed. I'm supposed to call Leo and let him sort it out. Or, if he's unavailable, Joao.

But it's late at night, and Leo is newly engaged. I don't want to bother him with my mess, so I call Joao instead.

"Tomas," he booms. There's loud music playing in the background, and he's almost having to scream into the phone to be heard over it. "What's up?"

"I need a cleaner."

"One sec." The line goes silent as he puts me on mute. When he returns, the music is much softer. "Did I hear you right?" he asks sharply. "You need a cleaner?"

Cleaner is code. "Yes," I reply. "Book her for two hours." Two hours equals two bodies. I seriously doubt anyone is listening to our phone calls, but it's always a good idea to take precautions. "It's a bit of a mess."

"Send me your location. I'll be there."

I do that and turn back to Ali. She's half-sitting, half-lying on the bench. I sit next to her in my sock-clad feet—the loafers are covered in blood and vomit and are a write-off—and put her head in my lap. The kidnappers chose this point to abduct Alina because the surrounding buildings are warehouses, abandoned at this time of the night. Had we been in a residential neighborhood... That would have been a much messier situation.

I got lucky. Really lucky.

Who would want to abduct Alina, and why? It doesn't make any sense. It's not Groff—Leo has a surveillance team on the man, and I know he's in London, trying to con some Russian heiress into investing in his nightclub venture. Could it be Ciro del Barba? That seems extremely unlikely. Del Barba might not like paying out a hundred grand, but he's not going to commit a crime in Antonio Moretti's city for something that's pocket change for a man as rich as he is.

So who could it be?

I'm still trying to puzzle it out when Joao shows up. He made really good time—it's been less than fifteen minutes since I called him. He's not alone, either. Paulina is with him, as are a couple of her cleaners. She takes one look at the scene and gets to work.

Joao surveys the carnage with expressionless eyes. "Is she okay?" he asks me, gesturing to Alina.

"I think so." The adrenaline drains out of me. The last time I killed someone was four years ago, when Leo needed backup during a gunfight, and I was the only person available. "Matteo is going to meet me in my apartment to make sure."

"Good. You should take her home. What happened here?"

"Two men were trying to abduct Alina." I nod in the direction of the man sprawled on the dock. "That's one of them. The other is in the canal."

"Why were they trying to abduct her?"

"I don't know."

"You should have left one of them alive for questioning," Joao says, stating the obvious.

"I wasn't thinking straight."

A smile twitches at the corner of his lips. "Clearly," he agrees, looking like he's trying not to laugh at me.

I ignore his mirth. "I don't think anyone heard anything." I look around at the surrounding buildings. "Nobody turned on a light."

"Don't worry—Paulina and I will handle the situation. Go take care of your woman. Dante wants to talk to you in the morning, by the way. He said the padrino will want a debrief."

I nod soberly. I killed two men tonight, and bodies are *inconvenient.* I'm going to have some explaining to do.

32

ALINA

I wake up in a strange bed, and three things dawn on me.

1. I'm completely naked.
2. There's a man sleeping next to me, wearing a pair of briefs and nothing else.
3. It feels like something crawled into my mouth and died.

I'm a second away from full-on-panic when I realize that the man in my bed is Tomas. Then, pieces of yesterday evening slowly start coming back. My mouth tastes like some kind of dead animal because I drank too much wine, and then I—

I threw up on Tomas's expensive, handmade shoes.

Oh. God. Kill me now.

I bolt out of bed—naked—and rush to the bathroom. I open cabinets until I find a toothbrush still in its pack-

TARA CRESCENT

aging. I brush my teeth vigorously and take a shower for good measure, scrubbing imaginary flecks of dried vomit off my hair and body. *Ugh.* It's been a long time since I've been drunk to the point of throwing up, not since my twenty-first birthday. I only remember drinking two, maybe three glasses of wine last night, and it shouldn't have hit me that badly, but it clearly did.

Ugh, ugh, ugh.

Did I text Tomas? No, I think I called him. A fragment of memory swims to the forefront. Did I call him hot? I'm pretty sure I did. I also draped my arms around his neck and drunkenly tried to shove my tongue down his throat. Another memory returns. He didn't want to kiss me, so I took off my clothes to seduce him. And when he started backing away, I burst into tears and demanded he sleep right next to me.

I groan out loud and cover my face with my hands. Running away from Venice has never seemed like a better idea. Or I could stay in the shower forever.

Unfortunately, the hot water starts to run out. I step out of the shower when it turns cold enough to be uncomfortable, dry myself off, and then realize that in my frenzy to cleanse the evidence of last night's sins off my body, I have no clothes to wear. With a sigh, I wrap my towel around me and tiptoe out of the bathroom. Perhaps if I'm really quiet...

Nope.

The instant I take a step into the bedroom, Tomas opens his eyes. He looks at me steadily for a moment, and then a smile tugs at the corners of his lips. His expression turns positively wicked. "Going somewhere, Ali? You weren't going to leave without saying goodbye, were you?"

"I absolutely was." I take a deep breath to apologize and feel my towel start to come loose. I grab it with a white-knuckled grip. "Can we just pretend last night didn't happen?"

He chuckles, the sound smooth and rich, like a fine aged whiskey. Which I'm never going to drink because alcohol is never passing through my lips again. "You want me to forget that you told me you want to sexy-wrestle with me?"

"I didn't say that." Oh shit, I did. *You are a colossal idiot, Ali.* More memories return from last night. Tomas holding my hair back while I retched into the toilet. Sitting next to me on the bed and feeding me spoonfuls of hot broth, wrapping his arm around me and holding me tight. "I am never drinking again. Ever. From now on, it's kale smoothies for me."

His eyes laugh at me for a moment, and then he props himself up on one elbow, his expression turning serious. "How do you feel?"

"Surprisingly good," I reply ruefully. "No headache, no hangover. I guess the universe decided that last night was embarrassing enough." I give him a sheepish smile. "Thank you for taking care of me, and I'm really sorry I threw up on your shoes."

He waves away my gratitude. "You said you had pizza with a friend. Who?"

"Gemma. She's a new member." Actually, now that I think about it, I can't remember if Gemma filled out the paperwork. I handed her a clipboard, but did we leave for pizza before she completed it? "She lives in Castello."

"How much wine did you drink?"

"Gemma ordered a carafe of vino sfuso," I say, frowning as I try to remember the specifics. "It was three-quarters of a liter, I think. She kept refilling my glass before it was empty, but even so, I couldn't have drunk more than three glasses. It just hit me harder than usual." I look at his face. "What?"

"When did you start feeling off?"

Is Tomas annoyed he had to take care of me? I don't blame him. He's acting a little strange, and I don't know what's going through his mind. I wish he'd just tell me.

"When it was time to leave. I stood up, and I was all woozy. Gemma offered to walk me home, but I shooed her off. Then I sat down on a bench..." My voice trails off. Did something else happen? I can't shake the nagging sensation that I'm forgetting something else. But as much as I try to remember what it was, the fog doesn't clear. My memory is happy to offer up every mortifying thing I said or did to Tomas, but it's pretty blank on everything else. "I think I texted you after that. And then I woke up here." Shit. Judging by the daylight flooding into the room, it's mid-morning. "The gym," I blurt out. "I wasn't there to open."

"Your priorities might be slightly skewed, dolcezza. Relax, I took care of it. Omar opened the gym this morning. He'll be there all day. As for your classes, your pretty boy instructor is going to cover them."

"His name is Luke," I reply on autopilot. Who's Omar? Not important now. I swallow and shuffle my feet. "Thank you for taking care of me," I say awkwardly. "And for putting up with Drunk Ali." We were supposed to go to

Casanova tonight, but I'm guessing Tomas isn't going to want to. He's not even looking at me—his attention seems to be fixed on the ceiling. After last night, I'm sure any sexual attraction he was feeling toward me is pretty much dead. "You were very kind. If you could help me find my clothes, I'll get out of here."

"What's the hurry?" He flashes me that smile again, the one that ignites a fire deep in my core. "You made a lot of promises last night, dolcezza. You're not going to stick around to fulfill them?"

He's being kind again, pretending he still wants me. But I know better. "Tomas, it's really nice of you, but you don't have to do this. You can't even look at me. I'm going to get dressed and—"

"I'm trying hard not to look at you," he interrupts harshly. "Because if I do, Ali, I'm going to want to yank that towel down. I'm going to want to press you against the wall, spread your legs and lick you until you're begging me to come. If I keep staring at the sight of you, dressed in a towel and nothing else, any bit of self-control I have is going to snap. I'm going to wrestle you to the ground and fuck you hard. That's why I can't look at you, dolcezza. Because I want you too damn much."

The sheet has fallen off his body during this impassioned speech. I stare at the hard bulge of his erection, and my mouth goes dry with need.

I don't want to wait until tonight.

I can't wait another moment.

I'm burning up inside.

I've been burning up inside from the day Tomas first came to my gym in his bespoke suit and handmade loafers, looking like the walking, talking embodiment of sex.

"Do it," I whisper, easing my death grip on the towel and letting it fall to the floor. "Fuck me hard." I take a step closer and tilt my head up. "Please?"

33

TOMAS

She doesn't remember the men trying to abduct her. I should tell her the truth, *and I will*. But not now. I'm not proud of myself, but when Ali drops her towel, every good intention of mine goes flying out the window. I've fantasized about this moment for a very long time. And now that she's naked, I'm not strong enough to resist.

She was drugged last night, asshole, my conscience says.

"How are you feeling?" I ask again. "Given what happened last night, it's probably not the best idea for us to—"

Ali's gaze travels from my face to my crotch. I'm obviously hard. "I don't know what you're telling me. Are you saying that you don't want to have sex with me?"

I laugh disbelievingly. "No, I'm not saying that. But given your reaction to the alcohol..."

I don't want to use the word drugged—that's going to open up a whole can of worms. I *should* tell her that she was drugged and almost abducted, but I skate around the topic because I'm a selfish bastard who wants to sleep with her. Who wants everything she's offering and more. My conscience just wants to be reassured that she isn't feeling the effects of the drugs in her system, and then, all bets are off.

"Of course, I want to sleep with you." I throw off the sheet and get to my feet. My erection is straining against my briefs. "That should be pretty obvious. I'm just trying—desperately—to do the right thing."

She huffs impatiently. "I've already told you. I'm not hungover, I'm not dizzy, and I don't have a headache. Stop being so goddamn chivalrous and fuck me." Her eyes meet mine. "Or do I have to beg?"

Fuck, yes. My arousal ratchets up several notches at that suggestion. I push the last of my reservations aside. "What an excellent idea," I say silkily. "I would very much like you to beg."

A shiver runs through her body. "It's a good thing I'm in an obedient mood," she replies in a whisper. She looks up at me, her eyes luminous. "What would you like me to do, Sir?"

I can't take my eyes off Ali. She's so fucking beautiful. Her hair is a little damp from the shower, and it hangs down her back, the tips beginning to curl as it dries. Her breasts are full and high, and her dark rose nipples are hard. Her pussy is mostly shaved, with the exception of a tantalizing landing strip that begs for my mouth. My cock aches for her. I can't wait to thrust into her sweet, hot cunt. I want to hear her breath catch as I slam into her. I want to hear her plead for more and beg for permission to come.

"Be sure," I say harshly, trying one last time. "Soft and

gentle is not for people like us, Ali. When I fuck you, it's going to be hard and relentless. Before you say yes, be very, *very* sure."

"That's good," she replies pertly. "If you treat me like I'm breakable, I will knee you in the groin." She straightens, the effect lifting her breasts out and forward. Toward me. "Do your worst. I can take it."

My conscience has heard enough to be satisfied. She's here, she's willing, and she's naked. And I want to see just how obedient she can be.

"On your knees, Ali."

A small smile touches her lips. "Yes, Sir," she says.

She sinks to her knees, slowly and gracefully, and sits back on her haunches. My throat goes dry. "Stay there," I order, my voice hoarse. "I'll be right back."

34

ALINA

Tomas disappears to take a shower.

Argh.

It's a test, I remind myself. *You promised you'd be obedient, and he's seeing if you'll follow through.*

But I don't have to wait long before he's back in the room. I sense his presence behind me, my shoulder blades prickling. He watches me for a long minute, and then his voice breaks the quiet. "Crawl to the bed, dolcezza."

I make the mistake of turning around. Can you blame me? I want to see him naked. On Sunday, when Tomas made me come, he'd stayed fully clothed. I catch the merest glimpse of his long, thick cock before he makes a disapproving noise in his throat. "I thought you promised to be obedient, Ali," he chides. His voice hardens. "Do as I say *and nothing else.*"

A shiver rolls through me at his tone. "I just wanted to see your cock," I grumble, turning my head away again.

His rich chuckle fills the room. "You'll be seeing

plenty of my cock soon enough," he promises. "That was your first warning, by the way. The next time you disobey, you'll get punished. Crawl to the bed."

"How would I get punished?" If he didn't want me asking questions, he should have specified that. "Are you going to spank my ass?"

"No, I think you'd like that too much." I hear his footsteps, and then his fingertips trail lightly over my spine. "If you don't start crawling, dolcezza, I think I'll blindfold you."

I feel his touch like a spark. Goosebumps erupt over my skin, and my arousal ratchets up another notch. *Blindfolded*. It's an intriguing punishment, and for an instant, I'm tempted to provoke him so he does it. With my vision cut off, every other sense will be heightened. I won't be able to see where he is. Where he's going to touch me.

But I also won't be able to see him part my legs. I won't be able to see the desire in his eyes as he thrusts into me. I won't be able to see him unravel.

Obedience it is.

I crawl forward, intensely aware of Tomas behind me. Watching me. I make my way on my hands and knees, elongating my body, trying to make my movements slow, unhurried, and sensual. I've never done this before, and something about this act feels so wicked and simultaneously so vulnerable. It's about trust. I trust Tomas to dominate me in bed without judging me for my desires. I trust him to dominate me without letting it spill over into real life.

I crawl to the bed, my pussy slick and throbbing, my breasts swaying from side to side, my nipples tingling with heat. "Get on it," Tomas says. "I want you on your back, head on the pillow, hands gripping the headboard."

Why do I like this? Why am I more turned on than I've ever been? I don't know; I don't understand. All I know is that desire rages inside me like an inferno. One touch from him, and I will combust.

Tomas walks to his dresser. When he appears in my line of sight, he's holding a green silk tie in his hands. "I promised to tie you up," he says, his voice rough. "And Ali, I always keep my promises."

A thrill shoots through me. *Yes.*

I hold my wrists together as Tomas ties them together and then to the headboard. He has to lean forward on the bed to do it, and his cock bobs only a few inches from my lips. He's intimidatingly large. Eight inches long and so thick that I don't think my fingers will close around him. It sticks straight out, hard and flushed, bobbing as he works to knot me in place, and my mouth waters for a taste.

He finishes tying me to the headboard. "Can you move?" he asks. "Test them."

The bonds aren't tight enough that they're cutting off circulation. I tug and flex my wrists, but I can't free myself no matter how hard I try. Tomas watches me struggle, a smile in his eyes. "You're not going anywhere, are you?" he says, all cocky and confident. "I have you *exactly* where I want."

"You've left my legs free," I retort. "That's a really bad idea."

He laughs. "But I want you to fight back, Ali," he says, his gray eyes gleaming. "That's part of the game." His expression turns serious. "Rules of the game. You say stop, and I'll stop. If you don't ask me to stop, I'm going to assume you don't want me to."

"No safe word?" I tease. "Pity. I've come up with a perfect one. Asset."

His lips quirk at the reference to his stage name. "No safe word," he says. "We're not in Casanova; we're in my bedroom. You ask me to stop, and I will. Okay?"

He's waiting for my explicit consent. If he's being so careful about making sure I'm on board with the rules, then he's planning to be rough, really rough. And I can't wait. "Okay," I reply. "If I want you to stop, I'll ask." I lick my lips, anticipation making my body throb. "You want to fight? Me too. Show me what you've got."

He doesn't immediately respond. He stands at the side and stares at me, as if I'm a gift laid out for his approval. I look, too, my gaze greedy. Tomas's suits do a good job camouflaging what's underneath. Naked, his muscles are impossible to hide. I drink him in. He's got tiger claws tattooed on his chest, along with a dragon sinuously draped around a faded scar. His stomach is hard, his abs chiseled. The first time I saw him, I thought he was male-model pretty. I was *so* wrong. Tomas hides who he is under his bespoke suits and his calm demeanor, and he doesn't let people see him. I feel privileged to be the exception.

His fingers close around my ankle. I try to kick free, but his grip doesn't slacken. "These toenails," he says, a delicious growl in his voice. "These pretty pink toenails have been haunting my fantasies from the first moment I laid eyes on them." He sucks my toe into my mouth, and a bolt of heat shoots straight to my core. "All fury and fire and these pretty pink toenails. So full of contradictions, cara mia, and I can't wait to find them all."

I'm burning up. This feels so sensual. So erotic. "I'm full of contradictions?" I manage to choke out. "What about you?"

"Pretty pink toes," he continues, ignoring my words. "And a pretty pink pussy." He lets go of my ankle and climbs on the bed, moving over me and wedging a knee between my thighs. He wants me to fight back? I'll fight back. I part my legs slightly, and then I bring up my right knee to his groin. But even though I've tried to disguise it, he's expecting my move, and his hand blocks my kick. "So predictable," he says mockingly. "Is that the best you can do?"

"Fuck you." My angry retort dies away in my throat as he rolls my engorged nipple between his thumb and forefinger. He's not gentle. A sharp burst of pleasure-pain shoots through me, and I suck in a breath.

"You were saying?" His mouth follows his finger, and he sucks my swollen nub into his mouth. "I didn't pay enough attention to your nipples on Sunday," he murmurs against my skin, his teeth grazing my tender flesh. Fresh heat fills my core. "A failure I intend to rectify." He pinches and plucks and sucks until my entire body is throbbing, aching for more. My head falls back, desire coursing through my bloodstream, and he holds me down and trails a line of kisses down my throat.

I shudder and shiver and try to buck him off. He *likes* that. His eyes flash fire, and his mouth curves into a smile. "Have you forgotten I have sixty pounds on you, dolcezza? You're not going anywhere."

He's right; I'm not. "If you're so confident about that, why did you tie me up?"

He laughs. "I'm just enjoying the visual."

He positions himself at the foot of the bed and lifts my hips up to his mouth. "All week, I've been waiting to do this again," he says, his voice thick with anticipation. "And I intend to feast."

My hips jerk as his fingers part my folds. His tongue meets my pussy. He savors. *He feasts.* There's tongue and teeth on my clit and my lips. He tongue-fucks my opening and slides his fingers inside, searching for my G-spot, and all thought flees my brain. Nothing is left except searing hot pleasure.

He twists and turns his fingers until he finds that pad of flesh inside and presses down on it, sending a fresh wave of heat through me. I writhe as he licks and sucks with obvious abandon, my muscles clamping down on his fingers, a tight spiral building inside me. I'm close, really close. My nerve endings are on fire. Just a little more pressure from his insistent, maddening tongue, just one more thrust of his fingers...

He stops.

"No," he says, wiping my juices from his chin. "Not today. Today, dolcezza, you're going to come on my cock and not before."

"No," I yelp, almost screaming in frustration. I was almost there. I try and clamp my legs together, hoping the pressure will send me over the edge, but he stops me, his strong fingers wrapped around my ankles, preventing me from reaching the climax I crave. "It's not fair."

His eyes fill with dark promise. "We're in my bedroom," he says. "You don't make the rules here." He looms over me, a threat and a promise rolled into one. "Now, would you rather kick my cock or take it down your throat?"

My pulse pounds. "Down my throat," I whisper.

"Say, please."

Anticipation surges through my nerve endings. I don't hesitate.

"Please."

35

TOMAS

Her eyes are the color of dark chocolate. She's half propped up against the headboard, her hair mussed, her lips soft and full and ready for my cock. She scrambles my mind until there's only raw need left. Raw, primal need.

I cup her cheek. "You want me to fuck your mouth?" I growl. "Are you going to wrap those pretty lips around my cock and take it all the way down your throat like a good girl?"

She sweeps her tongue over her lush lower lip. "Yes, Sir."

Fuck, yes. She's ready for it, ready and eager. Bring it on, her eyes say, and I want to. But she won't be able to ask me to stop if my cock is buried in her mouth. "Can you snap your fingers?"

She tries it. "Yes."

"Snap them if you want me to stop."

She nods her understanding. I straddle her, my legs on either side of her chest, my cock in her face. Her mouth falls open in response, and fuck me, that's hot. She leans forward and delicately licks precum off my head with the tip of her tongue. I groan out loud, and she licks me again, my little tease, before taking my head into her mouth, her lips closing around my shaft.

I need more, and I need it now. I hold the back of her head and slide in deeper, rolling my hips forward. She moans in her throat and swallows around my cock, and the vibrations jolt up my spine. I start to thrust, my fingers tangling in her hair. Her lips stretch around my girth, and her mouth envelops me in its hot, velvety sheath. "You're going to be my good girl, aren't you?" I rasp, hitting the back of her mouth with each thrust. She gasps for breath, and I pull back until she nods for me to continue. My heart is racing in my chest as I thrust again, deeper this time, and hold my cock until she starts to gag, her eyes leaking tears.

I pull out and wait for her to protest.

She doesn't snap her fingers.

She doesn't tell me to stop.

I pull her up and place my hand on the back of her head. "Such a good girl," I croon, thrusting steadily into her mouth, my hand holding her in place so she has to take me. She swallows against her urge to gag, and the muscles in her throat massage my thrusting cock. She's making wet, sucking sounds, and they just make me hotter. My breathing turns shallow and uneven. My balls tighten. I feel feverish. I'm not going to last. I'm about to blow my load—

I pull out. "No," I snarl. "I'm not going to come in your mouth, dolcezza. Not today. I'm going to come in that sweet, tight cunt of yours." I take a deep breath, trying to steady my hammering heart. "Turn around. On your hands and knees."

She laughs and licks her lips like a satisfied cat. "I would have enjoyed swallowing," she says. "But I'm going to enjoy getting fucked even more."

"Brat." She gets into position, and I press my hand between her shoulder blades until they meet the mattress. I step back, taking a moment to savor the view. Her round, spankable ass, her plump pussy lips, her lush breasts pressed into the bed.

My throat goes dry. She's irresistible. I reach for a condom and roll it on with shaking fingers. "Hard and relentless," I remind her.

"Do your worst." She wriggles her ass at me, and I spank it, the sound echoing around the room. She moans in pleasure, but before she can open her mouth to ask me to do it again, I grab her hips with both hands, rest my cock against her opening, and thrust deep.

She groans into the sheets and grinds her hips into me.

She wants more? I'll give her more. I pull back and slam into her, spanking her ass again. I grip her tight and stroke deep and hard, my skin slapping against hers. Ali's muscles clamp around me in a velvety sheath, and her moans, gasps, and grunts *inflame* me. "You want this, dolcezza?" I slap her ass again. I want her to feel my cock in her body and soul. "Tell me. Show me."

"Fuck me harder." She sounds as ragged as I feel. She thrusts her hips back and clenches her muscles, and they grip my cock hard. Oh, fuck yes. I'm so close I'm shaking. The air is filled with the sound of sex, and it's taking all the self-control I possess to hold off on my orgasm. Not yet. I need to see her face.

I spank her ass one final time before I pull out and flip her over. Her hair is tousled, and her eyes are hazy with desire. "Please," she whispers. "I'm so close, Tomas."

"Me too." I look into her luminous brown eyes as I position myself between her thighs. "Me too, dolcezza." I thrust forcefully into her. "Me too."

I haven't had my fill—I might never have my fill of her. Alina Zuccaro is a drug, and one hit has transformed me forever.

He thrusts deep inside me, his eyes on my face.

If I had to describe Tomas to a stranger, the first word I'd use is controlled. He's not controlled now. His famed composure has vanished. His face is contorted with desire, and his eyes blaze as they rest on me.

He's looking at me as if I'm the only woman in the world.

And it's addictive. I want to capture this feeling in my hands and never let go.

My arousal spikes dangerously. "Ali," Tomas says my name like a prayer. His mouth crashes down on mine, and his fingers pluck my nipples again. "You know what you told me last night?"

Oh God, what else did I say? What secret truth did I confess? "Tell me."

His eyes glitter. "You told me that you masturbate thinking of me." He reaches over my head and unties my hands. "I want you to do it now. I want you to pet your pretty little clit while I fuck you hard."

If it were a request, I might be too embarrassed to fulfill it. But it's not. It's an order, *and I promised to obey.*

I flex my wrists to ease their slight stiffness, and Tomas gently but firmly guides my right hand to my pussy. His eyes rest on me, hot and heavy and hooded, as I graze my wet folds with my fingertips. He pushes into me, slow and steady, as I touch my swollen clit, my hips jerking at the contact. Tomas got me to the edge with his mouth and his tongue, and I'm so sensitive.

"I'm going to come," I whisper, feeling the familiar tight spiral build inside me.

He cups my chin and looks deep into my eyes. "Yes," he says, his lips finding mine. "Come for me, Ali."

He speeds up his thrusts, his breathing harsh and labored. My muscles start to convulse around him, and he hisses. "Yes," he says, his fingers gripping my hips. "Yes, fuck yes. Keep your eyes on me, dolcezza. I want to see you fall apart."

My orgasm hits me with the force of a tidal wave. I roll from one climax to another, barely aware of Tomas grunting out his pleasure as he comes. I stare into his gray eyes, and there's only one thought in my head.

This didn't feel like casual sex. It felt entirely too real.

I MUST FALL ASLEEP. When I wake up again, Tomas isn't next to me. I get out of bed and look around for my clothes, but they're nowhere to be seen. My handbag is on a chair, but my phone is missing. I frown. Did I leave it in the restaurant? No, that's not right. I have a clear memory of talking to Tomas after dinner. I was talking to him when—

I draw a blank.

My mind offers fragments of images, but when I try to focus on them, they disappear into thin air. Have you ever tried to remember a dream after you wake up and find that the harder you try to hold on to the details, the faster they dissipate? This feels like that.

Except this wasn't a dream. Something happened last night. I was too distracted earlier to dwell on the maddening gap in my memory. After all, I did wake up next to a shirtless Tomas, his hotness overriding every-thing else. But now, the questions are piling up. I went to dinner in Castello. Got drunk, sat on a bench, called Tomas. But why did I end up in his house? Tomas lives in Giudecca; my apartment in Dorsoduro would have been much closer. Why bring me here? And what happened to my phone?

There's a folded T-shirt on the mattress that I'm assuming is for me. I put it on—it hangs to mid-thigh—and head downstairs in search of answers.

Tomas is in the kitchen, his cat Freccia sprawled in a heap next to him. I enter the room, and she gets up and comes over to investigate, sniffing the air near me before sniffing disdainfully and resuming her nap. Tomas laughs. "That's my cat for you."

"I think you're maligning her. She's hanging out with you, isn't she?"

"She's hoping that I'll drop a piece of pancetta on the

floor." He shakes his head wryly. "Give her a treat, and she'll become your new favorite person."

I bribe Freccia. She daintily eats the treat from my palm and then demands petting. I oblige, looking around the large, sunlit space as I do so. Tomas's kitchen is filled with plants and gleaming copper appliances. At home, mine is the size of a closet. One day... One day, after I buy Tomas out, I'll find a proper apartment. I'll fill it with plants in colorful pots, fragrant candles, and walls of books.

Freccia decides she's done with me and leaves the room, her tail held high. I straighten, and Tomas holds up a mug. "Coffee?"

"Yes, please. What time is it?"

"A little after noon."

"Noon?" I repeat, shocked. The gym has been open *for hours,* and I'm not there. In the two years it's been open, that's never happened. "I need to head to Groff's."

"Why?" He hands me a cup. "Omar is handling it."

"Omar?"

"You know him. Average height, curly black hair, hangs out in the weights area."

I do know Omar. He joined the gym more than a year ago and works out at least four times a week, but he's very quiet, and he's never said more than a word to me. "How do you know Omar?"

"He works with me. He's one of Leo's guys."

I freeze, my cup midway to my lips. There's only one Leo I know. "Leo Cesari, the same guy who's engaged to my friend Rosa? That Leo? He works with you in the mafia?" The dots start to connect. "Hang on. You told me Simon made a pass at the enforcer's fiancée, and that's how you got involved. It was Rosa, wasn't it? Which makes Leo the mafia enforcer."

"Yes." Tomas looks unfazed by my obvious shock. "To speed this up, Rosa's friend Valentina, who I believe you've met, isn't a web developer; she's our hacker. And Dante, her husband, is Antonio's second-in-command. Daniel handles our legal stuff, and Joao, who has visited your gym at least twice, also works for us. And the doctor last night..."

"What doctor?"

"Matteo was here when we got back. You don't remember him?"

Now that I think about it, there *was* someone here. I can't remember his face, but he was kind. He took my temperature and told me to pee into a—

"Why was there a doctor here?" I demand, shock jolting down my spine. "I don't understand. I drank too much, and I just needed to sleep it off. Why did you call a doctor, and why did he need to take a urine sample? He took a urine sample, didn't he? I'm not imagining that part?"

"He did," Tomas confirms.

My head is spinning. What the hell is going on? One minute, I'm in a pleasant sex haze, and the next, I feel like the foundations of my world are cracking. "What aren't you telling me, Tomas?"

He sighs, his eyes troubled. "You weren't drunk, Ali. At least, I don't think so. I think someone put a date rape drug into your wine last night."

"But that doesn't make any sense. The only person who came near my glass of wine was Gemma. Why would she want to drug me?"

233

He looks at me steadily. "Do you remember the men trying to abduct you?"

"Men?" A frisson of alarm runs through me, and a fuzzy memory drags itself to the forefront. A boat gliding into the dock, its engine cut off, its lights out. Two men dressed in black coming toward me. I start to tremble. "I don't understand... Who were they? Why would they want to abduct me? Why would *anyone* want to abduct me?"

He puts his arm around me, and I lean into his body. His strength. He smells like sandalwood and soap, a clean male aroma that's both comforting and a turn-on. I know this is just supposed to be about sex, and I've already overstayed my welcome, but I can't bring myself to pull away. Right now, I need comfort in the worst sort of way, and Tomas is here, as solid as a rock, offering his shoulder for me to lean on. "I don't know," he says. "But I intend to find out. Matteo should call me in the next hour with the results of your sample."

"What about the men? Can we ask them?"

"They're dead."

I pull away from his embrace and stare at him. "They're dead? How?"

"I killed them," he says flatly.

My vision turns fuzzy around the edges. "You killed them," I repeat in disbelief. I open my mouth and close it. Please let this be a bad dream because I can't quite believe what I heard. "Why?"

"Because they tried to abduct you," he replies, his voice hard.

He's being so matter-of-fact. He's acting like their deaths are no big deal, and it's never been more obvious to me that we live in two very different worlds. Those men were alive last night, and they're dead now. Tomas killed two men, and he doesn't seem to care. Not at all.

Who did I just sleep with?

The way I'm feeling must be visible on my face. "Alina," Tomas says quietly. "I know this is hard for you to understand, but—"

I take a step back. "It's not hard to understand." I feel sick. Bile fills my mouth. I slept with Tomas less than twelve hours after he murdered two men. Even worse, I liked it. *I liked him.* "Why didn't you tell me earlier? Before I..." My voice trails off, and I can't finish the thought. "Why did you hide it from me?"

An expression of hurt flashes over his face. "I didn't set out to hide anything from you," he says. "I was going to tell you everything when you woke up. And then you dropped your towel."

That's a reasonable explanation, but I'm in no mood to hear it. Right now, all I want to do is flee. I take another step back. "I need to go," I blurt out. "Where are my clothes?" I'm not looking forward to wearing the vomit-splattered garments, but I can hardly go dressed in Tomas's T-shirt and nothing else.

"I sent them to the cleaners," he replies. "Paulina went shopping this morning, so..." He disappears from the room for a moment and returns with a paper bag. In it, I find underwear, a pair of yoga pants, and a new Groff's T-shirt, all my size.

"Thank you," I say grudgingly. *Who's Paulina?* "So, you're a killer but a thoughtful one?"

His lips twitch. "Your phone ended up in the canal

last night. Here's a replacement. Valentina synced it up, so it should have all your info on it."

Damn it, he's making it really hard to dislike him. From the day he walked into my gym, I've been trying my best to hate Tomas Aguilar, and at every turn, he thwarts me.

"Thank you," I repeat stiffly.

And then I leave.

37

ALINA

From the moment I walked into a martial arts class for the first time and found structure and discipline there, I've wanted to run my own gym. It's stressful running a small business, and it's a lot of work. But every time I walk into Groff's—I really need to change that name—it's felt like home.

Until today.

Tomas wasn't lying; his fellow mafia henchman Omar is staffing the lobby. A young woman I don't recognize is at the smoothie stand, whipping up protein-infused smoothies for the gym goers with a cheerful smile on her face.

Tomas strikes again. Any other day, I'd be tempted to pull out my phone and text him with a snide reminder that, according to the contract, he can't make hires without consulting me. But today, my new phone is another reminder of the events of last night. Another reminder that the men who threw my phone in the canal are now *dead*.

Men who were trying to abduct you. If Tomas hadn't intervened, what do you think would have happened? Where do you think you would have woken up this morning?

I'm not saying I'm not grateful, okay? I am very grateful for Tomas's help. I owe him my life. But I'm in shock. Tomas told me he was part of the mafia, and I should have taken that as a sign that I needed to keep my distance from him. Instead, I let his calm, even-tempered demeanor obscure the fact that he's a killer.

A killer who saved your life.

Luke gives me a friendly grin when he spots me. "Hey, Ali," he says cheerfully. "How's it going?"

For one hysterical second, I wonder what his reaction would be if I answered with the truth. Let's see, Luke, I imagine myself saying. I had the hottest sex of my life with a man who turned out to be a killer. Oh, he also owns half the gym, and one of his mafia enforcer buddies is at the front desk. For all I know, the perky blonde making smoothies is an assassin.

"I'm good," I say instead. "Thanks for covering my class this morning. Sorry about the late notice."

"No worries," he says. "I was happy to help. I forgot how much I enjoy teaching. Like I told your boyfriend—"

My what? I almost blurt out, and then I remember my petty display of jealousy in front of Sara earlier this week. Of course, the news has spread. If there's one thing my members like more than protein shakes, it's gossip. I brought this upon myself.

Luke is still talking, saying something about how he's ready to take on more classes and would I also be interested in hiring one of his friends? I promise to look at her resume, excuse myself, and approach Omar.

"Hey," I say cautiously. "Thank you for opening this morning."

"Of course, signorina," he replies with a smile. "I did what I could, but some members asked me questions I couldn't answer. I took down their information and told them you'd be in touch." He hands me a notepad. I scan it quickly, and as I suspected, most of the questions are about the email I sent out about the double-billing issue. Thank you, Simon.

I have a ton of work to do. There are classes to teach, bills to pay, emails to write. Member questions to answer. But I can't focus on any of it. The events of last night loom large. If Tomas was telling the truth, someone tried to abduct me. But why? I'm neither rich nor famous. I'm just an ordinary person.

The application form. "Has Gemma come in?" I ask, rummaging through the paperwork to find her membership application.

Omar's expression turns grim. "No," he says. "She has not."

I'm half-expecting a blank form, but it turns out that Gemma *did* fill it out. I pull out my new phone and dial her number, the one she listed in her application, but the call doesn't connect. "This number is not in service," an automated message says. "Please check the number and try again."

According to the application, her last name is Ridolfi. I google Gemma Ridolfi, and an Instagram profile comes up. I scroll through her posts, growing steadily colder as I read. All the details match what Gemma told me about herself. Her favorite city is Paris. Her mother died four years ago. She works out at MMA Roma, and is considering a transfer to Venice, but wonders if there are too many tourists in the city.

But when I look at her selfies, they're of a completely different woman.

Everything 'Gemma' told me about herself is a lie. Every single thing.

"Omar, can you cover the front desk for another hour and a half?"

"Certainly," he replies agreeably. "Get some rest, signorina. Take all the time you need."

He thinks I'm going to take a nap, and I don't bother correcting him. Instead, I turn around and head back out the door. I'm going to return to the scene of the crime. I need answers, desperately, and that's where I'm going to find them.

THE OSTERIA IS *GONE*.

I stare at the empty storefront with a tattered For Rent sign stuck on the dusty window. I was here yesterday—I swear it. I sat in that far corner and ate bad pizza with Gemma. We talked about travel, her desire to blend in, and her attempts to learn to speak Venetian. I liked her. I thought she could be a friend.

But there's no furniture inside the storefront. Nothing to show that I had dinner here. The battered wooden tables, the rickety chairs, the photo of James Gandolfini on the wall—all of it is gone. It's like yesterday never happened.

I fight the urge to burst into tears.

"Ali," a warm, kind voice says. Tomas puts his arm around my waist. "It's going to be okay, dolcezza. We'll get to the bottom of this, I promise."

He killed the men who tried to abduct me. I should be intimidated by the way he took the law into his own hands and terrified by his remarkable lack of remorse. But right now, when the very foundations of my world are dissolving, Tomas is here, his arm around me, offering me the support I desperately need.

"It was here," I whisper. "The osteria I ate at last night. It was in this empty storefront. I swear it was. Am I losing my mind, Tomas?"

"No," he says. "Joao ran the fingerprints of the dead men. They're career criminals from Rome, available for hire to the highest bidder. They've both served time for assault. One of them had twenty thousand euros on his person. We think it's the down payment for your abduction." He clenches his right hand into a fist. "Your friend Gemma was smart enough to pay them in cash. There's no paper trail for Valentina to follow, nothing to help us understand *why*."

I stare at him helplessly.

"I checked the security cameras at the gym," he continues. "Gemma was there twice, but both times, she kept her head down and her face obscured. She knew where the cameras were, and she took care to stay concealed. And Matteo called me ten minutes ago to confirm that you were drugged. Your urine sample had GHB in it. This wasn't random. This was the work of professionals." He guides me to a bench and makes me sit down. "Why would anyone go after you?"

"I don't know," I burst out. "This doesn't make any sense. I'm *nobody*."

He laughs softly. "Ah, Alina," he says, turning into me and cupping my chin with his callused hand. "You are a firecracker. A meteor blazing across the night sky. A tempest, wild and powerful. You are many beautiful things, dolcezza, but the last thing you are is *nobody*."

I stare at him in disbelief. Those words... No man has ever seen me the way Tomas does. No man has ever looked at me the way he's looking at me now, as if I'm the most important person in his world.

And I don't know what to do with it. I don't know how to process any of it. The last twenty-four hours have been too tumultuous. I feel achy and needy and deeply unsettled.

I wet my lip with my tongue. I need to focus on the abduction. Not on Tomas or the way he's looking at me. I need to stop remembering how amazing this morning was. I need to ignore the ache in my core, the hunger in my blood. "Could it be Simon?" I don't know why my former partner might want to kidnap me. None of this makes any sense. "Or Ciro del Barba? Maybe he was angry that you bet on me?"

"Antonio talked to del Barba this morning," Tomas responds. He's still cupping my chin. I want to close the distance between us. Stand on my tiptoes and kiss his lips. "It wasn't him. As for Groff, Leo has him under observation. He's currently doing his best to seduce a Russian heiress, but he doesn't realize she's also a con artist. It's not him either." He drops his hand, and I feel its absence like a loss. "Think, Ali. Has anything changed in your life in the last couple of weeks? Anything at all, no matter how unimportant."

"You bought Simon's share of the gym."

"My enemies, such as they are, wouldn't target you. That's not how these things are done."

"Wait, you have enemies?"

He shrugs. "Not really. My former boss, Alonzo d'Este, wasn't happy when I announced my intention to leave Valencia, but he's retired now. His son Gabriel is in charge, and I don't think we're enemies. In any case, abductions aren't his style. If Gabriel wanted to target me, he would ruin me financially."

There's so much to digest there that I don't even try.

"I don't know what else is new. Lidya got me into del Barba's underground fight, but you've already dismissed him from the list of suspects. The only other thing that's happened is..." My voice trails off. It's not that, is it? It can't be.

Tomas's expression sharpens. "The only other thing that's happened is... what?"

"I heard from my father." Every nerve in my body is on edge. "My mother never told me anything about him, but two weeks ago, I got a letter from him." A letter that was hand-delivered to my gym. At the time, I hadn't thought much of it. *But now...* "He enclosed a photo of him and my mother, taken more than twenty-five years ago. He said he wanted to get to know me better, and he invited me to visit him in Palermo." Disbelief wars with suspicion, and disbelief wins. *Of course it's not my father.* All my life, I've dreamed about him finding me. Telling me he loves me. Telling me he wishes he could have been around while I was growing up, but he's going to make up for all his years of absence. All my life, I've wandered around with a tear in my heart, one waiting to be healed by his love. "He can't have anything to do with this. He just *cannot*. That makes no sense."

"What's his name?"

"Vidone Laurenti."

Tomas's shoulders stiffen, and his face wipes free of expression. "Vidone Laurenti," he repeats flatly. "Alina, Vidone Laurenti is part of the mafia. He's the underboss of VDL, a mafia organization in Sicily." He takes a deep breath. "I think you'd better come with me."

38

TOMAS

Thirty minutes later, Ali and I are seated around a conference table in our headquarters in Giudecca. Antonio Moretti, the padrino of the Venice Mafia, is here, as are Dante and Valentina. Joao is here, too. The only member of the inner team missing is Leo, our enforcer.

"Should we get Leo?" Dante asks as we sit down.

Antonio shakes his head decisively. "He doesn't need to get involved in this mess; he has enough going on right now." He turns to Ali. "The last few hours must have been quite a shock," he says sympathetically. "This can't be easy to process."

Ali's been silent the entire way to Giudecca. But at Antonio's words, her back straightens. "It's not true," she bursts out. "My father *invited* me to visit him. We discussed a trip in November. He told me he was going to try to visit Venice earlier than that. He can't be responsible for last night. He just can't be."

Her shock is completely understandable. The truth is, I'm reeling too. If Ali is Vidone's daughter, she's a mafia princess. *Just like Estela.* And her father needs to marry his daughter off to secure a business alliance. *Just like Estela.*

I've fallen in love with Ali, *but I have a dreadful feeling of déjà vu.* I feel like I'm on the edge of a precipice, and even the slightest breeze will send me falling.

"I'm sorry," Antonio responds gently. "I really am. Perhaps it'll help if I tell you what I know." He steeples his fingers. "Vidone Laurenti works for Il velo delle lacrime. VDL for short. He's the VDL underboss."

"Tomas said that," Ali murmurs. "I didn't really believe him."

Antonio gives me a searching glance before turning back to her. "He's not lying. VDL is a relatively new outfit, mostly composed of former Cosa Nostra members. Your father is no exception. He killed his first man when he was fifteen in a robbery gone wrong, and a trail of blood has followed him since. Valentina has a dossier."

"Oh." She bites her lip. Her hands shake as she takes the paper file from Valentina, and she makes no attempt to open it. "How do I come into the picture?"

"Vidone had a daughter, Sabrina. A little over a week ago, she was killed in a car crash in Tunisia. Sabrina was engaged to Damir Malinov. Damir's father, Gregori, controls the Kutuzovo OPG." He sees her look of confusion and clarifies. "Russian mafia."

She still doesn't understand. Why would she? In her world, fathers don't use their daughters as collateral for business deals with Russian mafia bosses. In her world, people marry for love.

I explain further. "Sabrina is dead," I say, my voice harsh. "But if you are also Vidone's daughter, he's going to want to marry you off to Damir Malinov to fulfill the terms of the alliance. That's why he tried to abduct you."

"No." She stares at me, a world of hurt in her brown eyes. "I don't believe you. Abducting me and marrying me off to a complete stranger? This is crazy. He wanted me to visit, *that's all.*" She pushes the file back to Valentina. "All of this is conjecture, and I don't buy it."

My heart aches for her. I hear it in her voice—how much she doesn't want it to be true. Growing up, it was just her and her mother. I hear the loneliness that she keeps hidden, the longing for family.

But not all family is created equal, and Vidone Laurenti isn't the father figure of her dreams.

Antonio leans forward, his face harsh. "It doesn't matter whether or not you believe us. Laurenti knows by now that his attempt didn't work. He's already desperate enough to try to snatch you off the streets of Venice, and things are only going to get worse. In Venice, I can put guards on you, but my reach is limited outside the city. I could try to protect you, but I can't promise I'd succeed."

"What should I do?" she whispers.

"Are you sure you don't want to marry Malinov?" I quip, keeping my tone light with effort. "After all, he's a rich and powerful man."

Her head snaps up, and she stares at me as if I were insane. "What the hell would I want to do that for?"

A weight seems to lift from my heart. Still, I keep going. "Money? Jewelry? Fancy vacations? Gregori Malinov owns a mansion in London, a villa in Barcelona, and more."

Fire flashes in her eyes. "You're joking, right?" she grits out through clenched teeth. "I'm wearing a T-shirt that's advertising my gym and yoga pants. No jewelry because it gets in the way during a fight, not even earrings. Do you think any of those things are important to me? And then, this morning—" She stops herself abruptly. "I'm not interested in marrying anyone, rich or not."

This morning... what? What was she going to say? How was she going to finish that sentence?

"I have an idea." Dante speaks up for the first time, and we all turn our attention toward him. Dante's nickname is the Broker—making deals is what he does. "Call your father. He won't come to Venice, so offer to meet him at a neutral venue. Someplace outside Italy. Valencia, for example." He looks pointedly at me before turning back to Ali. "And if he brings up Malinov, either now or when you're there, you'll know the truth."

"And if you're right?" Ali asks. "What's to stop him from kidnapping me in Valencia? What if I wake up in Moscow, married to a stranger?"

Kutuzovo is based in St. Petersburg, not Moscow, not that it's relevant.

"Two reasons." Dante counts off on his fingers. "First, Tomas will be going along for protection. And second, the two of you are going to get married first."

"What?" Her mouth falls open. "No way. I'm not going to marry Tomas."

Her response isn't a surprise, but it leaves a sourness in the pit of my stomach. I push her rejection down deep inside. "What about pretending we're engaged?" I suggest. "Dante's right. You can't go into that meeting alone. And the presence of a fiancé might give Laurenti pause."

There's a long moment of silence. Finally, she nods reluctantly. "Okay. I'll do it."

39

ALINA

Six hours later, I'm still reeling.

Valentina discovered an MMA conference that was going to take place in Valencia next weekend. Watched by Antonio Moretti and his henchmen, I called my father and told him I was going to be there. "I know it's short notice," I said hesitantly. "But I'm only planning on attending a few sessions. If you could make it to Valencia—"

I didn't even have time to finish my sentence before he cut me off. "I'll be there."

So that's done.

I'm back home in my apartment. I've lost track of time, but it's dark outside. I sit on my couch, a cup of herbal tea cradled in my hands, and stare into space. I should be thinking about Vidone and the fantastical story that Antonio Moretti told me about a business deal that will be sealed by my marriage to a Russian Bratva

Instead, I'm thinking about Tomas, and my insides are a mass of hurt.

We slept with each other this morning. We've worked together for two weeks. We've bickered and lobbied insults at each other. We've fought each other. He bet ten thousand euros that I'd win my underground MMA fight. He saved me from being abducted; he killed two men for me.

I thought we meant something to each other. I thought we were... friends, maybe, although friendship doesn't even begin to cover the complexity of our relationship. Friends with benefits? Enemies who bicker a lot but are secretly always there for each other and who also sleep together?

Whatever label you put on it, I thought Tomas *knew* me.

But then, less than twelve hours after the best, most intimate sex I've ever had in my life, he sat at that conference table, as calm as ever, and asked me if I was sure I didn't want to marry a complete stranger. Less than twelve hours after we slept together, Tomas implied I'd jump at the chance to marry someone because of what they could *buy* me. Vacations. Fancy cars. Diamond jewelry.

If Tomas really believes I'm tempted by the prospect of marrying Damir Malinov, he doesn't know me at all.

And whatever I thought we had was a lie. The affection in his eyes when he looked at me—I was imagining it.

I wanted someone to lean on so badly that I made it all up. Pathetic, needy fool that I am, I confused Tomas's support with caring. But he's been clear about the reason right from the start. It's all in the contract. If he's concerned about me at all, it's because I'm running Groff's. He's put more than a million euros into the gym, and, like any responsible investor, he's protecting his investment.

I want to curl up into a ball and cry. I want to jump into a ring and fight until my hands are raw and bloody, my face bruised, and my body aching from the repeated blows.

But even that won't hurt as much as my heart does.

If there's a story of my life, it's that everyone eventually betrays me. Simon swore that he was committed to the gym, but he never did a damn thing. He let me shoulder all the workload. In the grip of Alzheimer's, my mother forgot my face, forgot she even had a daughter. If Tomas is to be believed, my father doesn't even want to know me. He needs a daughter to marry off to a Russian Bratva prince, and I'm conveniently there.

And Tomas? There is chemistry between us and a definite attraction, but Tomas has always made it clear what he really wants from me. He needs me to run the gym efficiently. Even if we end up in bed together—like this morning—he's perfectly capable of compartmentalizing his emotions. It's just sex to him. An itch that needs to be scratched. Nothing more.

The problem is me. When I want something, I go all in. I ignore the warning signs and dive into the deep end. I did it with Simon—who goes into business with a vacation fling? But I wanted the gym so badly that I didn't do any due diligence on my partner. Same thing with Tomas. I told myself at the start that I shouldn't get involved with him, and then, what do I do? I watch him solve my problems, one by one, starting with the contractor, Marcelo, and then *I get involved with him.*

Even now, I'm burying my head in the sand about his mafia involvement. Even though he killed two men last night, that's not what's making me sick to my stomach. No, I'm sitting here fretting because I've fallen in love with him, and he clearly doesn't feel the same way about me.

Enough brooding. I take a deep breath. Somewhere along the way, I've forgotten I wanted to buy Tomas out as soon as possible. But I need to recommit to that plan. I need to raise one point three million euros as soon as possible. Rosa's fiancé Leo is rich—maybe he'll lend me the money. Then again, he works with Tomas, so he'll probably take his side. Jon Burke retired as a very wealthy lawyer and is only involved in the Legal Aid Society because he feels like he has to make amends for being a shark attorney. Maybe he'll want to become a partner in a gym. Worst case, I could ask Ciro del Barba. I've only met the man once, but I get the sense that he'd find it funny to buy Tomas out. Yes, that's like jumping from the frying pan into the fire, but I'm willing to do it anyway.

My trip to Valencia is next weekend. I'm going to meet my father there. If he turns out to be loving and supportive, the parent I've always dreamed of having, then great. If he's trying to get me married off to some Russian guy, then I'll firmly point out that he's being ridiculous. Once I've got that sorted, I'll come back home and focus on what's truly important.

My gym, and wrestling control of it away from Tomas Aguilar.

I'M SURVEYING the contents of my refrigerator bleakly when there's a knock on the door.

I open it to find Tomas.

I contemplate slamming the door in his face, but as satisfying as that would be, Tomas has done nothing wrong. He's never lied to me. If my heart is broken, it's my fault.

I step aside silently.

He comes into my space. "No dildo today?" he asks, looking at my bedside table, laughter coating his voice. "Pity."

Haha. I'm not amused. "What do you want, Tomas?"

His expression turns alert. "You sound angry."

I'm angry, but not with him. I'm furious with myself. "I'm not. Why are you here?"

He takes a step toward me, and I back away. He stops immediately. "Are you afraid of me, Ali?" he asks quietly. "Is this because of the men I killed? I'm not going to apologize for that." He clenches his hands into fists. "But I'm not capable of hurting you, dolcezza. I would rather tear my heart out first."

I have many complicated feelings about Tomas, but fear isn't one of them. "I'm not afraid of you. I don't know why, but I'm not. I've never been."

He stays where he is. "But you're angry. I hear it in your voice."

Because you want this to be just about sex, and I've

been stupid enough to fall in love with you. "You still haven't told me why you're here."

"Two reasons. First, there's this." He takes a small box out of his pocket and flips it open. "If we're pretending to be engaged, you need a ring."

The ring is *beautiful.* The central stone is a deep blue oval-cut sapphire surrounded by a halo of small, sparkling diamonds. The warm gold setting is intricate, carved filigree work that looks fragile and delicate and oh-so-beautiful.

My heart stops in my throat.

"Dante suggested that I ask you to marry me over dinner in a busy restaurant," he says. "The more witnesses to our engagement, the better. But I didn't want to make a production of it."

I wouldn't have wanted to make a production of it, either.

He looks into my face. "Yes?"

I nod wordlessly, trying to stop myself from crying.

He slips the ring over my finger. "It fits perfectly." Some unnamed emotion flashes over his face. "I don't know why I'm surprised."

I stare at the sapphire for a long moment. Everything is confusing. Nothing makes sense. I wish I understood what was going on. "Was this the ring you bought for Estela?"

Maybe it's the reminder of Estela, a woman he really wanted to marry. Maybe he's contrasting that actual proposal with this fake one. But when he answers, his voice is clipped. "No, it's not."

"You said there were two reasons. What's the second?"

"We had a date tonight, remember?" He surveys my

messy hair and crumpled T-shirt. "But I guess not. Casanova? Do you still want to go?"

This is what it must feel like to be stabbed through the heart. This sharp, specific pain that goes through me when Tomas invites me to go to a sex club with him.

I take a deep breath. And then another. There's a breathing routine I go through before a fight to clear my thoughts and focus my attention on the ring, and I deploy it now. Because I'm not going to cry in front of Tomas Aguilar. "I don't understand you," I say, my voice as light as I can make it. "We slept together *this morning*. Yes, it's casual, this thing between us. We're not dating; it's just about sex. But even so. Did you really think I would be interested in marrying some random Russian guy?"

His lips tighten.

"You thought I'd marry some stranger because of what he could buy me?" I continue. "Is that really what you think of me? Because if it is—"

"It's not," he cuts in, his voice harsh. "You have every right to be angry. It was an *unforgivable* thing to say."

I thought he'd deny it. Or bluster or defend himself. But I should know by now that that's not who Tomas is.

I still don't understand *why*.

"Then why did you say it?" I whisper.

His expression is strained. "Because of Estela," he says. "Her father was a high-ranking member of the cartel. She was meant to marry a man he picked out. When I found out who your father was..." He rakes his fingers through his hair. "I had to know."

I stare at him. I'd forgotten the details. He told me earlier this week, on that quiet, intimate drive back home from Milan, that Estela rejected him in favor of an arranged marriage with cartel royalty. It must have come as one hell of an unpleasant shock when I told him about my father. It would have felt like déjà vu in the worst possible way.

"I'm not Estela."

"I know." His eyes are affectionate. "You have more integrity in your little finger than she'll ever have. I'm sorry, Ali. All I can say in my defense is that I was reeling." He blows out a breath. "Do you want me to leave?"

Say yes, a cautionary voice whispers in my head. *To Tomas, this is still about sex, but you're falling in love with him. Turn him down. If you go to Casanova with him, it will only lead to heartbreak.*

But I'm not strong enough to resist the invitation in his eyes.

"What does one wear to a sex club?"

"Whatever you want." He smiles wickedly. "It's not going to stay on you for very long."

My cheeks color under the heat of his gaze. A warning bell rings in the back of my mind, but I don't hear it. My insides tighten with need. This morning was the best sex I've ever had, and I want more. Even if that's the only thing he's offering, I'm going to accept. I'm making a mistake, and I know it, but I'm not ready to stop. I want Tomas Aguilar too damn much.

"I like the sound of that," I reply, my pulse racing with anticipation. "Give me fifteen minutes to get ready."

40

TOMAS

Casanova? I don't give a shit about Casanova. I didn't come over to Ali's apartment because of our date—with everything going on, I'd completely forgotten all about it until she opened her door.

No, I came over to give her my abuela's engagement ring.

My grandparents were married for almost seventy years, and they were in love with each other to the end. I have fond memories of listening to my grandmother reminisce about meeting my grandfather for the first time. "Sebastian was such a good-looking man."

My sister Carlota, who had always been a romantic, would ask, "Did you fall in love with him right away, Tita?"

"No, mija," my abuela would reply with a laugh. "I didn't like him very much. He was polite but too reserved for me. Then, one day, we got into a fight—I don't remember what about—and I screamed at him at the top of my lungs. Then he kissed me, and that's when I fell in love."

Ana Isabel died the year before I left Valencia. In her will, she left my sister her wedding dress and me her engagement ring. I could have used her ring when I asked Estela to marry me, but I didn't. It was too old-fashioned, I reasoned, and Estela was the kind of woman who would prefer a large diamond.

But maybe, in my heart, I knew she wasn't the one.

And Ali is?

Carlota got married eighteen months after I left Valencia. She wore my abuela's wedding dress and looked radiant. I didn't attend the wedding. She has a son now, Adan, who is almost three years old. I've never met him in person. Valencia is a two-hour direct flight away from Venice, and I've never made it back home.

Until now.

The last time I asked a woman to marry me, things went spectacularly wrong. This isn't the same situation. This isn't a real proposal; Ali and I are just pretending to be engaged to thwart her father's plan to marry her off to Damir Malinov. And more importantly, Ali would never be as vicious as Estela. She might bristle with rage and bite my head off, my tempestuous dolcezza, but she's incapable of cruelty.

Still, I was nervous when I knocked on Ali's door. I made a joke about her dildo, and she wasn't amused. Worse, she was angry. And then, like an idiot, I mentioned Casanova.

Her words play in a non-stop loop in my mind. *It's casual, this thing between us. We're not dating; it's just about sex.*

Just about sex.

Casual.

She even flinched when I slid my grandmother's wedding ring on her finger.

I don't know why I'm surprised. Ali's been honest all along. She's made it clear from the first time we met that she wants me out of her gym. She even fought in Ciro del Barba's underground tournament so she could make enough money to buy me out. Neither of us can deny the chemistry between us, *but she doesn't want me in her life.*

And I don't belong there. My world is bloody and dangerous. I just killed two men without the slightest bit of remorse. I'm no good for Ali.

She disappears into her bathroom to get dressed. Fifteen minutes later, she emerges wearing a sleeveless black dress that clings to her curves. Her lips are red and full, and her hair hangs down her back in soft waves. "I'm ready to go," she announces.

She looks beautiful, and I want to tear that dress off her body. I'm about to tell her that when a disquieting thought strikes me. "You don't have to come to the club if you don't want to," I say gruffly. "You're under no obligation to me. I promised to help you with this situation, and that's what I'm going to do. My support isn't conditional on whether or not we fuck."

She gives me a very peculiar look. "I know that, Tomas. If I thought you were going to blackmail me into sleeping with you, I wouldn't want your help." She tilts her head to the side, an impish smile on her lips. "Maybe I'm just looking for a repeat of this morning, or maybe I want to know what you fantasize about."

"Isn't that obvious?" She's a drug in my veins, and I'm

craving another dose. "*You.* I fantasize about you. Always." I offer her my hand. "Let's go."

Her stomach rumbles loudly as we make our way down the stairs. "Haven't you eaten yet?" I demand with a frown.

"No," she admits. "I drank some tea earlier and got a smoothie downstairs for lunch, but—"

It sounds like she hasn't eaten all day. And this morning, instead of offering her breakfast, I fell on her like a starving animal. "In that case, we should stop for dinner first. What would you like to eat?"

"Anything except pizza," she replies with a wry twist of her lips. "After last night, I think it's going to be awhile before I crave it again."

I don't laugh. Her words are a reminder that I almost lost her last night. "I know the perfect place."

I TAKE her to a small tapas restaurant near the university. It's one I frequent fairly often. The decor is simple, but the food is Spanish and extremely good. The proprietor, Monica, greets me warmly. "Buenas noches, Tomas. ¿Qué tal?" Not waiting for an answer, she bustles away to get us water.

Ali looks at me curiously. "You come here often?"

"At least once a week."

Monica re-appears with a bottle of water and two glasses. She smiles at Ali. "You want to order from the menu or be surprised?"

"I don't know?" She looks at me for guidance.

"I always ask to be surprised."

"Then I'll do the same thing, thank you."

The proprietor nods in approval. "I'll be right back with some bread," she says and disappears into the kitchen again.

When she's out of sight, Ali smirks at me. "I would have thought you were too much of a control freak to allow yourself to get surprised."

"You're about to find out how much of a control freak I can be at Casanova."

If I'm expecting Ali to back down, I should really know better. Her eyes sparkle with anticipation. "I'm looking forward to it."

The conversation over dinner stays light. As always, the food is delicious. Ali particularly likes the tortilla de patatas. "This is delicious," she says. "Does the food here remind you of your mother's cooking? Is that why you come here so often?"

"Not my mom. My sister is the chef in the family. When Carlota was nine, she threw a tantrum, refusing to eat what my parents cooked and announcing that she could make a better meal. She's been handling kitchen duties ever since. My parents kept worrying that they were exploiting her, but Carlota loves feeding people."

She tilts her head to the side. "This might be the first time you've talked about your family. What was your childhood like?"

"Normal. Happy." I don't want to talk about my family right now. "Did you like being tied up this morning?"

She blinks at the sudden change in subject and glances around to see if Monica is within earshot before she replies. "Yes," she murmurs, her voice low. "I did. But you already knew that."

That's interesting—Ali is *shy*. And because I'm an evil bastard, I intend to have a lot of fun with that.

"What someone enjoys in the moment and how they feel about it afterward aren't always the same. No reservations?"

"None." She wets her lower lip with her tongue. "Are you going to tie me up at Casanova?"

I'm going to tie her up and so much more. Anticipation dances through my veins. Her plate is empty, and so are the dishes in front of us. "Are you done?" I ask gruffly, signaling Monica for the check. "Let's continue this discussion at the club."

41

ALINA

Casanova is nothing like what I expected. I knew the memberships were expensive, but it's still a sex club, and I guess I assumed it would look ever-so-slightly seedy.

I was very wrong. The space is luxurious but not ostentatiously so. Gold chandeliers offer dim but warm lighting. The carpet is plush, and people are elegantly dressed. If I didn't know what Casanova was, I'd assume this was an upscale lounge where the rich and beautiful hung out. "Nobody is walking around naked with a collar around their neck," I whisper to Tomas once we surrender our phones and enter the club. "In fact, nobody is naked. I thought there'd be a lot more of that."

He chuckles. "It's early by club standards. Give it time."

An attendant leads us to a booth in the back. I gawk as I follow her, drinking in everything. To my left, a long bar lines the wall. A man sitting there alone nods to Tomas in greeting. A pair of women chatting with the bartender stop their conversation and openly check him out as we pass by. My lips tighten at their blatant once-over, and I reach out and link my arm with his in a proprietary manner. *Back off, ladies. He's mine.*

Even if it's only for tonight.

We pass the dance floor and reach our booth. I slide in, and Tomas sits across from me. "Enjoy your evening," the attendant says. "Please ring the bell if you need service. Can I get you started with something to drink?"

"Sparkling water for me, please," Tomas replies. "Slice of lemon."

"I'll have the same."

I have so many questions for Tomas. I wait until our server delivers our drinks before peppering him with them. "How long have you been coming here?"

"Since I moved to Venice," he replies. "If you're looking for a certain type of sex, and you don't want a relationship, this is a good place to meet somebody."

My imagination throws up an image of Tomas chatting up some beautiful woman. I wipe my palms on my dress. "Do you have sex here, or do you take them back to your house?"

"There are private rooms in the back, so yes, I've had sex here. I don't take anyone back to my house. You're the only woman who's ever slept in my bed."

My head jerks up. "Ever?" It makes sense, in a twisted sort of way. Tomas has been pretty open about not wanting to be in a relationship. "She really broke your heart, didn't she?"

A pensive look fills his eyes at my mention of Estela. "At the start, that's what it was about. Now? It feels like a bad habit." The music changes to something with a slow, thumping beat. "The evening is yours, dolcezza. We could stay and have a drink, watch the floor show, and go home. Or, we could play." He leans forward. "Tell me what you want."

His smile is a carnal invitation, and I intend to accept. "I want to play."

"Tell me your safe word."

I wet my lips. "Asset."

"That's never not going to be funny to me," he responds, his lips twitching. "Asset, it is. Come here, Ali."

I get up to sit next to him. He pulls me closer, my back pressing against his chest. "You want to be tied up tonight, Ali?" he murmurs into my ear.

The low, pounding drumbeat of the music pulses in rhythm with the throbbing between my legs. "Yes, please."

"What else are you interested in exploring tonight?"

"I don't know." I've read books and watched porn, so I have some idea of all the things that could happen. But I feel like a kid in a candy store, overwhelmed with the choices. He could spank me and flog me, bind my breasts with rope, or use clamps on my nipples. He could do all that *and so much more.* How do I pick? Where do I even start?

"I like being spanked," I admit in a low voice. It's not much of a confession; Tomas saw exactly how wet I got when he spanked me this morning. "Maybe more of that?"

"Would you like to be spanked with something other than my hand?"

His voice is serious, but there's a gleam in his eyes that gives me pause. "Like what? A whip?"

"It's probably best if I show you." He presses the button that summons our server. "Could you bring us a set of impact toys, please?" He gives me a speculative glance. "I think my companion would be interested in trying a paddle, a flogger, and a crop."

Oh. My. God. My cheeks flame as the server writes our order on her tablet. "What kind of flogger would she like?" she asks, addressing her question to Tomas. "Our basic option is a cowhide leather with fifty falls, but we also have a twenty-fall version for beginners and one with eighty falls if you want a more intense experience. Then there are our petal floggers, which are made of recycled bicycle tires. The rubber is a stronger sting than the cowhide, and it leaves petal-shaped marks on bare skin."

"What do you think, Ali?"

I think I'm going to die of embarrassment. "I'll take the regular version," I mumble, unable to look her in the eye.

She punches it in. "For paddles, we have leather, wood, and fur. If you pick the leather, there's a looped option, a three-layer leather slapper—"

This goes on for a while. Tomas is clearly enjoying my squirming because he takes his time with the selection of toys. "People are going to see them," I hiss when the server *finally* leaves to fill our order. "She's going to bring the toys here, and everyone will be able to see them."

"So what?" he asks calmly.

I open my mouth to answer and then close it. I don't really have an answer to his question. The server was unfazed by Tomas's request. We're in a booth, mostly hidden from view, and nobody is watching us. So what if she deposits a collection of sex toys on the table? We're in a *sex club*.

Our server returns with a tray loaded up with floggers and whips. She sets the perverted display on the table with a smile. "Can I get you anything else?"

I can't look at her. My eyes lock onto a black leather flogger, its tails as long as my forearm. A shiver runs through me when I picture Tomas behind me, swinging it down on my bared, defenseless ass.

"Thank you, Natalya," Tomas says calmly. "We'll ring the bell if we need anything else."

Just then, the hostess escorts a couple to the booth behind us. The man is wearing a suit, and the woman is wearing a short red dress that barely covers her ass. Her eyes rest on our table, and a mischievous smile curves her lips. "Looks like you have a fun evening planned." She holds out a business card to Tomas. "Let us know if you feel like company."

I'm so mortified I can't even look up. Tomas takes it with a murmur of thanks. "Focus," he says when she's gone. "It's not your job to worry about what other people are thinking. I'm in charge. Tonight, you only have two responsibilities. You can obey, or you can use your safe word. Now, look at the toys on this table and tell me what you'd like to try."

Okay, I can do this. I take a deep breath, lean forward, and pick up the black flogger. "Can I test it on myself?"

"Go ahead." He leans back, stretching his legs out. He looks calm, but his eyes are hot and intent, and the look in them makes me shiver.

I swing the flogger on the inside of my forearm. The tails snap on my skin, hot and tight.

"What does it feel like?" Tomas asks. "Does it hurt?"

I don't know how to describe the sensation. It felt more ticklish than painful. "Not really. But I didn't swing very hard."

"No, you didn't," he says. He takes it from me. I half-expect him to swing it on my arm, but instead, he trails the falls through his fingers, an expression of appreciation on his face. "It's all in the wrist. I can make it hurt, or I can make it pleasurable." He gives me a closed-mouth smile. "Or both."

I shift in my seat, hot and restless and squirmy. "I want to try it." I pick up the crop and swing it on my arm. This time, the pain is sharp and immediate. "I'm a maybe on this."

"There's no maybe. Commit to it. Yes or no only."

I try everything and sort them into two piles, the ones that I want to try and the ones I don't. Tomas looks them over thoughtfully, and then his gaze moves back to me. "Are you wearing panties, Ali?"

What kind of question is that? "Yes."

"Take them off."

I start to get up to go to the bathroom, but he stops me by putting a firm hand on my thigh. "Perhaps I wasn't specific enough," he says. "Take them off here."

Oh God oh God oh God. I thought the toys were embarrassing enough, but this? I can't do this. "But there are people watching—" I start to say but make myself stop. My heart is racing, and butterflies are fluttering madly in my stomach. Tomas has me feeling dangerously off-balance, *and I like it.* "May I ask questions?"

"You may."

"Do I have to stand up to take them off, or can I do it

sitting down?" We're in a booth. I bet I can wriggle out of them without drawing attention to myself. Sure, if someone's staring right at me, they can probably figure out what I'm doing, but nobody is doing that.

"You can do it any way you want."

"Okay." I lift my butt off the seat, reach under my dress, and pull my panties down to my knees. I slide them off and ball them up in my hand.

"Give them to me, please."

I slide them to him under the table. He takes them from me without comment, and then he sets them down *on top of the table,* right next to his drink.

I swallow hard. They're *right there.* My black lace panties are right there on the table, and anyone passing by can see them.

Tomas rings for the server again. "Could you put these toys in a private room, please?" he says, indicating my 'Yes' pile.

"Of course, Signor." She starts to pick up the tray, hesitates when she sees my panties, and then continues her task, a small smile dancing about her lips. I keep my eyes downcast, my face red, unable to look her directly in the eyes.

Tomas waits for her to leave. "Are you turned on, Ali?" he asks, his long fingers absently stroking my panties.

God, yes. My face might feel like it's on fire, but I'm wildly aroused. My insides are clenched tight with anticipation. He's going to take me to a private room, he's going to run the tails of the flogger contemplatively through his fingers, and then he's going to bring them down on my bare ass, sharp and hard. I feel hot and cold and shivery all at once.

"Yes, Sir."

"Show me." I should have guessed that was coming. "Push a finger into your cunt and hold it up so I can see. And Ali," he warns. "No touching your clit. Tonight, your orgasms belong to me."

I shoot a glance around the room. Nobody seems to be watching us. The couple who propositioned us are having an intent conversation. Two women are on the dance floor, their hands roaming blatantly all over each other. At the bar, a man passionately kisses a woman, sticking his hand down the front of her dress at the same time. Everyone here is absorbed in their own private world. At least, I hope they are.

As unobtrusively as I can, I shove a finger into my pussy and hold up the evidence of my arousal, the wetness gleaming in the dim golden light.

"Good girl." He captures my wrist and sucks my finger into his mouth. "Delicious," he murmurs. "Do you want to come tonight, Ali?"

"Yes, Sir," I respond promptly. "More than once, I hope."

His smile turns amused. "Greedy." He sits back in the booth, lets his knees fall open, and pats his lap. "But I'm in a good mood tonight. Go ahead. Sit on my knee and rub yourself to an orgasm."

You ever start out floating in the shallow end of the pool and suddenly realize you're in the deep end and the bottom's dropped out from under your feet and you're drowning? That's how I feel.

"In front of everyone?" A shiver rolls through me. "I can't."

"I wasn't asking, dolcezza," he replies. "That was an order."

He waits. For my compliance or for my safeword. Either will be okay, I know. If I'm truly uneasy, I don't have to do this. This is an unsettling game, and Tomas is keeping me off-balance, but it is, in the end, just a game.

And I *hate* backing down from a challenge.

I inch backward and straddle his powerfully muscled thigh, giving silent thanks for my choice of dress. The silk bodice hugs my breasts, but the skirt has enough ease that I don't have to hike it up.

Even so, I feel *exposed*. And painfully aroused.

"Good girl," he says, his voice warm. "You're being so obedient that I think I'll help you out." He pushes his hand between my legs from behind until his wrist rests on top of his thigh, and his palm is pressed against my pussy. I grind into it, my body needing—craving—his touch, and he puts his thumb on my clit, rubbing it in a circle. "There you go," he says, wrapping his other hand around my throat. "Ride my knee. Rub yourself on my thumb. Show me how much you want this."

I start slow, my cheeks aflame, but soon speed up. I stop caring about whether someone's watching and surrender to sensation. I'm slick and wet and oh-so-needy. I ride his knee because he's given me an order, and tonight, all I have to do is obey. I get off on the freedom of submitting, grind my hips on his thigh, and press my clit into his thumb, my eyes fluttering shut as I take my pleasure.

My orgasm hits me with the force of a tsunami. I ride it out, every last quiver, with Tomas's thumb against my clit and his hand on my throat. When I'm done, he doesn't let me relax. "On your feet," he orders, his voice hoarse. I slip out of the booth, and he follows, a big wet stain on his knee. I blush, looking at the evidence of my arousal, and his gaze follows, and a smile touches his lips. "Look at what you did," he says sternly. "You've ruined my pants."

Hot anticipation runs riot through me. The flogger I chose, the leather crop, the feathered tickler and the fur-lined paddle. He's going to use them on me now.

"I'm sorry, Sir," I whisper, my eyes downcast.

"That's not good enough, is it, Ali?" Laughter coats his voice. "Do you think your juices are going to come off the linen?"

"No, Sir," I say as meekly as I can. "I was very careless. Please punish me."

Tomas hurries me to a private room. It's a small space, but it looks bigger than it is because three of the four walls are covered with mirrors. There's a wooden bench on the far side of the room, my tray of toys on it. In the center of the room, lit by a spotlight, a large wooden contraption dominates the space.

It looks like some kind of diabolical torture device. I say that to Tomas, and he laughs. "This is a Y-frame. It's called that because of the shape of the wooden frame. It's a bondage device."

"You're going to tie me up to this?" I swallow back the rush of lust. "Yes, please, Sir."

"So polite," he says approvingly. "Should I be worried? Is this really the same woman who spends the majority of her time plotting to poison me?"

"Don't flatter yourself," I retort unwisely. "Poisoning you is only the third or fourth most important thing on my to-do list."

He laughs. "I see you really want to get punished," he

says, smooth and dangerous. He pats the bondage frame. "Take off your clothes and hop up here."

I reach behind my back and unzip my dress. The fabric falls in a pool by my feet. I unhook my bra and teeter over to Tomas on shaky feet, my throat dry with anticipation.

Tomas kisses me on my neck. "Are you going to be a good girl for me, Ali?"

Sometimes, before a fight, there's a brief moment when I stare at my opponent and wonder if I know what the hell I'm getting myself into. But then the bell rings, those thoughts wipe away, and I'm all in.

That's me right now. I'm all in.

"Yes, Sir."

"Remind me of your safeword."

I'm certain he hasn't forgotten it. The words instead serve as a ritual, a way to build the tension in the scene. And it's working. I answer, my heartbeat galloping in my chest. "Asset."

"Asset," he repeats. He cups my breasts from behind, sliding his thumbs across my nipples. "You wanted to come more than once, didn't you, dolcezza?" His hand trails down my stomach, and his fingers find my folds. "I'm in a generous mood. I'm going to give you exactly what you're asking for."

My legs fall open instinctively, giving him more access. "Yes, Sir. Thank you, Sir." I'm not an idiot—of course there's a catch. But my pussy is swollen and slick, my clit craving his touch, and I just don't care.

He lets go of me and pats the leather top of the frame. "Get up. Face down, that luscious ass of yours in the air."

He helps me up on the padded frame. The frame

holds me horizontally, parallel to the floor, about waist-high off the ground. The trunk of the Y is wide enough to support my hips but narrow enough that my breasts hang down. My legs are spread wide open, leaving me shamefully exposed.

Tomas moves around me, binding me in place with thick velcro straps. A strap goes around my waist, holding me down, and my wrists are cuffed together behind my back. More straps tighten around my thighs, the back of my knees, and my ankles. With each restraint, my arousal builds higher. This feels... I don't have the words to describe how this feels. Exhilarating. Addictive. It feels like there's been an *absence* in my life, and this is the missing part. *He's* the missing part.

"Good?" Tomas's voice comes from behind me. His tongue swipes through my folds, and he laughs softly. "So wet. I think you like this, Ali. Are any of the straps too tight? I don't want to cut off your circulation."

"Nothing's too tight," I say breathlessly to assure him, wriggling my fingers and toes. "I'm good."

"In that case..." He comes around. His fingers tweak my already swollen nipples, and then something bites down on one of them. "Nipple clamp," Tomas answers my unasked question. "I'm going to tighten it. Tell me when it's too much."

The pressure grows. My nipple throbs in its grip. It's painful, but it's the kind of pain that's turning me on. My breathing comes faster as Tomas tightens the clamp. More, more, more, until... "Too much," I gasp.

He eases the pressure a notch. I exhale through my teeth, letting the pain flow through my body. "Ready for the next one?"

"Yes." I'm so wet. So aroused.

He fastens the next clamp, and the endorphins rush through my body, leaving me almost light-headed. "Now," he continues. "About those multiple orgasms." There's a whirring noise, and he puts a vibrator between my legs, parting my folds, and carefully positions the head until it's buzzing against my clit, its touch maddeningly light. "You're going to work for them, dolcezza." He nears my mouth, unzips his trousers, and pulls out his thick cock. "Get me hard."

He's already hard; he doesn't need my help. But I'm not complaining. I part my lips and take him deep, moaning in my throat as he grows even harder in my mouth. He pumps deep a couple of times, and then he pulls out and disappears from view.

I watch his reflection in the mirror in front of me. He rolls on a condom and picks up a flogger, and then he's back between my legs. He thrusts into me, his full length sliding deep into my wet heat.

I almost scream.

He fucks me, his fingers gripping my hips, his strokes deep and fast. With every thrust, my breasts sway, and I feel the nipple clamps all over again. Our gazes connect in the mirror, and a jolt goes through me. A smile curves his lips, and then...

The flogger lands on my back.

Heat sears my skin, and I bite my lips to keep from crying out loud. The tails connect again, a thousand points of fire, but the pain fades quickly, leaving warmth behind. Oh God, this is so good. The vibrator continues to buzz, attacking my clit with steady insistence. Sensation comes at me from every direction, and it's over-whelming in the best possible way.

I can't take my eyes off Tomas. His face is distorted with pleasure as he fucks me and flogs me. I start to quiver, my muscles tensing. My skin beads with sweat. "I'm going to come," I gasp. The vibrations, the slap of his skin against mine, the hard perfection of his cock, bottoming out with each harsh thrust. "I can't hold on..."

He pulls out and jerks the vibrator away. He tears the straps off and repositions me so I'm facing up. *Facing him.* "Ask for permission," he orders, his voice ragged. "I own your orgasms. Ask me for permission to come."

Oh, fuck. I know this is a game people play, but I hadn't realized how much focus it involves to actually keep track of that perfect moment right before you come. Tomas puts the vibrator back on my clit and starts thrusting again, and it doesn't take long before need is clawing through me once more. My insides are twisted in a tangled mess, hot and achy, painful yet pleasurable, and it's too much to bear. I need release, and I need it *now*. "Please," I sob, my thighs shaking, my insides wound tight. If he says no, I won't be able to hold off. I'm on the precipice, and the slightest touch will push me over. "Please let me come."

He buries himself to the hilt and holds himself there. He stares deeply into my eyes. "Yes," he says, leaning forward and tugging the nipple clamps free. "Yes, dolcezza. Come for me."

Blood comes rushing back to my nipples. I scream at the sudden pain and shatter, quivering around him, falling from one orgasm into another, wave after wave of pleasure, until it's all just sweet, perfect, endless bliss.

TOMAS SITS on the wooden bench and pulls me onto his lap, wrapping a soft blanket around me. I cling to him like a limp kitten. "Did you enjoy that?" he asks, pressing a kiss on my forehead.

"Couldn't you tell?"

He laughs softly. "I wasn't sure how you'd feel about being tied down on the frame," he says. "Well, after this morning, I knew you'd enjoy it at least a little, but this was a lot more restrictive."

"I liked it." I lace my fingers in his. "The frame wasn't the scariest part. I almost balked when you asked me to ride your knee in the booth." I laugh softly. "But it was really hot. It felt good to give up control. You knew that, didn't you?"

"It was a gamble. You take so much pressure on yourself. You're running your gym single-handedly, you're busy from morning to night, and you don't take any time for yourself. I figured you'd enjoy giving up control for a little while."

He calls it a gamble, but I've learned that Tomas only bets on a sure thing.

"And what about you?" I survey him thoughtfully. "Why do you like control? Because you felt powerless in Valencia?" The moment I say those words, I wish I could take them back. It's a very intimate thing to say, and Tomas doesn't want that from me.

He stiffens. "That's very insightful." I wonder if he's going to shut me down, but after a long pause and a heavy sigh, he says, "Insightful, and more than a little true. But it's not the only reason." He kisses me softly. "You trusted me enough to let me tie you up, dolcezza. That's a pretty big ego rush."

I could stay in his arms forever. That realization sends a shock through me, and it forces me to get up and get dressed. Tomas isn't interested in a relationship, whatever label I want to put on this thing between us. One thing I know for sure is that there is an expiration date built in. I can't let myself forget that.

43

ALINA

T omas insists on accompanying me home after Casanova. "Invite me up," he says when we reach the gym. "I'm going to spend the night."

"What? But I thought Signor Moretti was going to assign me bodyguards. Aren't they outside?"

"Yes," Tomas replies. "And if an attacker makes it past them, they'll have to deal with me."

"Aren't you being somewhat paranoid?"

"It's only paranoia if you have no logical reason to believe you're in danger," he points out. "Given that Laurenti has already made one attempt to abduct you, I'd say that, no, I'm not being paranoid. I'm taking appropriate precautions."

"Won't Freccia miss you?"

He laughs shortly. "Dolcezza, I love Freccia, but I'm under no illusion about my importance to her. Agnese, Antonio's housekeeper, has agreed to feed her. As long as my cat has a steady supply of sardines and pasta, she will

I can't help smiling as I picture Tomas's tiny ginger cat gorging on a plate of spaghetti. "She eats pasta?"

"She is Italian," he responds lightly. His expression turns grim. "I'll sleep on the floor if you'd like. But I am not going to leave you alone."

"There's plenty of room in my bed." It's weird that I'm blushing. After what we just did, spending the night together shouldn't feel particularly intimidating, but somehow, it does.

Maybe because it's a lot more intimate.

And letting myself be intimate with Tomas is a very bad idea.

TOMAS EXAMINES my locks disapprovingly before propping a chair under the door handle. "No offense, Ali, but your locks are trash," he says. "I'll get someone to change these tomorrow."

I roll my eyes. "Have you ever noticed that when people start their sentence with 'no offense,' they're about to say something extremely rude?"

We get ready for bed. I usually sleep in a ratty T-shirt, but I'm too vain to let Tomas see me in that, so I change into a nightgown Rosa made me last year as a birthday present. It's periwinkle blue, floor length with two long side slits, and a plunging neckline that shows off my cleavage. It's subtly sexy, not overly so, and it's the prettiest lingerie I've ever owned.

Heat flares in Tomas's eyes when I come out of the

bathroom. "Very nice," he says, his voice a low growl. "Very sexy. I want to rip it off you."

"You better not," I retort, a thrill running through me at the blatant masculine possession in his gaze. "It was a present from Rosa." I climb into bed, my skin tingling. It feels dangerous to share a bed with Tomas. "There's a new toothbrush on the counter."

"Thank you." He goes into the bathroom. I hear the tap run, and he emerges a few minutes later, still fully clothed.

"Are you planning on sleeping in your suit?"

"No." He takes off his jacket and lays it over the back of the couch. He starts removing his cufflinks, and I watch him, my mouth dry. I lost track of how many times I orgasmed at Casanova, but it was *a lot*. I should be sated, but when Tomas unbuttons his shirt, my desire comes raging back. "I usually sleep naked." His eyes meet mine, and there's a laughing challenge in them. "If you're comfortable with that?"

Yes, please. I'm *fully* on board.

I'm opening my mouth to say that when Tomas pulls out a gun tucked in the back of his waistband. I jerk up in bed. "That's a gun," I squeak. "A real gun."

He gives me a puzzled look. "Of course. If someone bursts into this room with a weapon, my jujitsu skills are hardly going to help."

He tucks the weapon under the pillow on his side of the bed. I stare at the spot warily. "Is it safe? What if it goes off by accident?"

"The safety is on," he replies, unbuckling his leather belt. "Have you ever fired a gun before?"

"No. Why would I? In case you haven't noticed, I'm a

gym instructor, not a member of the mafia. This is so far outside my experience—"

I stop talking as Tomas lies down next to me. The mattress sinks under his weight, and my awareness sharpens. I'm not used to sharing a bed. I try to remember the last time I spent an entire night with a man, and my memory offers nothing. This is extremely intimate. I can feel the heat radiating off his body. He's close enough that I can reach out and touch him. Stroke those hard muscles, run my fingers over his tattoos. Follow them with my tongue. I could straddle him, and he'd wrestle me down, his weight over mine, holding me anchored in place.

Tomas mistakes my silence for disquiet. "For what it's worth, killing people isn't an everyday occurrence in my world either," he says, his lips twisting in a grimace. "I'm the money guy, not the assassin. Most of the time, my life is very boring."

"There's an assassin?" I blurt out.

He gives me his blandest look. "I didn't say anything about an assassin." He turns on his side, facing me. "I'll teach you to shoot this weekend if you'd like."

There's definitely an assassin, but the less I know about it, the better. I spend a minute wondering who it could be and then let it go.

Tomas wants to teach me to defend myself. My heart warms. Maybe it makes me a bad person, but it's stopped bothering me that he killed two people last night. Without his intervention, I could have woken up in Moscow this morning, the unwilling, captive bride of a Bratva boss. He protected me last night, and he's protecting me now.

"Thank you." I reach out and touch his arm. "I don't think I said that. Thank you for saving me last night."

Something unreadable passes over his face. "You're welcome."

My entire body is alight with desire. *Stop staring at his crotch,* Ali, I scold myself, but it's not working. He's in my bed, and I want him to make love to me. "And yes," I manage to say through the haze of lust drowning my brain. "I'd like to learn to shoot a gun."

"Good," he responds. "Now, onto more pleasant things. You look stressed, dolcezza. What would help you feel better? A hot drink? Something to eat?" His gaze slowly slides over my body. "An orgasm?"

"An orgasm?"

"It'll help you relax." He strokes the lace, his touch setting me on fire. His fingers are inches away from my taut, aching nipples, but he avoids them intentionally, the jerk. "Ask me nicely."

A ripple of excitement runs through me. I *like* this game. "And if I don't? Are you going to throw me out of bed?"

"Oh no," he says with a smile that's positively carnal. "If I throw you out of bed, Ali, it's because I want to fuck you on the floor. No, your punishment will depend on how much of a brat you are." He plucks my nipple between his thumb and forefinger, and the rush of pleasure leaves me speechless. "I could put you over my knee and spank your ass. Or I could make you bring me your vibrator. Like this morning, I'll tie your hands up so you can't touch yourself, and I'll edge you with your own toy, over and over, until you're begging for release."

Every nerve in my body is screaming in anticipation. "Yes," I whisper. "Yes, please. Do all of that."

And he does.

THE NEXT DAY, as promised, Tomas takes me to a gun range that Antonio owns to teach me to shoot. It's a large, brightly lit room with a row of targets at the far end, and no one's there except for us.

"You look nervous."

"I am, a little," I admit. Tomas, on the other hand, looks relaxed and confident. He's wearing a pair of beige linen pants and a white linen shirt, and the effect is making me drool.

"It's good to be nervous," he replies. "Guns aren't toys; they're dangerous weapons. Better to be wary than complacent." He opens the case he's carrying and pulls out a black handgun. "This is a Beretta M9. It's a good beginner pistol."

"Can I hold it?"

"Not yet," he says. "Let's go over the basics of gun safety first. Most important: always treat every gun like it's loaded."

That makes sense. "Got it."

"Never point your gun at someone unless you mean it," he continues. He gives me a stern look. "But if someone's threatening you, you shoot, got it? I don't want you to feel sorry for the scum that tried abducting you."

"I don't know if I have what it takes to shoot someone in cold blood, Tomas."

"It won't be in cold blood," he says, cupping my cheek in his palm. "It's you or them, dolcezza. Don't let it be you."

When he puts it that way... "What are the rest of the rules?"

"Keep your finger off the trigger until you're ready to shoot." He demonstrates the motion. "Got it?"

I nod. He walks me through the different parts of the gun, showing me how to load and unload it, and then it's time to actually fire the gun. Tomas makes me wear protective glasses, puts earmuffs over my ears, and then positions himself behind me. His hands cup my waist. "Aim for the bullseye," he murmurs into my ear.

A shiver rolls through me as he kisses the side of my neck. "You're distracting me," I accuse. "How am I expected to be able to fire if you keep doing that?"

"Real life doesn't come with perfect conditions, dolcezza." He slides his hands up my sides and squeezes my breasts. "Focus."

Things take a detour after that, but eventually, we return our attention to shooting. I raise the gun, aim for the target, flip the safety off, and squeeze the trigger. The recoil takes me by surprise, but I get used to it. By the time we're done, I'm hitting the target every single time.

WE'RE SUPPOSED to leave for Valencia on Thursday morning—Tomas found someone to cover his accounting class—and we're meeting with my father on Friday night. If all goes according to plan, we'll return to Venice on

Sunday. Tomas and I discuss the details over dinner at a Thai restaurant after the gun range.

"I know a couple of reliable people who can staff the front desk," he says when I fret about being away from the gym. "I'll send you their resumes."

"I'm too stressed to review resumes," I reply, massaging my temples with my hands. "Let's just hire them. Your recommendation is good enough for me."

He pretends to be shocked. "You're agreeing to do something I suggest instead of arguing about it," he marvels. "This is a first."

"Don't get used to it. I'm still plotting—"

"To buy me out." He surveys the menu, sounding remarkably unfazed. "Yes, I know."

Hmm. Come to think of it, something's not right. Tomas agreed to take a smaller share of the profit because I was teaching all the classes. But now Luke's an instructor, and I'm going to hire Luke's friend Naima as well, so technically, I'm not holding up my end of the deal.

And Tomas has never once mentioned renegotiating the contract.

"Why haven't you insisted that we change the profit distribution?" I demand.

"What are you talking about?"

"In the gym. If I'm hiring instructors, I shouldn't be taking eighty percent of the profits. Why haven't you renegotiated?" I start to put bits and pieces of information together: his quietly luxurious house, the bespoke suits, the expensive car he drives. Tomas is rich, rich enough that the profits from my gym don't matter. "You don't care about the money at all, do you?"

"Most people that tell you they don't care about money are lying," he responds, avoiding my question adeptly and pouring me some tea. "Do you know what you'd like to eat?"

I do. We order our food. The red curry is truly excellent, but I'm too distracted to enjoy it. Tomas is avoiding answering my question, and I'm left even more confused than before. If he isn't worrying about me because of the money he's invested in Groff's, then why is he protecting me?

Because he cares about me?

I wish I were brave enough to ask.

44

TOMAS

Time has an uncooperative way of speeding up when you want it to slow down. Before I know it, it's time to fly to Valencia.

Antonio loans us his private plane. "How are you doing?" he asks me when I see him Thursday morning, his eyes searching my face. "You haven't been back to Spain in a while."

"I'll be okay." But even as I say it, a whirlwind of emotions churns inside me. I've been homesick for five years, but faced with heading back to Valencia, I realize something's changed. Home is the tiny office where Alina and I work together; it's the gym she spends all her waking hours in. It's the octagon we fought in.

Home is wherever Alina is.

"You like this girl, don't you?"

"Yes." I have no idea how she feels about me, and I'm too afraid to tell her how I feel about her, but I've fallen in love with Ali. I was closed off from the world, drifting through existence like a zombie, and she brought me

293

back to life. She makes me laugh every single day. Sparring with her, betting on her fights, drinking the café bombon she made—it's a vision of a future that I want so badly it hurts.

I love her drive. Her passion. I love that even though her father is a piece of shit, she still searches for the good in him. I can be vulnerable with Ali and know that she's there for me. I've always known, on a subconscious level, that she's a kind, empathetic, loyal person. After all, I never hesitated to tell her about Estela, and I've kept that betrayal a secret from almost everyone I know. But with Ali? There was never any doubt that she'd have my back.

Antonio nods, unsurprised. "Be careful, Tomas. Laurenti is desperate, and Malinov is a wild card."

"What have you heard?"

"Nothing concrete, just whispers. Gregori murdered his way to the top. His son Damir drinks hard, races Formula 1 cars, and pretends to be a rich, spoiled playboy. But underneath, he's cut from the same cloth as his father. Valencia is neutral ground, and I trust Gabriel to enforce the rules. Even so, don't get complacent."

"I won't." Where Alina's safety is concerned, complacency is the last thing I'd risk.

He has one final bit of parting advice. "Have you told your family that you're going to be in Valencia?"

I shake my head. It's a four-day trip. What are the chances I'll run into them?

His eyebrows slant in a frown. "That's a mistake," he says. "I'm going to give you some unsolicited advice, Tomas. You have to close the door to the past in order to move toward the future. If you like Alina Zuccaro, don't just tell her. Take her home, introduce her to your family. Show her that she matters."

He's not wrong. "I'll think about it."

"Good luck."

ALI IS TOO nervous to appreciate the private plane. She sits forward in her chair, her body taut with tension. She passes up the attendant's offer of a drink and stares out of the window without saying a word until we're in the air.

Then she turns to me. "I'm sorry," she says. "I've been so wrapped up in my own stuff that I've completely forgotten. You haven't been home in five years, have you?"

"No, I haven't."

"Are you looking forward to it? Have you told your family you're going to be in town?"

"Not particularly," I admit. "And yes, I texted my mother before we took off."

"And what did she say?"

"I don't know. I turned off my phone."

She gives me a probing look. "This is a private plane, and nobody's asked me to turn off my phone. You don't think they'll be happy to see you?"

"No." I take a deep breath. "I've missed so much. My sister's wedding and my nephew's birth. My mother's sixty-fifth birthday and my father's seventieth. Every year, the Aguilar clan gathers to celebrate Christmas in my grandparents' villa on the outskirts of the city. Not just my immediate family either. The entire extended clan.

Aunts, uncles, cousins. Everyone. It's a family tradition that dates back decades."

Ali's face softens. "And you haven't been back because of Estela."

"I thought she was the reason, but I think I've been lying to myself. It was a bad working environment, and I should have dealt with it head-on by quitting. Instead, I distracted myself with Estela." I clench my hand into a fist. "I missed my only sister's wedding. How do I come back from that? You just can't. Too much time has passed, and the hurts have hardened. My family won't be happy to see me back. They're going to find it difficult to forgive me."

She puts her hand on top of mine. My grandmother's ring is on her finger, the sapphire glowing softly under the cabin light. "I don't know your family," she says, lacing her fingers in mine. "But they sound great. If you love them and they love you, you have to try. My mother died young, and toward the end, she didn't even remember me. You never know how long you have with your loved ones. You have to make every moment count."

This feels like a very weighty topic. "You say that now," I quip. "You'll change your mind when you meet them. They're loud, opinionated, and nosy."

Her expression is wistful. "It was just me and my mom growing up," she murmurs. "I've always wanted a loud, meddlesome, opinionated family. I'd have loved a sister. Are you the older one or the younger? Do you have any other siblings?"

"No. It's just Carlota and me. She's two years older than me."

"An older sister." She smiles. "I was such a lonely kid

that I used to make up siblings. Sometimes, it was an older sister, Paola. Paola had great clothes, and she'd lend them to me and teach me how to apply makeup. Then there was my brother Christian. He'd punch anyone who made fun of me."

"Why would anyone make fun of you?"

"I was the odd one out at school," she replies. "I didn't know who my father was, and my mother kept to herself. When the other parents invited her to their parties, she declined. She didn't even like me attending my class-mates' birthdays." She shrugs as if it doesn't bother her. "After a while, the invitations stopped coming."

That's why she's going to Valencia. That's why she's burying her head in the sand about what kind of man her father is. I can relate. God, can I relate. There were plenty of warning signs that Estela Villegas was not who I built her up to be. That she was superficial, selfish, and materi-alistic. But I needed a reason to feel hopeful, and I latched upon Estela as the answer to all my problems. Who am I to judge Ali for ignoring the truth? After all, I did exactly the same thing.

Two hours later, the plane touches down in Valencia. We have a brief tussle over Ali's duffel bag—she insists she can carry it herself, and I'm just as adamant that she isn't going to. I win the fight. I'm laughing at the death glare she gives me as we turn the corner...

Loud, excited shrieks fill the air.

I freeze in shock.

My mother is holding one end of a huge banner that says, "Welcome home, Tomas!" and is jumping up and down in glee. My father holds the other end, beaming from ear to ear. Carlota has Adan in her arms, and at her side, her sheepdog Biel is busy barking her head off, just adding to the general commotion.

My brother-in-law Ramon grins at the look of utter shock on my face. "Did you really think we wouldn't make a fuss?"

Then, my father starts forward. "Cómo estás, Papá?" I have time to ask before I'm enveloped in his arms.

"It's so good to see you, mijo," he says, his voice thick with emotion. "I'm so glad you're home." My mother hugs me tight, her eyes wet with tears, and Carlota thrusts her son into my arms. "Look, Adan," she says. "This your tío Tomas."

I genuinely didn't know what kind of reception I was going to get from my family, but here they are. With less than three hours of notice, they've all shown up at the airport. They're hugging me in their arms and talking at the top of their voices, and it feels like I've never been away.

I swallow the lump in my throat. I'm happy in Venice, but there's always been a raw spot in my heart when I think about Valencia. It's not the parks I miss, and it's not the long afternoons in the sun drinking caña after caña, debating the fortunes of Valencia CF in La Liga and cursing its foreign owner for chronic underinvestment in the club. It's not the café bombon, and it's not the paella. No, it's this. It's the absence of my family that has scraped my heart.

But as I hug my mother tight, I finally feel that wound heal. I finally feel whole.

The padrino was right. I needed to face the past first, and now I can look to the future. A future that hopefully has Ali in it.

She's standing off to the side, looking a little dazed at the commotion. I laugh and grab her hand, tugging her closer. "Meet my family, Ali." I can't stop smiling. "What did I say about them? Loud, opinionated, and nosy."

And I love them.

45

ALINA

A m I a little overwhelmed? Yes. Tomas's family is noisy, boisterous, and a little over-the-top. I mean, a banner welcoming him home. What's next, a parade?

And I love it.

I stand to the side, not sure what to do with myself. Tomas has the family I've always wanted, and it's hard not to feel a little envious. Then he catches sight of my face, and he smiles at me, wide and happy. "Meet my family, Ali," he says, lacing his fingers in mine. "What did I say about them? Loud, opinionated, and nosy."

That's when his mother catches sight of the ring on my finger.

Her eyes go very wide. For a long moment, she doesn't say anything, and then she squeals in delight and pulls me into a tight hug. "Tell me everything," she says, her voice high and excited. "How did you meet? When did you get engaged? Have you set a date for the wedding, and what about a venue? It's going to be in Valencia right?" She turns to Tomas, her arm still around me. "Mijo, if you tell me you want to have the wedding in Italy, I will be very mad."

Oh shit. I give Tomas a horrified look. His mother thinks we're really getting married, but of course we're not. This is a fake engagement, and its only purpose is to convince my father that I'm not interested in marrying the Russian groom he's lined up for me. And I don't know what to say to his parents. I feel awful lying to them.

"Tomas," I start hesitantly.

"Ali," he replies calmly. "Mamá, let her go; you're smothering her. Ali, this is my father, Jose Antonio Aguilar. My mother, Carina Cetrone. My sister, Carlota Aguilar Cetrone, her husband, Ramon Torrente, and their son, Adan. Everyone, this is Alina Zuccaro. My fiancée."

Wait, he's introducing me as his fiancée? I wish we had time to get our story straight. Had I known we'd be ambushed by his family, I would have insisted. "It's good to meet you."

Tomas's sister gives me a warm hug. "Welcome to the family," she says. "It's so good to meet you." She gives her brother an arch look. "Tomas hasn't visited in five years. I'm assuming you're the reason he's finally here." She beams widely. "I like you already." She takes her wriggling child back from Tomas. "Tell me everything about yourself. What do you do for work, what do you do for fun, and what's the most annoying thing Tomas does?"

"Umm..."

Tomas thankfully comes to my rescue. Again. "Carlota, enough with the inquisition." He gives me a rueful smile. "Want to go to our hotel and get settled?"

"A hotel?" Tomas's mother sounds horrified. "You're staying in a hotel when you're home? Nonsense. I readied your room when you told me you were coming. I'm not taking no for an answer, mijo. Family stays at home."

I have to bite back my chuckle. "Your room?" I love this. Tomas is calm and collected all the time, and nothing ever seems to get under his skin except, from the look of it, his family. It's funny. I'm seeing a whole new side of him, and I like it.

"My childhood room," he replies, giving his mother a look of fond exasperation. "I moved out when I was eighteen, and yet Mamá still hasn't got rid of my stuff." He gives me an inquiring look. "What do you think? Stay with this lot, or opt for peace and quiet?"

"Hey," Carlota says indignantly, punching him on his arm. "We can be quiet." She seems to notice her barking dog for the first time. "Biel, cállate."

Stay with Tomas's family. I don't hesitate; my answer is instantaneous. "I'd love to stay with your family."

I HALF-THOUGHT I'd find posters of bikini-clad women in Tomas's bedroom. After all, he says he moved out when he was eighteen. Sadly, there are no half-naked blondes gracing his wall.

His bed, though? It's small. It's not quite as small as a single, but it seems narrower than a double. Tomas notices me looking at it and grins. "It's going to be a tight squeeze. Scared?"

He's baiting me, but I'm not going to fall for it. "I'm

just thinking that it'll be hard to ignore your snoring in a bed this size," I say repressively.

"I don't snore," he replies with a grin, unzipping his garment bag and hanging up his suit jacket. "You, on the other hand…" His voice trails off suggestively.

When I first saw the garment bag, I was tempted to make a joke about how he couldn't go a weekend without wearing a suit. Then I remembered the reason we're in Valencia. My father has indicated that he wants to take me out to a fancy restaurant for dinner, and though he doesn't know it yet, I'm not going anywhere without Tomas. He's going to need the suit.

"I do not snore," I say indignantly.

He winks at me. "Don't worry, dolcezza. It's adorable, not annoying."

I frown at him. "You're in a very good mood. What's going to happen when your family finds out we're not really engaged? Should we tell them the truth?"

"No," he says immediately. "My mother is the worst actor in the world. If she knew the truth, she'd never be able to pretend. It's not a big deal. Once we're back in Venice, I'll tell them about the ruse."

"They seem really excited about your engagement." When she finds out it's not real, Carina is going to be crushed. And I can't bear to be the one who puts that look of disappointment in her eyes. "I feel like I'm abusing your mother's kindness."

"She won't hold it against you, dolcezza."

TOMAS'S PARENTS live near the beach in a neighborhood called El Cabanyal. It's warmer than Venice, but the ocean breeze makes the heat manageable. Carlota announces that we're going to eat outside. "Can I help?" I ask when I head back downstairs.

"No, no, just enjoy the lovely weather. Ramon and I can handle it."

"Are you sure?"

Tomas comes up behind me. "Carlota is the head chef at one of the best restaurants in the city," he says, his voice proud. "According to her sous-chef, she's very temperamental. There's lots of screaming and throwing things. It's best to stay out of it. You wouldn't want to be hit by a flying knife."

Her eyes narrow. "My sous-chef said that, did he? Just wait until I find him."

"Who's her sous-chef?" I ask in a low voice.

Tomas gives me a wicked smile. "Ramon. This ought to be fun."

Lunch is amazing. Carlota and Ramon bring out dish after delicious dish. Patatas bravas, olives stuffed with anchovies—Tomas tells me they're called gildas—Brie baked with caramelized onions with a dollop of raspberry sauce on top, paella, croquettes, a cuttlefish stew, warm bread, olive oil, and so much more. I eat *everything*. By the time I'm done, I'm so stuffed that it hurts to breathe, and I regret nothing. I lean back in my chair and let the conversation flow around me.

Carlota watches me approvingly. "You should come to my restaurant for esmorzaret tomorrow," she says. "It's in the central market. Have you been to Valencia before?"

"No, it's my first time." And probably my last. Once

Tomas's family finds out about my deception, they're not going to want to see me again. "What's esmorzaret?"

"Valencian brunch," Tomas says from across the table. "Usually, a sandwich—a bocadillo—followed by cremaet, which is basically coffee with rum. It's a Valencian specialty."

"Like café bombon?"

Tomas's father leans forward with interest. "You've had café bombon?"

"She made it for me," Tomas replies. "She thinks it's disgustingly sweet." He gives me an amused smile. "She'll come around."

Lunch lasts three hours. Adan, the baby, is a little restless by the time we near the end, so his father takes him to the beach. Tomas's mother stirs reluctantly at the end of the meal. "I need to stop by the hospital," she says. "I told them I wouldn't be coming in today, but there are a couple of patients I want to check in on. Tomas, will you give me a ride, mijo?"

Tomas gives me an inquiring look. "Will you be okay by yourself, dolcezza?"

I blush at the nickname. He's called me that dozens of times, but this is in front of his *family*. "Of course."

"You should take a siesta," Carina says with a smile. "It's my favorite Spanish tradition. Dinner here is a little later than in Italy. We don't usually eat until ten." She turns to her daughter. "Carlota, don't clear up, mija. I'll do it after I get back."

"No, you won't," Jose Antonio says firmly, demonstrating where Tomas gets his stubbornness from. "I'll do it."

"No, Papá, your hip is bothering you," Carlota protests. "It's no big deal. I'll take care of it."

I jump to my feet. "Please let me do it. It's the least I can do to thank you for this delicious meal."

"No, Alina, you're our guest—"

Tomas winks at me. "I thought you told her she's family," he says teasingly. "Which is it?"

Carlota makes a face at her brother. "Don't you have to give Mamá a ride?" she asks pointedly. "Maybe you should do that." She glances at me, a smile tugging on her lips. "How about we do it together? That's my best offer."

"I'll take it."

The kitchen is large and modern, and cleaning up takes very little time. It's just a matter of loading everything into the industrial-strength dishwasher. Carlota and I chat companionably as we work. Mostly, she tells me all the places I must visit in Valencia. "The market, of course," she says. "La Llotja de la Seda is a UNESCO World Heritage Site, and Mercat de Colón is in a really beautiful building. And, of course, you can't miss Turia, the park that runs through the city."

"I'm only here until Sunday." I handwash a beautiful jade green ceramic platter that won't fit in the dishwasher. "I don't know if I'll have time for everything."

"It's a small city, just like Venice. Everything's really close together. You can do it all in a few hours and then settle in the square with a glass of wine and people-watch. Have you set a date for the wedding?"

She's good. One moment, she's telling me about the tourist attractions, and the next moment when my suspicions have been lulled, she throws in a personal question.

307

I'll have to be careful how I answer; Tomas and I still haven't got our stories straight.

Come to think of it, Tomas's family's questions are good practice for the meeting with my father. Under the circumstances, I'm sure he'll have as many questions about my engagement, if not more.

"No," I reply. "Not yet. We're not in a huge hurry." I flash her a smile. "And before you ask, we also haven't picked a venue."

She grins. "Only my mother will be mortally offended if the wedding isn't in Valencia. I wouldn't mind visiting Venice. I've only been there once."

I'm dying of curiosity. "I know Tomas hasn't visited in five years," I say carefully. "Can I ask why you haven't traveled to see him?"

"We wanted to," she replies, her expression pensive. "He asked us not to. I'm afraid that when Tomas told us he was going to marry Estela, our reaction wasn't the best. None of us liked her." She makes a face. "When she turned him down—the evil bitch—he didn't want to discuss it. He shut down every attempt to talk. Maybe he felt like we'd gloat. I don't know. Tomas doesn't love often, but he loves deeply."

I can believe that.

"Anyway, that's all in the past where it can remain. What's important is that he's found you, and you're a zillion times nicer than Estela. And if you want to borrow my wedding dress..."

Umm, okay. "Is that another Valencian tradition?"

She bursts into laughter. "I'm so sorry," she says when her giggles have died down. "I should explain since Tomas clearly didn't. Our abuela, Ana Isabel—my father's mother—left Tomas her engagement ring, and she left me her wedding dress. It's my most cherished possession." Her expression softens. "Although Adan's first pair of socks might rival that. Anyway, Tomas never gave Estela our abuela's ring, so deep down inside, he obviously knew she was the wrong woman for him. And he gave it to you—"

"What?" I yelp.

"He didn't tell you?" She shakes her head in disbelief. "Typical guy. Yes, you're wearing the Aguilar engagement ring. We haven't spent a lot of time together, but already I can tell you're going to make my brother very, very happy." Her voice is warm. "So, if you want to wear my wedding dress, I'll be happy to lend it to you. But please, no pressure. Your mother might want you to wear her dress, of course—"

My throat feels thick with tears. "My mother is dead. If she had a wedding dress, I never saw it." I don't even know if she was married to my father when she ran.

Carlota takes in my expression. "I've made you cry," she exclaims in dismay. "Tomas is going to kill me. Oh God, Alina, I'm so sorry. I didn't mean to bring up a difficult memory—"

"No, it's not that." Well, it is that, a little. I miss my mother. It's been two years, but some days, the grief feels as fresh as ever. But it's not just her absence that's making me cry. It's Tomas's perfect, lovely, kind family. Throughout lunch, I sat there, surrounded by their warmth and laughter, and it was everything I'd always wanted.

But it's not real. None of it is.

Is it all fake, though? A hopeful voice inside me whispers. *He gave you his grandmother's engagement ring. That's got to mean something.*

Two stories are happening here. One where reality intrudes and I get my heart broken, and the fairy-tale version with a handsome prince and a happily ever after. But I don't know which version to believe.

46

TOMAS

My mom insists on dragging me inside the hospital to meet a couple of her coworkers. I'm walking back to the car when a man steps into my path. "Welcome back to Valencia," Gabriel d'Este says. "How are you, Tomas?"

Gabriel d'Este is an intimidating man. I haven't seen him since I left Valencia, but I've followed his career from afar. He wears his power lightly, but it exists all the same. He used to divide his time between Italy and Spain, but ever since he got married, he's called Valencia home.

His reach extends far beyond the city. When criminal organizations around the world need their money laundered, they come to Gabriel. He's ruthless and focused, vicious if you cross him. Not too many people are stupid enough to try it.

I shake his outstretched hand. "Do you really monitor everyone coming into your city?"

"Yes," he replies. "Also, Antonio called and gave me a heads-up that you'd be here."

I'm not surprised. Gabriel doesn't launder Antonio Moretti's money—I do—but the padrino doesn't believe in making unnecessary enemies.

"And you left your estate and drove into the heart of the city to find me?" I ask dryly. "I'm touched. What can I do for you, Gabriel?"

"I came by because I wanted to meet your fiancée. But more importantly, I owe you an apology that's long overdue." There's genuine remorse in his eyes. "I am sorry, Tomas. I deeply regret everything my father put you through. I knew he wasn't a good person, but I didn't realize how bad it was until he targeted Cici. My wife," he adds. "We got married a couple of years ago."

"I heard. Congratulations. And you don't owe me an apology, Gabriel. It's not your fault that Alonzo is an abusive jerk."

"We're going to have to disagree on that," he says. "I hear your fiancée, Alina, is Vidone Laurenti's daughter."

Of course he knows. "Did the padrino tell you that?"

"He filled me in, but he didn't have to. Laurenti told me himself when he dropped by."

"To kiss the ring?" Gabriel is an introvert to the extreme. I can imagine how much he enjoys having everyone drop by to pay obeisance. "That must have been fun."

His expression turns sour. "I'm glad you find this funny."

"So Laurenti's already here." My stomach twists uncomfortably. Ali still wants to believe that her father had nothing to do with her abduction attempt. She is still clinging to the illusion that she'll tell him we're engaged, and that'll make the whole problem go away. I know better. Laurenti has too much riding on the alliance with the Kutuzovo OPG. He's backed into a corner, and he's desperate. This situation is a powder keg.

But Valencia is neutral territory. Gabriel will not tolerate violence in his city, and that's the biggest reason I'm here.

"Not just Laurenti. Damir Malinov is here too." There's a note of distaste in his voice, and I make a mental note of it. "I've told them both to abide by Alina's decision. That should be sufficient, but if they refuse to cooperate, I'll get involved." He grins. "I hear Alina showed up at one of Ciro's underground tournaments and walked away with the big prize. Cici is dying to meet her."

The tension in my shoulders eases. Gabriel doesn't offer to get involved very often. By doing so now, he's telling the world that Alina and I have his protection and that if anyone harms us, they're risking his retribution. Laurenti might be stupid enough to risk pissing off Antonio Moretti, but nobody wants to be on Gabriel's blacklist. Even if they survive the immediate aftermath—which is not guaranteed—nobody in the world will clean their money for them.

This is the leverage Alina needs to make her father back off.

"Thank you," I say gratefully. "I truly appreciate the help." From the moment those goons tried to abduct Alina, I've been on edge, braced for violence. But with Gabriel's intervention, we might be able to solve this thing without any further bloodshed.

"It's the least I can do."

"I don't hold what Alonzo did against you, Gabriel, I

never have. The truth is, I should have quit a long time ago."

A shadow passes over his face. "I remained ignorant about a lot of things my father did, and that's on me. If you ever wanted to come back, I would value your expertise."

"I'm happy in Venice."

"I figured you'd say that, but it was worth a try." He turns to leave, but I have one more question. "Where is Alonzo these days?"

His expression turns frosty. "In Mexico City. He thinks he's beyond my reach there. He's wrong."

I really wonder what Alonzo did to provoke Gabriel's fury. It sounds like it involved his wife. I can relate. Because if Laurenti tries to hurt Alina, I will snap. No matter what the consequences of breaking the peace in Valencia, I will hunt him down.

47

ALINA

Tomas is in a really good mood when he gets back from dropping his mother off, but we don't get a chance to talk until after dinner that night. "Did something happen this afternoon?" I ask him when we're in bed. "You look a lot less stressed than you did at lunch."

"Am I really that transparent?"

No. In fact, the first time I met him, I couldn't get a read on him at all. But somewhere along the way, I've become much more attuned to Tomas's emotions. Maybe it comes from falling in love with him.

"You're an open book," I quip. "I can read everything on your mind. I bet you'll make a terrible poker player."

His eyes heat. "You should put that theory to the test," he suggests. "Let's play strip poker."

Sure. I can predict how that'll go. Tomas will be fully clothed, dressed in one of his impeccable suits, and I'll be utterly naked.

The thought shouldn't send a bolt of heat through my body.

But it does.

You can't make out with Tomas—his parents' bedroom is next door. "Are you going to tell me what happened?"

"Gabriel d'Este offered us his protection." He fills me in on the conversation that he had with the other man. "We'll meet Laurenti tomorrow night, as planned. But if my existence isn't enough to convince him to leave you alone, Gabriel's support will be. There's only a small handful of people in the world with enough power to challenge him."

"My father is already in Valencia, then," I say, my heart breaking a little. If Gabriel d'Este isn't part of the mafia, he's mafia-adjacent. And Vidone went to see him. Kiss the ring, as Tomas put it. I can't bury my head in the sand any longer and pretend that my father is unconnected to this dangerous world.

He hugs me into his body. "I'm sorry, dolcezza."

I breathe in the warm, comforting smell of him. "It's okay. I didn't know him anyway. I just hoped…" My voice trails off. I bury my head in his neck, and it's a minute before I can speak again. "It's fine. I'm fine."

He brushes a soft kiss over my lips. "What can I do to make you feel better?"

He asked me that question Friday night after we got back from Casanova. He told me I looked stressed and asked me if I'd like an orgasm to help me relax.

And it had.

Tonight though, it's not going to be enough. Tonight, even Tomas can't distract me from my thoughts.

It's dark. I can't see his expression. Maybe that gives

me the courage to finally ask the question that's been uppermost on my mind all week. "Why are you here?" I whisper. "Why are you helping me? Why do you care?"

He laughs disbelievingly. "Ali, do you even have to ask why? Isn't it obvious?"

My lonely, hopeful heart offers me an answer, but I don't trust it. It's desperate and greedy for everything Tomas has to offer. It wants love and togetherness, family and laughter. It wants it so much that it will believe anything.

I need the words I want to say. *Tell me why. Please don't make me guess.*

But I've used up all my bravery for the night, and I can't make the words leave my mouth. The silence stretches between us, long and fraught, and eventually, we both fall asleep.

TOMAS IS up before I am the next morning. I wander downstairs to find him laughing and in a rapid-fire Spanish conversation with his father. "My mom had to go in early," he says. "But she left behind pretty specific instructions. I'm to show you around the city, paying a special emphasis on potential engagement party venues." He grins. "Want to start with the beach?"

Venice has a beach, all the way in Lido. In the last two years, I've managed to visit it *once*. There's always something to do at the gym.

Tomas says 'potential engagement party venues' without flinching. I can either spend the next few days fretting about what he's feeling toward me, or I can put all that angst on hold and enjoy the extended weekend.

This is my first vacation in two years. The circumstances are far from ideal, but I'm going to make the best of it. Starting with the ocean right outside the door.

"Let's go."

We get coffee and croissants at a restaurant overlooking the beach. "Restaurants on the water are tourist traps," Tomas grumbles as we stand in line.

"I don't care."

We find a spot on the sand for an impromptu breakfast picnic. Tourist trap or not, my croissant is delicious. "Remember, you have to save room for esmorzaret," Tomas warns as I contemplate standing in line for another one. "Carlota will never let me hear the end of it if I don't bring you to the market."

"Oh God, not another meal," I groan. "Don't get me wrong. I love everything I've eaten so far, and I'm pretty sure I'll devour everything your sister is going to put in front of me. But at the rate I'm going, I'm not going to be in any shape to fight next week."

He gives me a slow once-over. "There's nothing wrong with your shape, dolcezza. Nothing at all. Your shape kept me up all night with a hard-on."

I feel a blush creep up my cheeks. "I had a sex dream about you," I admit.

"Did you now?" His eyebrow quirks up. "What were we doing?"

"I'm not going to tell you. How far away is the market if we walk?"

"A little over an hour. Want to do it?"

"Yes, please. I really need the exercise."

"It's that way." We cross the road and set off in the direction of the market, and Tomas wraps his arm around my waist and pulls me close. "Tell me about your dream."

He's not going to let it go. "We were in the gym," I tell him, my face flaming. "And we were wrestling. Naked."

He laughs softly. "I never gave you a tour of my place," he says. "But if I had, you'd have seen my home gym." He gives me a sidelong look. "It has a ring. Want to wrestle there when we get back home?"

Ask him to explain what he meant last night, a voice prompts. But now's not the right time for that conversation. Especially if his answer isn't the one I want. And I really want to sexy wrestle in Tomas's ring. All that crackling anger turned to passion... A wave of pure heat engulfs me. "I'd love to."

48

ALINA

Esmorzaret is *delightful.* Tomas wants to show me the Llotja de la Seda afterward because it's right around the corner from the central market, but unfortunately, the Gothic-style trading hall, one of Valencia's biggest tourist attractions, is closed for renovations. "I can see it from the outside," I assure Tomas.

"It looks like nothing special from the outside," he replies a little grumpily. "But the trading hall..." He shrugs. "Ah, well. Let's go see the Mercat de Colón."

"Another engagement party venue?" I tease.

He rolls his eyes. "Mothers," he says in good-natured exasperation.

"I'm surprised she hasn't been texting you demanding updates."

"She might be," he grins. "I have, however, turned off my phone, so I can't get them."

I'm having such a good time with Tomas that I almost forget I'm here to meet my father for the first time. M absentee father, who works for the mafia and who might or might not have arranged to have me abducted.

But before I know it, it's time to leave for the restaurant.

My father is staying in a villa in a small town an hour south of Valencia, and we're eating at a seafood restaurant in the vicinity. I ask Tomas about the villa on the way over. "Does he own it, do you know, or is he renting it?"

"VDL is renting it," he replies. "A lot of mafia outfits have a presence in Spain now. Altea, which is an hour and a half south of Valencia, is filled with Russians. Marabella, Barcelona... if you're a certain class of criminal, Spain is *the* place to be. But it's not cost-effective for every high-ranking member of a mafia to rent a villa here, so they often share."

"Does Antonio Moretti have a house here?" I ask, curious despite myself. "Is there a Venice Mafia presence?"

"There is a house south of the city," he replies. "I've never been to it. But when Antonio visits, he stays with Gabriel."

"Are they friends?"

"I think so. But friendship is a complicated thing in their world."

"Their world, not yours?"

He grins easily. "Me? I'm just a low-level drone."

I somehow doubt it. "Does Antonio Moretti usually loan his private plane out to his low-level drones?" I ask pointedly. "From what I've heard, he's not the altruistic sort."

It's a rhetorical question; I'm not looking for an answer, and Tomas doesn't offer me one. "Valentina looked into Laurenti's finances. He's done pretty well for himself, but his expenditures have increased substantially in the last six months. He really wants the top job, and he's been going through money like water to get it. He's gambling that if his alliance with the Russians goes through, it'll catapult him to the top of the shortlist."

"And what do the Russians get out of it?"

"A foothold into Italy. Whatever that's worth. Valentina couldn't find the specifics of the agreement, unfortunately, but your father's getting the better end of the deal."

"And marrying his daughter to Damir Malinov, where does that factor into the equation?"

"A marriage is the old-fashioned way to seal these sorts of contracts," he replies, his mouth twisting into a frown. "Most people have moved on, but Southern Italy..." He shakes his head disapprovingly. "They treat their daughters like property there. It's barbaric." He gives me a sidelong look. "This is the world Vidone Laurenti lives in. Be prepared. He's bet everything on becoming the next VDL boss. If he doesn't pull it off, he's in a very precarious position. He's going to try really hard to get you on board."

"I can't imagine what he thinks he could tell me that will make me marry a stranger."

"He'll point out what a catch he is," Tomas says. "Malinov is very rich."

"I've already told you I'm not going to marry some random guy because he can buy me things."

He squeezes my hand. "Tonight, it's not me you have to convince, dolcezza," he replies. "It's Vidone."

I exhale in a long breath. My stomach is churning

with nerves. "I don't understand why he invited me to dinner," I complain. "What if he takes one look at me and is disappointed by what he sees? What if he doesn't like me? I should have treated this like a first date and insisted we meet in a coffee shop."

"Why would he be disappointed by what he sees?" Tomas demands.

"It can happen. Not everyone likes me."

"Then they're clearly out of their minds. My family loves you. My father was very impressed that you went through the trouble of making me a café bombon." A smile plays about his lips. "I didn't tell him about the rat poison. Why destroy his illusions?" He slides the car in front of a large white building with a terracotta-tiled roof and turns off the engine. "We're here."

He gets out of the car and comes around to open my door. I'd normally point out that my hands aren't broken, and I can do that on my own, but today, I'm glad for the delay.

I've been waiting all my life to meet my father, and it turns out I'm still not ready.

A hostess leads us to a small private room in the back of the restaurant. We barely step into the doorway when a man jumps to his feet.

Ali's father. Vidone Laurenti himself.

"Alina," he booms. "Daughter." He opens his arms wide and folds her into a hug. "I've waited so long to meet you."

That's a strange thing to say, given Laurenti just found out about her existence less than two weeks ago. I file that away for reference and focus my attention on Ali. She's a little stiff in his embrace, and she pulls away as soon as she can without being obvious about it. "I'm so glad you were able to make it to Valencia. It was such short notice, so I thought—"

"As if I'm going to pass up the chance to see you." He directs his attention toward me and his eyes narrow. "Who's this?" he asks, his voice significantly less warm than before.

"I'm Tomas Aguilar," I reply, holding out my hand

with a cordial smile. "Good to meet you, Signor Laurenti. When Alina told me you were coming to Valencia to meet her, I couldn't stay away. I'm her fiancé."

We've decided that, at least today, we're going to approach this meeting without any threats. I'm not planning on telling him that I know who he is, and I'm not bringing up Gabriel's support, either. Tonight, I'm going to give Alina's father one chance to just be a parent, and it's up to him if he takes it.

Sabrina Laurenti might have died in a car crash, but she wasn't Laurenti's only daughter. If he can put his agenda aside, he'll have a chance to have Alina in his life.

"Her what?" Vidone's face turns red. He pivots to Alina. "I thought you said you were single," he says accusingly.

She wets her lower lip with her tongue. "No, I said that it was complicated." We've rehearsed this answer, so the lie comes easily to her lips. "I wasn't sure where our relationship was going, and then Tomas asked me to marry him. When that happened, I knew he had to come to Valencia. I wanted the two of you to meet."

She smiles happily, and for a moment, my heart wants to believe it's all real. That she's delighted to marry me, that she cannot wait to spend the rest of her life with me.

But last night, when I more or less confessed my feelings, she didn't say anything. And this afternoon, when I suggested naked wrestling in my house, she was on board.

She wants to keep things casual. How much more evidence do you need?

It's not casual for me. I don't know if it's ever been.

And if we want different things, we should part ways. As much as it's going to wreck me to never see Ali again, I cannot be in another one-sided relationship. I was able to bounce back from Estela because deep down inside; I knew she was the wrong woman.

Ali though...

My dolcezza entered my life like a hurricane, and she's laid my heart to waste. And even if she never feels for me what I feel for her, it's worth it. Even knowing the outcome, I would do it all again. I wouldn't trade the time I've had with her for anything.

Focus, Tomas. I drag my attention back to Laurenti, who is looking from me to his daughter and back at me again. He realizes I'm still holding out my hand, and he shakes it quickly. "Good to meet you, Tomas." There's a smile on his lips, but it doesn't reach his eyes. "Alina, you didn't tell me you were bringing your fiancé when we talked."

"I didn't?" She blinks innocently, which is again part of the plan. "I'm so sorry. I guess I was so overwhelmed that we were finally meeting that I forgot to mention him." She offers him a conciliatory smile. "It's not every day you find the father you never thought you'd meet."

"No, it isn't." He finally gathers himself. "Where are my manners? Please, sit down, both of you."

This isn't my sort of restaurant. The furniture is starkly contemporary, all white leather and metal. Alina sits on a straight-back chair, her shoulders stiff and her jaw tense, and I settle on the chair right next to her and lace her fingers in mine. She squeezes my hand back.

I'm here, dolcezza. Lean on me.

In the light, I examine Laurenti. He looks like he's in

his mid-fifties. He's lean, almost thin, average height, his black hair liberally peppered with gray. A pair of gold wire-rimmed glasses are perched on his long nose. He's dressed all in black. Add a clerical collar, and he'd pass for a priest.

I'm not the only one staring. Laurenti is examining his daughter with narrowed eyes. "How old are you?" he asks abruptly.

"Twenty-five."

"That's not—" He stops himself. "What can I get you to drink? Some prosecco to celebrate the engagement? Or cava since we are in Spain?"

When we were discussing how to approach this meeting, Alina asked me if her father would try to drug her again during dinner. I reassured her that Valencia is neutral ground, and Gabriel would consider any attempt to abduct her as an act of war. It all seemed a bit fantastical to her—no violence at all because Gabriel d'Este deemed it so—but she went along with it.

She still doesn't trust him, though. "Just water for me, please," she replies. "I'm not drinking tonight."

He shoots her a sharp look. "Are you pregnant?" he demands.

Seriously? He might have contributed the sperm that helped give her life, but he's been absent ever since. He hasn't earned the right to ask her personal, probing questions. Alina seems to agree because her grip on my hand tightens. "No," she says tersely. "I'm not."

Okay, time to lower the tension. I lean forward, pasting an idiotic smile on my face. "I would love some prosecco or cava," I tell Laurenti cheerfully. "Whatever you have open is fine."

Dinner gets underway shortly after that. Laurenti seems to realize he's doing a great job pissing off Alina, so he eases up during the meal. He keeps the conversation light and does his best to be charming and funny. It's only when we're lingering over dessert and coffee does he return to the topic of our engagement. "When's the wedding?" he asks, leaning back in his chair. "Have you set a date?"

"No," Ali says. "We just got engaged." She sips her coffee. "I'm sorry your wife couldn't be here tonight. I'd have loved to meet her."

"She's very disappointed to miss you," he replies. "Serena is on the board of the art museum, and there was a meeting this weekend that she couldn't miss. She's hoping there will be other chances to connect." He attempts a paternal smile. "As do I."

Ali glances down at her coffee. "Tell me about my mother," she says softly. "How did you meet?"

"At the beach in San Vito Lo Capo," he replies. "Do you know the town? It's in northwestern Sicily. I was there for work. I went to the beach during a break, and there she was. Your mother."

"She was young when the two of you met."

He nods. "Seventeen," he says. "I wanted her the moment I laid eyes on her. She was beautiful, with her hair blowing in the wind and laughter in her eyes."

In his letter, Laurenti said he fell in love with Teresa the first time he saw her. Today, he says he wanted her, and that's a lot closer to the truth. I spent a long time staring at the photo he sent Ali, looking for anything that might be a clue. Vidone was smiling widely into the camera, blissfully happy, but Teresa wasn't. Her eyes were haunted.

I haven't told Ali my suspicions. What's the point? Her mother is dead, and she's having a difficult enough time with things as they are. Telling her now would only cause her distress.

But it seems like I can't keep my mouth shut. "She was seventeen," I say casually. "How old were you?"

His grip on the wine glass stem tightens. "Thirty-one. There was an age difference, yes, and her parents didn't approve of me at first, but I won them over."

Ali is following the conversation, her forehead furrowed, but at the mention of her grandparents, she leans forward eagerly. "You know her parents? Do they live in Sicily too? I'd love to meet them. Do you know how I can get in touch with them?"

"They're dead," Laurenti says shortly.

Her face falls. "Ah well," she says. "It was worth a try." She gives him a forced smile. "What was my mother like as a young woman?"

"She cooked well," he replies.

Two years together. Two of the happiest years of his life, if I'm to believe what he wrote in his letter. And the first thing that comes to mind to describe her is, 'She cooked well?'

"She loved the water," he continues. "She was always on the beach, staring out at the ocean."

"That never changed," Ali says sadly. "She loved the beach. We went to Ostia at least once a week. Even when she got sick, her best days were when I'd take her there. What did she cook?"

"I can't remember. It's been twenty-five years." He sets

his glass down. "Enough of the past. Tell me more about yourself, Alina. How did you and Tomas meet?"

"We own the gym together."

"That's interesting." His eyes rest on me, a little too aware, and I wonder if he's looked up when I bought my share of the gym from Simon Groff. Daniel promised the records wouldn't be made public, and the lawyer is ferociously competent. "It's not usually a good idea to mix business with pleasure. Do you like working with Tomas?"

Alina laughs for the first time. "We clashed at the start," she admits. "A lot." She exchanges a smile with me. "But Tomas won me over."

Did I? Hope raises its head again, and I quell it. Ali and I really need to talk. At this point, I have no idea what's real and what's fake.

"But, of course, you won't still be involved with it once you're married," he says. "I can't imagine that fighting will be good for your body when you're pregnant."

Ali blinks, stunned. "I have no intention of giving up the gym. I won't fight if I'm pregnant, of course, but that's a long way off. I'm only twenty-five. I'm in no hurry for children."

"And what does Tomas think of that?"

Is he trying to drive a wedge between us? Is that what this is? Wow, he is *not* good at it. Then again, Vidone Laurenti rose to power by being the most violent and unhinged man in the room. You take away his biggest weapon, and he is *floundering.*

"It's Ali's body," I reply blandly. "Ali's decision."

He shakes his head in disgust. "Young people nowadays."

Before he can launch into a rant about how my generation is failing him personally, Ali changes the subject. "I'm so sorry about your daughter," she says softly. "You must miss her very much. Do you have any photos of her?"

Grief clouds his expression. He didn't love her enough to let her marry whoever she wanted, but he did love her a little. Or maybe he's just mourning his lost alliance with the Russians. "Yes." He pulls out his phone and flips through it until he finds the photo he's looking for. "This is Sabrina and Damir. They were going to be married."

Ladies and gentlemen, Damir Malinov has entered the chat.

Alina looks at the screen and then passes it to me. I've seen photos of the Malinov heir before, so I focus on his former bride. Sabrina is pretty in a washed-out way. Malinov's got his arm around her waist, and she's smiling at the camera, but to my eyes, her smile looks more than a little strained.

To be fair, I'm not exactly an impartial observer.

I hand the phone back to Vidone. He looks at the screen once more before setting it down. "While you're in Valencia, Alina, I'd like you to meet Damir."

Of course you would. "Why?" I ask bluntly.

He gives me a hostile look and addresses his remarks to his daughter. "He's a good friend of the family," he says. "And he is grieving. I thought seeing you would bring him solace."

"I understand," Alina replies. "But I only have this weekend here, and I'd like to focus on us."

Vidone's expression softens. "I'd like that too."

Nicely done. If I didn't know who Vidone Laurenti was, I'd almost be convinced. He's mostly doing a good impression of a father awkwardly meeting his grown daughter for the first time.

But I know how much hinges on his alliance with the Russians.

Laurenti desperately needs Alina to marry Damir Malinov. He's met her now. He's taken her measure. As soon as we leave here, he'll be plotting his next move.

This is the kind of strategic chess game that Gabriel, Antonio, and Dante live for.

Me? I don't care about the machinations. I have just one goal, and that's to keep the woman I've fallen in love with safe.

50

ALINA

By the time dinner is done, I *know*. This is not a man who wants to know me. Maybe he does, but his main goal is to find a way to marry me off to Damir Malinov.

Everything the Venice Mafia told me about my father is true.

I'm silent on the long drive back. It's a perfect time to continue the conversation we started last night, but I'm too drained. Tomas doesn't say anything, either. We get to his parents' house well after midnight, tiptoe up the stairs to our bedroom, and fall asleep.

The next morning, I'm in the middle of my first cup of coffee when my phone rings. It's my father. "Alina," he says, his voice strained. "I need to talk to you urgently. Can we meet somewhere this morning?"

Tomas is sitting at the table across from me. "It's my father," I mouth, and his lips twist wryly. He doesn't say anything, but it's obvious what he's thinking. *Here we go.*

This is my father's attempt to convince me to marry

Damir. I'm about to agree when I remember the conference I was supposed to be attending. "I have to be at a
demonstration at eleven," I lie. "But I'm free until then."

We pick a restaurant near the port. I'm about to hang
up when my father says, "Don't bring your boyfriend. I
need to talk to you without him there."

My heart sinks. Even after everything, there must
have been a small part of me that was still hopeful.
"Whatever you have to say can be said in front of Tomas.
And he's not my boyfriend. He's my fiancé."

"Please, Alina. If it wasn't important, I wouldn't ask
you. Please do me this favor."

I just want this all to be over. I want to return to my
real life in Venice. I want to be in my gym, stuck inside
that tiny office with Tomas, the two of us trading insults
at each other. And the fastest way to do that is to hear my
father out. "Okay, fine." Tomas's expression turns thun-
derous, and I know we're going to have a fight about my
decision. "See you in an hour."

I hang up. "Before you say anything about how it isn't
safe for me to go alone, remember that you repeatedly
assured me we'd be safe in Valencia."

Tomas continues to frown at me. "We are safe in
Valencia," he says, an exaggerated note of patience in his
voice. "That still doesn't mean you should take unnecessary risks."

"He's not going to talk if you're there," I say wearily.
"You know that as well as I do. If you join us, it'll just be a
repeat of last night. Let's just cut to the chase." Tomas
opens his mouth to argue, and I add, "I want you to come
to the restaurant. Just stay out of sight."

He considers it for a minute and then nods tightly. "I still don't like it. But fine."

TOMAS GOES to the restaurant early to stake it out. I take a taxi there half an hour later. I arrive a couple of minutes early, but my father's already there, seated at a table by the window, cradling a cup of coffee in his hands.

He gets to his feet as I approach. "I'm glad you could come." He waves to the chair across from him. "Sit. You want something to eat? They make a good sandwich here. The Valencians have this mid-morning meal—"

"The esmorzaret," I cut in. "I'm not hungry." I smile at the hovering waitress. "Could I get a glass of orange juice?" Valencians are very big on freshly squeezed juice. Even the tiniest cafe I've passed has a juicer.

She nods and disappears to fill my order. When she's out of earshot, I direct my attention to my father. "You said you wanted to talk about something important...?"

"I did." He hesitates. "I don't know how to say this. I've gotten myself into a bit of a mess." He takes a deep breath. "A big mess. I entered a business arrangement with a Russian named Gregori Malinov. Gregori is Damir's father. Sabrina's future father-in-law."

I try and look confused. "Okay?"

"When Sabrina died... it complicated things. Gregori only entered the deal with me because we were going to be family. Now that we're not, he wants out. And if he pulls out of our agreement, I will be ruined."

"What does this have to do with me?" I ask, though I already know the answer.

"You're my daughter," he says. "If you were to pretend to be engaged to Damir—"

"What?" I spit out.

"It's just for a month or two, that's all. I just need enough time to convince Gregori to honor his word. Once he signs on the dotted line, you can break off the engagement."

I stare at him in disbelief. "You want me to pretend to be engaged to some stranger?"

"He was engaged to Sabrina," he replies, as if that makes his idea sound less crazy. "He's not a stranger. You saw his photo last night."

"What difference does that make? I've never met him."

"He's in Valencia. I can arrange a meeting this afternoon."

"No!" I take a calming breath and then another. "I can't do this. First, what you're asking me to do is crazy. Second, I'm engaged to someone else. And finally—"

"Tomas," my father cuts me off with a sneer. "I saw the car he was driving last night. Damir can provide so much better than that for you."

Not that it matters, but we were driving Tomas's father's car. Jose Antonio had generously loaned it to us when he heard us talking about getting a rental. For Vidone Laurenti to sneer at it, to dismiss Tomas based on the car he's driving...

Hot rage builds up in my heart. "I don't care about Damir's ability to provide for me," I snap. "This isn't real. You can't seriously expect me to put my life on hold for a couple of months just so your business deal can go through."

"Just so my business deal..." He splutters in outrage. "Do you think I'd ask for your help for a trivial matter? If this doesn't go through, I will be ruined. Everything I've worked for all my life will be in shambles. *I'm your father.* Where's your family loyalty?"

He reaches inside his jacket and pulls out a check-book. "I looked into your gym," he says. "It's small. You can't make more than twenty thousand euros in profit every year." He scribbles a number on the check, signs it with a flourish, and pushes it toward me.

It's a check made out to 'Alina Zucaro' in the amount of twenty thousand euros.

He spelled my last name wrong. I want to laugh hysterically. He's trying to bribe me into breaking my engagement with Tomas and entering this arrangement with Damir Malinov, and he hasn't even bothered to spell my name correctly.

Two weeks ago, Tomas bet on me winning Ciro del Barba's underground tournament. He confidently wagered ten thousand euros on the fight, and when he won, he deposited all his winnings, all one hundred and twenty thousand euros of it, into my gym's bank account.

I've wanted a family all my life. But family is more than blood. Maybe our family is who we want it to be.

I push the check back to my father. "I'm not interested."

"You want more? Fine." He tears up his first check and writes another. "Here."

This time, it's one hundred thousand euros.

I swallow the lump in my throat and get to my feet. "I

came to Valencia to meet you," I whisper. "All I ever wanted was a father. A family. I've waited for you all my life. But you just want your business deal to succeed. You don't want a daughter, and you don't want me."

Then I walk out of the restaurant.

I can barely see through the tears that fill my eyes. I stumble forward, and I walk into a solid figure. Strong arms wrap around me, and Tomas pulls me into a comforting embrace. "I'm here, dolcezza," he says, his eyes filled with concern and tenderness. "I've got you."

51

ALINA

Tomas steers me into an empty cafe. For a few minutes, I just cry, and he holds me, his expression concerned. Finally, my sobs die down. "I'm sorry," I mumble. "My mascara ran on your jacket. It's ruined."

"I don't give a damn about my jacket," he responds. "What did he say to you?"

"Nothing new. He offered me money to pretend to be Damir Malinov's fiancée. His first offer was twenty thousand euros, and then when I turned him down, he increased it to a hundred thousand." I smile bitterly. "He didn't even spell my last name correctly. That's how little he cared."

Tomas's lips tighten, but he doesn't say anything.

"So I told him I was done." I wipe the last of the tears away impatiently. "You knew who he was all along. You told me, and I didn't listen. I should have."

"I'm sorry," he says quietly. "I wish I had been wrong.

I wish, more than anything else, Ali, that he was worthy of you."

He's looking really worried, and I don't want him to be. "Forget him. I still have some Valencian things on my to-do list. Your sister told me I had to drink horchata and eat fartóns. I have no idea what fartóns are, but I'm in." I force a smile on my face. "Besides, I can't go back to your parents' house with red eyes."

"Don't forget your red nose," he quips, though the concern doesn't fully leave his eyes. "If we're heading toward the market for horchata, I have a fun surprise. I texted Gabriel about La Llotja yesterday, and he used his influence and arranged for us to visit." He gets to his feet and holds out his hand for me. "Want to go see it?"

LA LLOTJA IS SPECTACULAR. It's also completely deserted. Since the building is under renovation, there should be workers there. Maybe they're all at esmorzaret because there's no one to be seen. I wander through the large trading hall with its carved pillars and high arched ceilings, marveling at the five-hundred-year-old building, but my favorite part is the courtyard filled with orange trees.

"Thank you for bringing me here," I tell Tomas, sitting on a bench in the courtyard and taking it all in. "This is... special."

"It is," he agrees, but he's not looking at the building.

He's looking at me.

My heart leaps in my throat. Suddenly, I have to know.

It doesn't matter if the answer is going to break my heart —I can't take the uncertainty any longer. "Why did you come to Valencia with me, Tomas? Why are you helping me?"

"You asked me that two nights ago," he replies. "My answer is the same now as it was then. Isn't it obvious?"

This time, I don't chicken out. "Not to me," I whisper. "Tell me why, Tomas, because I need the words. I need to hear them."

"Ali," he murmurs, pulling me into his arms. *And it feels like home.* He brushes a kiss over my lips, a warm kiss that makes my hopeful heart flutter to life. "Dolcezza, I'm crazy about you. I've been crazy about you from the moment you stared at me from across the gym, fury in your eyes, and told me to step into the ring. I love you. I love you when you're plotting to poison me—"

His declaration takes my breath away, and a big, happy smile breaks out on my face. I take a deep, orange-scented breath, joy exploding inside my heart. "I wasn't going to actually do it."

"Always good to hear," he quips. "I love you so much that I'm here in Valencia, braving my terrifying family—"

"I'm going to interrupt once again to tell you that your family is perfect, and I won't tolerate any slander of them."

"They showed up with a banner to the airport," he points out. "My mother has us searching for engagement party venues. Has she stopped to ask us if we want an engagement party? No, she has not." A smile softens his eyes. "They already like you much more than they like me."

"That's not true."

He laughs. "Yes, it is. You're the reason I'm finally back in Valencia, and they know it." He laces his fingers in mine and brings my ring finger up to his lips. "I gave you my grandmother's ring, Ali. This might be a fake engagement, but what I feel for you is real."

The sun is out from behind a cloud. It's warm and quiet and peaceful, and it's just the two of us here, and I still can't quite believe it. I've fallen in love with him, and he feels the same way. He loves me. Tomas Aguilar, with his bespoke suits and those grey eyes that see far too much, *loves me.* I want to pinch myself and scream for joy and run around in giddy circles, giggling madly in sheer happiness.

"I thought you wanted something casual."

"I thought *you* wanted something casual," he replies accusingly, and then we both start to laugh. "Why didn't you just ask?"

"I wasn't ready to hear the answer," I admit sheepishly. "You kept doing nice things—"

I hear a loud, sharp sound, and an unripe orange in the tree directly above me explodes into pulp. I barely have time to react before Tomas pushes me to the ground and throws his body over mine.

"Sniper," he says into my ear. I can feel the thump of his heartbeat against my chest. "From one of the upper floor windows. Stay down."

Someone is shooting at us.

In a supposedly safe Valencia.

How is this possible?

52

TOMAS

A sniper is shooting at us.

In *Valencia*.

I roll us under the nearest stone bench. The sniper is firing from one of the large, arched windows on the upper floors. The tree foliage is interfering with his or her line of sight and the fountain in the middle of the courtyard acts as another barrier, but we've still been immensely lucky not to have already been hit.

He fires again, and a piece of marble chips off the fountain. My heart spikes in panic. My thoughts race. Gabriel d'Este does not allow violence in his city. Who would be stupid enough to ignore his edict and risk his wrath?

Is Vidone Laurenti truly this desperate? But he has to know that this attack won't do anything. Even if he succeeds in getting rid of me, Ali isn't going to meekly offer herself up as Damir Malinov's bride. Even if I die here, she will not be unprotected. Antonio Moretti will not stand aside and watch her get married off to Malinov against her will. Of that, I'm sure.

Or is this Gabriel's doing? That unwelcome thought burrows in my head. Is this payback because I don't want to work for the d'Este family any longer? But that doesn't make any sense. If Gabriel d'Este wanted me dead, I'd already be rotting in the ground. And if the padrino believed that d'Este was still holding a grudge, he would have never let us come to Valencia.

Who, then? Who do I have to kill? Laurenti, d'Este, or someone else?

My thoughts are churning so much that I don't realize at first that the shots have stopped. But they have. I wait for a good five minutes and then roll off Alina. "Sorry," I murmur, every nerve in my body on edge. "I didn't mean to squash you."

"You didn't." Her breathless voice makes a lie of her words. "Is it safe to get up, do you think? Or is the sniper biding his time?"

"The sniper is dead," a man's voice says calmly. "It's safe to get up."

Gabriel d'Este. I spring to my feet and *move*. Before he can say another word, before he can even react, I have a knife to his throat. "Tell me," I growl. "Was this you? Are you responsible for this?"

He freezes. "There are three guns trained on you right now, Tomas," he says. "You won't survive this. Put down the knife, please, unless you want to die."

"I might not survive it, but neither will you. Answer my question."

"No, of course I didn't have anything to do with this," he says, the impatient edge in his voice hard to miss. "I understand your fiancée has been shot at and you're not thinking clearly, but come on. Do you really think I'm stupid enough to send a sniper after you, watch them fail, and then show up in person, putting myself at risk, all for the dubious pleasure of shooting you myself? Don't be a fucking idiot, Tomas, you're better than this. The hospital your mother works at bears my name. I'm the biggest investor in your sister's restaurant. If I wanted you dead, it would have already happened."

The adrenaline slowly fades. Gabriel's right; it's not him. Then who? I let my hand drop and slacken my grip around his throat.

He pulls away from me, putting some distance between us. "Please drop the knife," he says. "My security team can be somewhat trigger-happy, and I really don't want to be responsible for your death."

I let the knife fall to the ground and kick it toward him. D'Este picks up the weapon and makes a covert hand sign. I half-expect a hail of shots to ring out, but to my shock, nothing happens. He must have asked his security team to stand down.

Gabriel turns to Alina. "Senorita Zuccaro," he starts, but Alina isn't paying attention. Her eyes are fixed on my arm. "You're bleeding," she gasps. "One of the bullets must have hit you."

I look down. "It's just a flesh wound."

"It's just a…" Her eyes widen in outrage. "Tomas, you got *shot*. Why are you so calm about it? Is this a daily occurrence for you?"

"Every other day," I quip. I turn to Gabriel. I pulled a weapon on Gabriel d'Este in the heart of his city. What the *hell* was I thinking? "Sorry about that. You're right, I wasn't thinking clearly." I start thinking now. I've been assuming that I'm the target. But it doesn't add up. Laurenti is many things, but he hasn't survived over three decades in the mafia by being stupid. If Gabriel black-listed VDL, they wouldn't be able to get their money laundered, and the organization would be in deep trouble. Vidone wouldn't make such a rookie move.

But if I wasn't the target, *it was Alina.*

Then, it all comes to me in a flash. All the information was right there—I just had to put it together.

The Kutuzovo OPG had a deal with Vidone Laurenti, but Antonio had been surprised by that. What were his exact words? 'I'm surprised Kutuzovo has time to flirt with Italy; I thought they needed all their resources to keep the Sidorov Bratva at bay.'

And Vidone's daughter Sabrina died under suspicious circumstances.

Of course. It was Kutuzovo OPG—and their pakhan Gregori Malinov—who had Sabrina killed so that they could get out of the deal with Laurenti. When they found out that Vidone had another daughter for Damir Malinov to marry, they targeted her, too.

"Under the circumstances, your reaction was understandable," Gabriel says with a wave of his hand. "I take it from your expression you've figured out who's responsible for this attack."

It's not the father; Gregori Malinov is in Russia. It's the son.

I nod tightly. "I need Damir Malinov's address."

53

TOMAS

Of course, it's not that simple. As ready as I am to take Damir Malinov down, I know I can't do it by myself. And Gabriel flat-out refuses to let Antonio send troops to Valencia.

"Fine," I snap, feeling my grip on my temper slipping. "Then I'll do it by myself." I'm aware I'm acting recklessly, but I don't care. Damir Malinov tried to kill Alina. I will not let him survive.

"And then you will die," Gabriel replies. "You need a plan, Tomas." He turns to Alina. "I deeply regret that you've been placed in danger in my city," he says. "Please let me make amends."

She lifts her head. "Do these amends include a doctor to look at Tomas's arm?"

"Of course."

"Then let's go."

Gabriel whisks us away to his house. His on-call doctor cleans my wound and puts a bandage on it without blinking an eye. Alina hovers near me while that happens. "I hate this," she says. "You'd think I'd be used to blood, but when it's yours..."

I squeeze her hand. "I'm fine."

She takes a deep breath. "I know you want to kill Damir Malinov," she says. "And I understand. I want to kill him, too. But tell me why we can't just go back to Venice."

"This isn't about revenge." The hot flash of anger has evaporated, leaving behind a cold resolve. "Your father is desperate to honor the contract, and Gregori Malinov is just as desperate to end it. We can go back to Venice, but neither of them will leave you alone. Vidone Laurenti wants you married to Damir Malinov, and Gregori wants you dead. There's only one way to end this."

Realization dawns on her face. "Kill Damir Malinov."

"He's Gregori's only son," I reply. "If he's dead, the alliance between VDL and Kutuzovo is done. And you get your life back."

"But you can't storm his compound by yourself," she whispers, her expression desperately worried. "And if Gabriel won't let Antonio Moretti send you help..."

"Antonio can't help," Gabriel says, walking into the room and overhearing that last part. No such thing as knocking for d'Este, I see. "But here's someone who can." He steps aside, and I suck in a breath as I see the face of the man behind him.

Andrei Sidorov. The pakhan himself.

What the fuck?

The Sidorov Bratva controls large areas of Russia, Belarus, Romania, Hungary, and Croatia. For Andrei to be here in person...

"Damir Malinov killed one of my emissaries," he says

grimly. "He put out word that the Kutuzovo were interested in negotiating for peace, and when Vassili
approached him under a flag of truce, he tortured and
killed him." His eyes are blocks of ice. "My sister Natalya
was in love with Vassili. Damir sent her the footage of
him being tortured." He holds out his hand to me.
"Andrei Sidorov. Let's go kill the bastard."

54

ALINA

The man I love is going off to war, and there's not a damn thing I can do about it. "I want to come," I say, but even as the words leave my mouth, I know what Tomas's answer is going to be.

"Dolcezza, no." Tomas's expression is anguished. "Please don't ask again because I can deny you nothing. But it's not safe for you."

He's right. I know he is. The only time I've shot a gun has been in a training range. If I go with Tomas, his focus will be split. Rather than concentrate on taking out Malinov, he'll be worrying about me.

I want to go. God, I don't want to let him out of my sight. But if I do, I'll be putting him in danger.

"I'm not going to ask again." I pull him close and press a hard kiss on his lips. "But come back to me, you hear that? You promised me sexy wrestling in your home gym, and I intend to hold you to that promise."

"I'll be back before you know it," he murmurs into

mouth. He pulls back and looks into my eyes. "Don't worry, dolcezza. If I die, it'll be of rat poisoning under suspicious circumstances."

A reluctant smile forms on my lips. "I already told you I'm not planning on poisoning you," I tell him. "Not until I find out who'll inherit your share of the gym."

He laughs softly. "It's you, Ali. I had Daniel draw up the papers earlier this week. You are now the sole owner of Groff's." A look of distaste flashes over his face. "And the moment we go back to Venice, we're renaming the gym." He kisses me again, a slow, lingering kiss that feels like he doesn't want to leave. Like a promise for a long and happy future. "I love you, Alina Zuccaro."

I've wanted to hear those words for so long. But he says them to me, and my heart clenches with worry. "I love you, Tomas Aguilar." The words spill out in a rush. I didn't say them to him earlier, when we were at La Llotja. I was going to, and then the sniper shot at us. And this isn't the right time for grand declarations of love, but I can't let him go without telling him how I feel. "I love you so much. I was ready to murder you when you walked into my gym, but what I didn't know then was that that day was the best day of my life."

His eyes soften. His gaze locks onto mine, and there's so much emotion there that my heart begins to swell. He lifts his hand and strokes my cheek, and I turn into his touch, nuzzling into it like a kitten searching for comfort. I want to cling to him and beg him to stay, but I make myself be strong. "Be safe. Please."

"I promise," he says again. His fingers linger on my face for a long, infinite moment, as if he's trying to memorize every detail of my face, and then he slowly lets go. "I love you and you love me, and that's all that matters. This is a blip, Ali. I'm going to take care of Malinov, and then I'm going to come back, and then we're going to live happily ever after. That's a promise."

And then he's gone.

W e've decided that while Tomas is gone, I'm going to remain in Gabriel d'Este's house. A butler—of course, there's a butler—shows me to a small living room where I can wait. The walls are covered from floor to ceiling with bookshelves. Normally, I'd be snooping—you can learn a lot about a person from their reading tastes—but I'm too stressed.

I pace back and forth, clutching my phone, looking at the screen every few seconds as if Tomas is going to stop in the middle of killing someone to text me. I've done one hundred and twenty-seven laps of the room when there's a knock on the door.

My heart jumps into my throat. "Come in," I call out. Is it Gabriel? Is it over? It can't be; it's only been twenty minutes since Tomas left with Andrei Sidorov and his two bodyguards. Is it bad news?

A woman enters the room. She's of medium height and build, dressed in a red T-shirt and cream shorts, with chestnut-colored hair falling in lustrous waves around her shoulders. "Alina, hello," she says with a warm smile, holding out her hand to me. "I'm Cecelia d'Este. Gabriel's wife."

"Good to meet you," I reply, though I'm really not in the mood for pleasantries.

"No, it's not, is it?" Her expression is knowing. "I've been in your shoes. The last thing you want to do is make small talk. But when the same thing happened to me, it helped that I wasn't alone." She kicks off her shoes and curls herself into a deep blue armchair. "Please feel free to pretend I'm not here."

I think I already like her. "This is my battle," I blurt out. "I should be fighting it. Instead, Tomas is putting his life in danger because of me. His life was perfectly peaceful until I came along."

"Ah, but was it?" She tilts her head to one side. "I don't know Tomas, but from my understanding, he left Valencia and stayed away from his family for a long time. And if you hadn't entered his life, he might have never come home."

"Oh God, his family." I can't believe I forgot all about them. "If they're in danger..."

"No, Flurin is on it. Gabriel's head of security. He's got a team on them." She gives me a reassuring smile. "He's very competent. They will be okay."

"Thank you."

She waves away my gratitude. We lapse into silence. I resume wearing a tread in the carpet, and she flips through something on her phone. Five long minutes go by. "How will we know what happens?"

She looks up. "Gabriel and Andrei are in contact," she

says. "If something happens, he'll know, and he'll come find us."

"Okay, good." I resume my worrying. "This is all my fault," I blurt out after another ten minutes go by. "If I'd never responded to my father's letter, none of this would have happened."

She puts her phone away. "Do you really believe that, Alina? Can I call you Alina, by the way?"

"You can, but I prefer Ali."

She smiles. "Ali, my friends call me Cici. By now, you have to know that the moment Sabrina was killed, Vidone Laurenti focused on you."

There's something about the way she words the sentence that sets off an alarm bell. "You know something about him, don't you?"

"I know more about Southern Italy than I ever wanted to," she says wryly. "VDL is on my family's radar. When did Laurenti tell you he discovered your existence?"

"A few weeks ago." I clench my hands into fists. "It's not true, is it?"

Her expression softens. "I'm sorry," she says. "No, it's not. Laurenti knew the moment you took the DNA test. He was furious when he found out."

I can't believe it. "I took that test two years ago. You're saying he's known about me for two years but never once reached out?"

"Your mother wasn't supposed to get pregnant. After all, she was his mistress, not his wife. An illegitimate child clouds the line of succession." She smiles. "Also, when she ran, she managed to steal a good bit of money from him."

That explains the money in my mother's bank account. One mystery solved. "My mother was his mistress?"

"You didn't know?" Regret washes over her face. "I'm so sorry."

"I don't think she had much of a choice." Something Tomas said at dinner with my father comes roaring back. "She was seventeen. He was thirty-one." Bile fills my mouth. "That's why she never talked about him. She just wanted to forget that part of her life."

All those times I asked her about my father, was this what she was trying to forget? That she was groomed by a man much older than her, a violent man who would do whatever it took to possess her?

I'm going to be sick.

She would never discuss the past. She's dead now, and I'll never be able to prove it, but my heart knows. *She wanted to forget.*

And she had. Those memories never came back. If one good came out of her Alzheimer's, it was this. The wretched disease that took my mother far too young helped Teresa Zuccaro forget the things she never wanted to remember.

Tears fill my eyes, and I wipe them away. "I'm sorry," Cici says again, her expression distressed. "Ali, I'm so sorry. I should have kept my mouth shut. Please don't—"

"No, it's okay." Cici thinks I'm crying because my father ignored my existence for two years and only contacted me when he needed something from me. But that's not really a surprise. No, my tears are reserved for my mother. The woman who was there for me every single day of my childhood. "I'm okay. I met with my father again this morning." God, was that really only a couple of hours ago? It feels like *forever.* "I'm under no illusions about who he is."

She gives me a careful, assessing look. "You also know he tried to abduct you from Venice?"

"We suspected."

She hands me a USB key. "Here's proof. Can you give this to Antonio when you get back to Venice? I'd email it, but I don't want Valentina to intercept it first because the woman he sent—"

"Gemma?"

"Her real name is Stefania Freitas. She's an assassin. Extremely competent, never fails to finish a job."

An assassin. I *liked* Gemma.

She takes a breath before she continues. "She's also Joao Carvalho's wife."

Tomas's friend Joao? The one who also works for the Venice Mafia? I'm about to open my mouth and ask when Cici's phone rings, loud and shrill. I glance down at my own device and realize that it's been an hour since Tomas left.

There's news.

56

TOMAS

The address Gabriel gives us is in Eixample, a few streets away from the Mercat de Colón. The four of us drive there in Andrei Sidorov's Land Rover—two of Sidorov's grim-faced men in the front, and in the back, the pakhan himself and me.

We ride in silence. Andrei Sidorov has a distant expression on his face. He's not here—he's in the place you go to before battle. I close my eyes, and unsurprisingly, Alina pops into my head. She's in the ring, and her eyes are spitting fire. "Come, show me what you've got."

My fiery dolcezza. She almost died today. I almost lost her *forever.* I meant every word of my promise. She loves me, and I love her, and we're going to live happily ever after. I want a future with her, one filled with banter and good-natured insults *and love,* and I won't let anyone— her father, the mysterious Gemma, Damir Malinov—get in the way of that.

"I know you want to kill Malinov." My voice is harsh. Almost a snarl. "But you can't. *He's mine.*"

The men in the front stiffen, but Andrei Sidorov is too much of a professional to react. "According to Gabriel's idiotic rules, you're the only one with a *claim*. I'm tempted to tell him to stuff it, but my wife will never forgive me if I start a feud with d'Este. Kill the bastard."

"It's just as well," he continues. "If it were up to me, I wouldn't be quick, and I wouldn't be merciful. I would do to him what he did to Vassili." His face stays expressionless, but his voice turns vicious. "I would cut off his tongue so he couldn't scream, and then I'd chop his balls off and feed them to him."

I swallow back the bile in my mouth. "He did that?"

"He's unhinged. It's common knowledge in Russia."

I'm used to violence. I have no stomach for torture, but I recognize that sometimes, there's no other way to get information. But if Sidorov's emissary went under a peace flag, and if Andrei Sidorov is telling the truth, Damir Malinov killed him as painfully and viciously as possible.

This is the work of a disturbed, deranged mind.

And Vidone Laurenti was going to marry Ali off to him.

Fury builds in my chest. Laurenti would have known exactly who Malinov was. If the abduction attempt in Venice had worked, Ali would have woken up in St. Petersburg, the captive plaything of a crazed killer.

And her father didn't give a damn. He was prepared to do this for what? Money? Power? I will make sure he has neither. When I'm done with Malinov, I'm going to make it my mission to ruin Vidone Laurenti.

WE ARRIVE AT THE HOUSE, tucked away at the end of a cul-de-sac. Gabriel told us there were six Kutuzovo foot soldiers in the house with Malinov, but no one is patrolling outside, which is odd.

Even odder? The front door is ajar.

"Kolya, stay in the car," Sidorov instructs the driver. "We might need to make a quick getaway."

He starts to get out, but the other man in the front seat turns around and shakes his head. "I will check it out, pakhan," he says respectfully but firmly. "Please wait in the car until I give the all-clear."

Andrei sits back in his seat. "I pay the bills, but my wife has Tima wrapped around her little finger," he grumbles. He doesn't sound too put out by it. "And Mira gets cranky when she thinks I'm taking unnecessary risks."

A brief smile flashes on the soldier's face. He gets out, weapon in hand, and moves toward the open front door. He steps inside. He's wearing a mic, so we can hear him as he moves through the house. A long moment passes, and then he says, "It's clear. Malinov is the only one here."

Sidorov exchanges a glance with me. He has questions, and he's not the only one. Why is Malinov alone? Where are his foot soldiers?

But none of that matters. All that matters is killing Malinov.

I shrug, tighten my grip on my gun, and get out of the car.

WE FIND Damir Malinov inside his study in the back of the house. "Welcome," he slurs. There's a glass of whiskey in his hand and a half-empty bottle on the desk in front of him. He looks up and sees the man next to me, and recognition sparks in his eyes. "Ah, the Sidorov king makes a personal appearance. I quake in fear."

I keep my gun on him. So does Tima.

Andrei Sidorov moves into the room and sits down in the chair across from Malinov. "Where are your men, Damir?" he asks conversationally.

"Gone." He downs his whiskey and pours himself another glass from a shaky hand. "D'Este called my father and gave him a choice. If Gregori wanted to keep doing business with him, he needed to disown me. Naturally, the bastard chose to protect himself. He called off his soldiers and told me to go honorably to my death." He laughs bitterly. "Paternal love, what can I say?"

Sidorov doesn't sound surprised. "If it makes you feel better, Gregori won't survive this either."

"It does, actually." Malinov turns his attention to me for the first time. "You're not one of Sidorov's people. Who are you?"

"My name is Tomas Aguilar." I don't take my eyes off his hands. "Your sniper targeted my fiancée." Ali and I haven't talked about our engagement. It might have started out as a ruse, but no more. I want it to be real. "In La Llotja a couple of hours ago."

"Oh, her. The bastard daughter of Vidone Laurenti." He laughs without humor. "I didn't know she was engaged." He gives me a dismissive once-over. "I also didn't know that d'Este would get so bent out of shape about an attack on a nobody." He lifts his glass to me. "A bad miscalculation, as it happens."

I almost shoot him right then, but I have one more question. One more thing I need to understand. "Your contract with Laurenti would have had an exit clause. If you didn't want to marry his daughter, why didn't you just buy him out? Why target an innocent woman?"

Malinov looks genuinely confused by my question. "The exit clause would have cost ten million euros," he says. "The sniper cost ten thousand."

I ease back the safety. "The woman you targeted has a life," I say quietly. "She has people she loves and people who love her back. She didn't choose to play this game. She's an innocent."

Malinov's mouth twists into a sneer. "She's a nobody."

"Not to me," I reply, my voice as cold as ice.

And then I put a bullet between his eyes.

57

ALINA

Tomas is okay. That's what Cici tells me. Malinov is dead, Tomas is safe and unhurt, and they're on their way back to Gabriel's mansion.

I run outside. I'm waiting in the driveway when a Land Rover pulls in twenty minutes later. Tomas gets out, and I immediately throw myself onto him, my hands around his neck. "You're here," I whisper, my tears wetting his collar. "You're not hurt?"

"I told you I'd be fine." He holds me, his touch warmly reassuring. His heart beats in his chest, steady and unhurried.

He's alive.

I cling to him like a barnacle to a rock. "Is it over? Please tell me it's over because my heart can't take much more of this."

"It's over," he says. He pulls back and looks steadily at me. "I'm the numbers guy, Ali. This never happens. I usually leave the fighting to Dante, Leo, and Joao. But this time..." He cups my cheek with his callused hand. "This time, it was personal."

I stare into Tomas's gray eyes. He went to war *for me*. So that he could protect me. I love this man so much. "Want to go back home? After all, you did promise to show me your private gym."

"I always keep my promises." His expression turns grim. "I want to see Laurenti first."

My father. That reminds me of Cici's revelation. I tell Tomas what Cici said about how Vidone has known about my existence since I took the DNA test two years ago, and he nods, unsurprised. "You knew?" I ask.

"I suspected."

"Why didn't you tell me?"

His face softens. "You wanted him to be a good person so badly, cara mia. I wanted it to be true for you."

"Cici also implied that my mother wasn't with my father of her own free will." I look up at his face. "You knew that too, didn't you?"

"Again, I didn't have any proof. But the difference in their ages suggested it. Plus, your mother chose to live in Rome, the most crowded and anonymous city in the country, and she never once talked about your father. None of that suggests a happy story."

"I don't want you to kill him."

"I'm not planning to. I want him to live to regret every decision he's ever made." His voice is a block of ice. "I'm going to take great pleasure in ruining him financially."

I want nothing more than to go back to Venice, cocoon myself in my gym, wrap myself in Tomas's love, and leave this whole episode behind. But it turns out I, too, have a vindictive streak in me. "Does he know that Damir Malinov is dead? Would he have found out?"

"No. It's too soon."

"Good," I tell him, a vicious smile on my face. "I want to be the one who delivers the news to him."

He pinned everything on this alliance with the Russians going through. I want to see the look on his face when I tell him it's over.

AN HOUR LATER, I knock on the front door of Vidone Laurenti's rental villa. My father smiles widely when he sees who it is. "Alina," he exclaims, opening his arms wide to hug me. "I was just about to call you. Tell me you've changed your mind." He sees Tomas at my side, and his smile falls away. "What are you doing here?"

Tomas doesn't reply. I ignore my father's outstretched arms. "After we had coffee today, I had a long conversation with Cecelia d'Este."

Vidone Laurenti's face turns expressionless.

"She told me something very interesting. She said that you've known about my existence for two years."

"She's lying," he splutters.

"She's not the one lying, *father*. Why did you wait to contact me? The truth, please."

Vidone must know I'm not buying his paternal act any longer. "You want the truth?" he spits out. "Here it is, then. Why would I contact you? You're a bastard. You should have never been born. Your existence is an insult to my wife, to my family. If your bitch of a mother hadn't taken off, I'd have killed her."

At my side, Tomas stiffens. "Say the word," he says, calm on the surface, a seething mass of fury underneath. "And I will kill him."

I wait for pain to wash over me at Vidone Laurenti's words. It doesn't happen. This man will never be my father—not in any way that counts. And I refuse to give him the power to hurt me any longer.

"No. That's too easy." I lace my fingers in Tomas's and stare Laurenti in the eyes. "Damir Malinov is dead. Tomas killed him an hour ago. Your alliance with the Russians is over. When you lie awake at night, wondering where it all went wrong, *know this*. Two years ago, I was grieving. I was lost, and all I wanted was a crumb of affection. I wanted a family so desperately that if you'd given me that, I would have done anything you asked me." I start to turn away from him. "When you confront the wreckage that is your career, remember that it wasn't the daughter who should have never been born who did this to you. *You did this to yourself.*"

And then I walk out of Vidone Laurenti's life for good. With each step, the weight on my shoulders lifts. I shut the door behind us, and the sun comes out from behind a cloud, and it feels like a new beginning.

All my life, I dreamed of finding my father. But it turns out I don't need him. I've never needed him. I close my eyes for a second, and send an apology to my mother. *I'm sorry,* I whisper. *If my questions ever brought you pain, please forgive me. And thank you for bringing me up. For being a strong, steady presence in my life every single day. For showing me how to always being kind. For teaching me to persevere in the face of overwhelming odds. For being the only parent I ever needed.*

"You okay?" Tomas asks me, his eyes warm and kind.

I've spent a long time feeling alone. But I'm not alone, not anymore. I have Tomas. He sees me like nobody else does. He believes in me even when I doubt myself. He's my infuriating partner, my rock, *my everything.*

"I will be." I slip my hand in his. It's time to leave the past behind and embrace the future, the one with Tomas in it. "You know something? My mother would have really liked you."

IN THE CAR, I lean back in the passenger seat. "What now?" I ask, shutting my eyes and letting the adrenaline drain away.

"We could head to the airport. Antonio's private plane is gassed up and waiting. We could be home in three hours."

I jerk up in my seat. "Your parents would never forgive you. Or me."

"For leaving without saying goodbye? *Please.* My mother will forgive this and a lot more." A smile creases his face. "As long as we let her throw us an engagement party in Valencia."

"Engagement party?" My heart leaps. Our conversation got cut off when a sniper shot at us. Does this mean... "Really?"

"Of course. I'm crazy about you, Ali." His eyes fall on the engagement ring I'm still wearing, and he pulls off the road and into a deserted parking lot with spectacular views of the ocean. He lifts my hand up and slides the ring off my finger. "We might have been pretending to be engaged," he says quietly, "but it never felt fake. Not for a single minute. It always felt real."

He takes a deep breath. "We haven't known each other for very long. It's soon. We can wait if you'd prefer, but it's going to change nothing in my heart. I love you, Alina Zuccaro, and I want to spend the rest of my life with you. Will you marry me? We can have a long engagement—"

Nothing's going to change for me either—my heart swells with certainty, *and I know*. I've found more than love with Tomas. I've found a deep sense of belonging. He is my safe haven, my family, and my home. We might drive each other crazy. We might spar and banter and threaten to poison each other. (To be fair, it's mostly me threatening to poison him.) But underneath, he's my person. He's my forever. He's my happily-ever-after.

"Yes," I reply, cutting him off and launching myself into his arms. "I don't need any more time. I'm sure. So, yes. Yes, yes, yes."

EPILOGUE
ALINA

Three months later…

The grand reopening party for the newly renamed Zuccaro's happens on December thirtieth.

Everyone shows up. And when I say everyone, I mean *everyone*. Tomas's whole family flies in from Valencia for the event.

For me.

Because this is my dream.

It's not just Tomas's parents. My friend Rosa and her husband Leo are there too. Leo's not the only one of Tomas's coworkers in attendance. No, they're all here, starting with the padrino himself, Antonio Moretti. Dante, Joao, Omar, and Daniel all crowd in, too. My instructors, Naima, Julian, and Nova, are here—yes, I finally hired more teachers, and it's working great—as are my regulars, Sara, River, Sergio, and the others.

Prosecco flows like water, and the smoothie machine works overtime. Everyone troops upstairs to take in the expanded weight room. "I love it, Ali," Sara exclaims, hugging me tight. "You were living here, weren't you? Did you move in with your hottie?"

My hottie is saying something to Luke, who is nodding along animatedly. Tomas still calls him my pretty boy instructor, but the two of them get along well. At least, when they're not beating the crap out of each other in the octagon.

Tomas notices I'm staring at him. He looks from me to the new ring Marcelo installed, and his lips curl into a wicked smile. I feel myself blush as I remember his promise to me this morning in the shower. "There's a new ring in the gym," he said, pushing me against the wall and caging me in with his body. "After the party, when everyone's gone, I'm going to drag you there, dolcezza." He winked at me. "And you can show me all your special moves."

Sara clears her throat. "My God," she says. "The two of you have been together for three months already. You're past the honeymoon stage, Ali. Stop eye-fucking him already."

My cheeks flame. "I wasn't eye-fucking him." I totally was. "Yes, I moved into Tomas's house in Giudecca." He talked me into it a week after we came back to Venice from Valencia, though, to be honest, I didn't take much persuading.

I thought it would be pretty great living with Tomas, but it's even better than I imagined. Freccia is a snuggler, and she's decided her new favorite nap spot is my lap. Many of the mafia members live in Giudecca, and

Tomas's coworkers and their partners have become the family I've always wanted. Antonio and Lucia regularly host dinners at their palazzo. Dante and Valentina are a two-minute walk away, and their daughter Angelica, who has started taking classes with me, is a delight. I even enjoy the thirty-minute commute from Giudecca to Dorsoduro. When I lived above the gym, I never got to really leave work behind. I can now, and I'm much happier for it.

Joao also lives in the neighborhood, though we don't see very much of him. When Tomas and I got back to Venice, once the dust settled down, I remembered Cici's words about Gemma, and relayed them to him. Tomas was shocked. "I didn't even know he was married," he said.

I know he told Joao what Cici told me. Shortly after I moved in with Tomas, Joao had come over for a visit. "I'm sorry about Stef," he said. "I didn't know. We've been estranged for a very long time." His eyes turned hard. "I'll take care of it. She'll never threaten you again."

And after that, I haven't heard anything.

Tomas walks over and drapes his arm possessively around my waist. Sara laughs. "I think that's my cue to get more prosecco," she says. "Great party, Ali. And the space looks fantastic."

He waits for her to get out of earshot. "Did I tell you that I finally tracked down Groff's crooked bookkeeper last month?"

I'm wearing three-inch heels, and I still have to look up at his face. "You did? Please tell me you didn't do any murdering."

He rolls his eyes. "Felicity Fletcher is alive and well.

377

As I keep telling you, Alina, murdering opportunities are sadly few and far between these days. A great pity." He reaches into his jacket pocket and extracts a thick bundle of one-hundred-euro notes. "Turns out Groff convinced her that he'd fallen in love with her. And, of course, once he ran away to London, she never heard from him again." He hands me the cash. "I strongly suggested that she return your money. She'd already spent some of it, but there's more here than I thought there would be. Fifty-eight thousand, three hundred euros."

"In cash?" I hiss, pushing the giant wad of bills back to him. "Tomas, you can't just give me that much money. What if I lose it? What if I get robbed on the way to the bank?"

He laughs openly at my reaction. "Are you or are you not Ciro Del Barba's underground champion?"

"Okay, fair," I admit grudgingly. I think back to the day Tomas first discovered the theft. "I never thought I'd be grateful to be stolen from, but if it hadn't happened, we wouldn't have had any reason to spend time around each other. We might not have ended up together."

He gives me a wry smile. "Remember how I volunteered to fix your books? I told you it was a complicated job, and it wouldn't be easy to find someone to do it, so I offered to do it myself?"

"Yes?"

"It wasn't that hard. I could have found someone to do it, but I didn't want to. If anyone was going to spend hours with you, crammed into that ridiculously tiny office, it was going to be me."

I put my hand over my heart. "I think that might have been the most romantic thing I've ever heard."

"You're mocking me, dolcezza," Tomas says. "Sounds like you're in need of a good spanking."

A shiver runs through me. "In the new ring?" I ask hopefully. "Because someone promised to drag me there."

He grins and pulls me close, so my back is against his chest. "You look hot in this dress, Ali," he says into my ear. "I want to tear it off you. Tell me again what time this party ends."

Goosebumps break out on my skin, and I glance discreetly at my watch. "Another hour."

"I can hold off for one more hour," he says. "And no longer. After that, I'm tearing off your dress, party guests or not."

My knees turn weak. "Is that a threat or a promise?"

He laughs and lets me go. "You'll find out."

ONE HOUR LATER, the last guests leave, and I lock the door behind them. I shut the blinds and go in search of Tomas. I find him in the office, looking at something on the screen. "That was a very successful re-opening," he says. "Add in the New Year rush, and I'm predicting you'll soon need to open a second location."

"You think?"

"I know." He looks up. "Is everyone gone?"

"Yes. Your mother asked me again when we were going to set a wedding date. She hates that we're taking our time."

"She'll live," Tomas says with a shrug.

"I felt bad about disappointing her," I continue. "So I committed to a formal engagement party in Valencia." I make a rueful face. "Sorry."

He laughs. "She wore you down, did she? You're too soft-hearted, that's your problem. Don't worry about it— the party will be fun."

He seems unfazed at the idea of a big Valencian celebration. Phew.

I pull my hair loose from its ponytail and slip off my fiendishly uncomfortable heels. "Onto more fun things. Now that everyone's gone, you promised you're going to drag me into the ring, Signor Aguilar."

He leans back against the wall, his posture relaxed. "Do you need to change into something more comfortable before I kick your ass?"

Before he kicks my ass? Oh, he's going to regret that. I reach behind my back and unzip my dress, letting the fabric fall to the floor. "Why bother to change?" I lose my bra and panties as well and give him a cocky grin. "Show me what you've got."

His eyes turn heated. He laughs and shrugs off his jacket. His hands move to his belt, and my gaze follows. The thick bulge of his erection is clearly visible underneath his trousers. "As you wish, dolcezza."

Thank you for reading The Fighter.

More Tomas & Ali?! Our happy couple heads to Valencia for the engagement party Tomas's mother insists they have, but then they run into Estela! How does Tomas react, and does Alina tear into Tomas's evil ex? *You've got to read the scene to find out.*

Sign up to read it by scanning the QR code below or going to:
https://taracrescent.com/bonus-the-fighter/

Want more Venice mafia?
Lucia and Antonio fall in love in **The Thief,** which kicks off with Lucia stealing a painting from Antonio. Read this mafia hero+art thief heroine romance with second chance vibes today!

Valentina and Dante banter, hack, and stab their way to love in The Broker. Enemies-to-lovers, with a mafia hero and a single mom hacker heroine? Yes please.

Leo and Rosa are forced to get married to save Rosa's brother. Love a broody hero, arranged marriages, and an age-gap romance? You're going to want to read The Fixer.

The next book in the series features **Joao and Stefania,** and will be out early 2025. My newsletter is the best way to find out when it goes live, so sign up by scanning the QR code above.

Turn the page for a preview of THE THIEF, Antonio & Lucia's story.

THE THIEF

I stole from Venice's mafia boss...
But when I get home with his painting,
He's there in my bedroom, *waiting for me*,
And he says...
"Hello, little thief."

In the dark and shadowy underworld of Venice, one man rules with an iron fist.
Powerful mafia boss. King of Venice. **Antonio Moretti.**
Ten years ago, he was the stranger who emerged from the shadows to protect me on the worst night of my life.
But when I return to Venice to steal a priceless painting from Antonio, intent on returning it to the museum it belongs to, I realize...
The king of Venice has set a trap for me, and this time, *he's not letting go.*

A PREVIEW OF THE THIEF

LUCIA

I am very drunk, and everything is hazy.

It's a dark night—cloudy, moonless, and foggy. I've been wandering for hours, not paying attention to where I'm going, and I've ended up in a neighborhood I don't recognize. Venice is a safe city, but this section of town is far from the tourist core. The boats aren't pleasure yachts; they're working fishing vessels. Warehouses dot the docks, and there are more rats than people this late at night.

A week ago, I was working on my senior thesis in Chicago. I didn't know my mother was dying of cancer because my parents had kept her illness a secret from me. Which meant I didn't know she'd gone into hospice either.

I never got the chance to say goodbye.

I lift the bottle of vodka I'm clutching like a lifeline to my mouth and take a healthy swig.

Three days ago, I got a call that destroyed me. My mother had succumbed to the cancer ravaging her body. My father, unable to contemplate life without his wife, put a bullet in his brain. One day, I was wondering if I could convince my art history professor to grant me an extension for my final paper. The next, I was flying back home to bury my parents.

A hint of movement jerks me to the present. Something rustles to my right. Before I have time to react, three bodies coalesce from the fog and surround me. One of them holds a knife to my throat. "Don't move, and don't shout, signorina," he growls. "I don't want to hurt you. Give me your purse."

I'm being robbed.

Numbly, I hold out my bright green bag. I bought it on Calle Larga XXII Marzo from a *vu compra* who'd set up shop opposite the Dolce and Gabbana store. Mama and I did a bunch of tourist things before I left for college: we visited St. Mark's Basilica, listened to musicians at the *piazza*, rode a gondola, and ate at a restaurant a stone's throw from the Ponte di Rialto. The vendor insisted that the bag was actually Prada, not a fake, and my mother laughed at him. "We're not tourists," she said and haggled with him for the next fifteen minutes.

I should have realized she was sick. She'd lost weight, and for the last couple of months, she wouldn't FaceTime me. "My cell phone broke," she said. "I have to go buy a new one."

I should have suspected that something was badly wrong.

One of the men snatches the imitation Prada bag

388

from my hand while another shines a flashlight in my face. "Your necklace too."

Things are moving too fast for me to process, but those words penetrate my drunken stupor. The necklace I'm wearing, a filigreed ruby pendant dangling on a gold chain, belonged to my mother. My father gave it to her as a wedding present, and she never took it off. She's gone now, and this is all I have left of her. It's my most cherished possession.

"No."

"Don't be stupid, signorina," the man with the knife snaps. "It's not worth your life. Take off the goddamn chain and hand it to me before you get hurt."

"Someone's coming," Flashlight Guy says, his voice nervous. "We're not authorized. . . We need to get out of here." He makes a lunge for my necklace. The chain digs into my neck, and I yelp in pain.

A tall, lean man glides out of the shadows, his face obscured by the brim of his hat. "Stop," he says, his cold voice slicing the moisture-laden air like a whip.

One word. Just one word, but the reaction is electrifying. The man holding my purse takes one look and bolts. "Fuck," the guy who made a grab for my chain swears. The knife clatters to the ground, and the thief who held it holds up his hands in a gesture of surrender. "I'm sorry," he says, his voice trembling. "I didn't mean to. . . I didn't know—"

"You didn't know I was here. But I'm always watching. You should remember that." My rescuer's voice is ice. "Leave."

The remaining two criminals flee.

The man turns in my direction. He studies me for

what seems like an age, his gaze lingering on the side of my neck. "You're hurt."

"I am?" I reach up, and my skin stings where the necklace cut me. "Yeah, I guess." The pendant is safe, though, and that's all that counts. "It'll heal."

He moves closer, his breath warming my face, and he touches the cut with a feather-light touch. "Who did this to you? Which one of them?"

A shiver runs down my back. Once again, everything is moving with bewildering speed, events rushing past me like leaves in a windstorm. The vodka has scrambled my thoughts, and this man isn't helping. His voice and touch aren't supposed to permeate my numbness, but they are, and I don't know how to react.

"The guy holding the flashlight."

"Marco." My hero's voice promises death. His eyes settle on me again, and his tone softens. "You're cold, signorina." He pulls off his jacket and drapes it around my shoulders, and warmth descends over me like a blanket. "This isn't a good part of town to be in alone. Alone and drunk."

My gratitude evaporates in a rush. He's judging me? What the hell does he know about my life? "You shouldn't offer unsolicited advice either, but here we are." Okay, that's quite rude. Mama would be shocked. "But thank you for your help," I add grudgingly, turning to leave.

"You're welcome," he replies, falling in step with me.

"What are you doing?"

"Escorting you home," he says, as if it were obvious. "Like I said, this is a dangerous neighborhood, and I would hate for you to get hurt again."

Home is filled with memories I'm trying to obliterate with a bottle of vodka. "I don't want to go home," I mutter sullenly. "And I don't care if I get hurt."

There's a long pause. "But *I* care, signorina."

Why? "We're at an impasse, then." I take another deep drink of my vodka, and then, out of some strange impulse, I offer the bottle to him.

I expect him to turn it down. I'm even prepared for him to do something dramatic, like fling it into the canal. But shockingly, he does neither. He pries it gently from my fingers. His lips wrap around the mouth of the bottle, the way mine did a second earlier, and he drinks. Then he hands it back to me, his fingers brushing mine.

Heat blossoms in my chest.

We walk in the darkness, taking turns drinking from the emptying bottle, neither breaking the silence. "I buried my parents today," I finally blurt out.

He glances in my direction. "I'm sorry."

"I'm not sad." It's not exactly a lie. *Sad* is too simple an emotion to describe how my world has been shattered. "I'm angry. I'm *furious.* My mother was sick, but she hid it from me. And when she died, my father blew his brains out."

He doesn't say anything.

"It wasn't just my parents who lied," I continue. "They all did. My best friend didn't tell me either. Did they think they were protecting me?" I take another healthy swig. "Because I don't feel protected." My voice comes out defiant, shrill, and bitter. "I feel abandoned. I *hate* them for that."

He remains silent, but this time, the silence prickles at me. "What are you thinking?" I demand. "Are you going to give me the same advice the priest did? Are you going to tell me to forgive them?"

"I would never presume to tell you how to feel."

I stumble over a coil of rope. I'm about to fall, but his arms are around me before I do. His touch feels. . . solid. Reassuring. *Shockingly male.* "So, what then?" I persist. He's a tall body in the darkness, a warm presence at my side. I still can't see his face, and maybe that's what loosens my tongue. Or maybe it's the vodka. "You don't have any advice for me?" I keep stabbing at the open, bleeding wound. "If you were me, if your parents abandoned you like mine, what would you do?"

"I didn't know my parents," he says without inflection. "I was left at a church as a baby."

Oh. *Oh.* "I'm so sorry."

"I don't need your sympathy, *tesoro.*" The easy, relaxed set of his shoulders is replaced by stiffness. This is clearly not a welcome topic, and it's obvious he'd much rather talk about my problems than his own.

"Give me advice, then," I breathe. "Tell me what to do. Tell me how to move forward from this."

He still has his arm around me, and I've made no effort to pull away. It's nice to be held. His touch is a portal into a fantasy world where I'm not suddenly alone. A world in which there's someone who cares for me. Someone who will catch me before I fall.

"Did your parents love you?"

I nod wordlessly. That's why their betrayal hurts so much.

"We don't make our best decisions under pressure," he says quietly. "When we are hurt, when we are in pain, we don't think. We hide, we lash out. I can't pretend to understand your parents' decision. Maybe they thought they were protecting you. Or maybe they didn't want your last memories of them to be filled with pain."

I make a scoffing sound, but he's not done.

"As for moving forward," he says softly. "You just do. You remember that you were loved, and you put one foot in front of the other. Until one day, you think about them without pain. The anger and grief will fade, *cara mia*, and you'll be left with the good memories."

We've been walking steadily toward civilization. The Ca'Pesaro looms before me, casting ornate shadows into the canal. I drain the rest of my vodka and fling the bottle into the water.

He tracks the angry movement. "Where are you staying?"

I cannot go to my parents' apartment. I just cannot. I can't be in the place where they died. I can't run into the neighbors, and I cannot cope with their sympathy and concern. "I don't know." I reach for my phone and realize it's in the bag the thieves took. "My purse is gone." I take a deep breath and fight the urge to burst into tears. "I have no money."

He puts his hand on the small of my back, a comforting gesture that tells me I'm not alone. "Come with me, signorina. Let's get you settled for the night. We'll find your purse in the morning."

My rescuer takes me to a hotel. The lobby is brightly lit, and I turn to him to finally see what he looks like, but all that vodka has caused me to see double and triple of everything. I get the sense of a firm jaw and full lips, but that's it.

"A room," he says to the clerk behind the counter.

The man jumps to attention. "Si, Signor," he says. There was respect in his voice but also a trace of fear? Or am I imagining it? I can't tell.

A key is produced. The well-dressed stranger steers me to the ancient elevator. Can I really call him a stranger if I've spent the better part of the last hour pouring out my troubles to him? I slump against him, my bones turning to liquid. "You smell nice," I tell him. It seems important that he knows that. "Like the ocean." I sniff him again. "And something else. Pine, maybe? I like it."

He doesn't reply, but his grip on me tightens slightly. I like that too.

We reach the room, and he follows me in, heading to the bathroom. I collapse on the bed, feeling his absence like a loss. I hear water running, and he returns with a glass, motioning me to sit up. "Drink this," he orders. "It'll help with your hangover."

"I don't get hangovers."

He laughs shortly. "Oh, you will, *cara mia.*" It's the second time he's called me that. He cups my cheek with his hand and looks deep into my eyes. "Go to sleep," he says, his voice gentle. "Things will look slightly less bleak in the morning."

He turns away from me. I stare blankly after him. Only when he's almost at the door do I realize he's leaving. "Stop!" I don't want him to go. "I don't want to be alone tonight." I grip the bedspread with my fingers and take a deep, shaky breath. "Please?"

He hesitates for a long moment, then he relents. "Okay." He turns off the lights, and the room plunges into comforting darkness. A minute later, the mattress sags with his weight as he gets into bed with me.

My eyes close. Sleep tugs me under, but I fight it. I want one more thing tonight. "I don't know your name."

"Antonio."

"Antonio." I try it on my tongue. "I'm Lucia."

"A lovely name for a lovely woman." The words feel trite, but the weight in his voice makes me believe him. "You're safe here. Sleep well, Lucia."

When I wake up the next morning, I'm alone. There's no sign that anyone was ever with me. In fact, if I wasn't in a strange hotel room, I'd be convinced I imagined the whole thing.

I get out of bed and wince. Antonio was right. My head feels like it's going to explode. This is what I get for drinking an entire bottle of vodka in one evening.

I go to the bathroom and splash some water on my face. The skin around my neck is abraded and raw where the thief tried to yank my chain off. I finger the pendant absently, a complicated cocktail of emotions churning through me. Antonio's words from last night ring in my head. *The anger and grief will fade, and you'll be left with the good memories.*

There's a knock at the door. I open it to a staff member wheeling in a cart of food. "Breakfast, signorina."

I'm starving, but I have no money to pay for the food. I'm about to tell him I didn't order anything when he adds, "Also, this was left for you at the front desk."

The *this* in his hands is my bag. The green, imitation

Prada bag my mother bought for me before I left for college. And it's untouched. My passport, money, and phone are all in there.

My gallant rescuer strikes again.

Tucked in a front pocket is a thick, cream-colored card.

A phone number is printed on the front, and there's a handwritten note on the back. *Call me.*

I stare at it for a very long time.

Last night, Antonio took care of me. Stayed with me, listened to me. He made sure I was safe. When everything around me was crumbling, when I desperately needed someone to lean on, he was there.

But safety is a myth. Your world can shatter in the blink of an eye. People betray you. They hide illness from you and die. They shoot their brains out and leave you bereft.

The last three days have taught me I can't afford to lean on anyone.

I take a deep breath and tuck the card back into the purse. "Can you call me a cab in an hour?" I ask the man.

"Of course, signorina. Where to?"

"The airport." There's nothing left for me in Venice. Not anymore.

Ten years later. . .

When you're a museum curator moonlighting as an art thief, having a hacker for a best friend is a pretty good deal. Especially when it's time to plan your next heist.

It's Friday evening. I pour myself a glass of cheap red wine, settle in front of my laptop, and call Valentina. I feel the familiar stirring of excitement as I wait for her to connect. My first art heist was a mad impulse, but recently, I've been targeting rich and powerful people who knowingly acquire stolen art. People who think their wealth provides them immunity. It gives me great satisfaction to steal from them and return the paintings to their original owners.

And I can't wait to kick off this year's project.

The last time Valentina and I talked, I presented her with a list of seven potential targets, compiled by scouting through news reports, auction listings, and talking to my parents' old fence, Alvisa Zanotti. Signora Zanotti might be retired, but she keeps her finger on the pulse of the art world and stays updated on the ins and outs of black-market art. Valentina promised to look into the seven and narrow it down for me.

Italy is six hours ahead of Boston, so it's midnight in Venice. When Valentina logs on, she looks exhausted. "Long day?" I ask sympathetically.

Valentina and I have been best friends since kinder-garten. Growing up, we spent practically every waking hour together. Valentina often took refuge at our house because her parents fought constantly. Some of my fondest memories are of the two of us spending long afternoons doing homework at our battered kitchen table, my mother supplying an endless stream of snacks.

"You could say that." She fills her wine glass right to the brim. "Some of the other children have been bullying Angelica, so I pulled her out of school."

After the death of my parents, I didn't talk to Valentina for two years. I blamed her—unfairly—for the secrets my parents kept. But Valentina didn't give up. No matter how often I ignored her, she kept reaching out. Our friendship finally resumed when she sent me a picture of a newborn. "This is Angelica," she wrote. "My daughter. Will you be her godmother?"

Anger stirs in me now. "Why were they bullying her?"

Valentina shrugs wearily. "Because she doesn't have a father."

"Ah." She's never once talked about the guy. I asked about him once, and she shut me down. Since then, we've reached a tacit understanding that neither of us will talk about the past. She doesn't mention my parents, and I don't ask why Angelica's father doesn't play a role in his daughter's life.

"I'm sorry," I tell her, wishing I had something more helpful to say. Something I could do, something more useful than offering support from afar. "That sucks."

"Yeah." She drinks deeply from her glass. "I haven't had time to look at your list."

"Forget the list." Valentina looks like she's at the end of her tether. I can't blame her. It's been one thing after another the entire year. Angelica broke her ankle in January. Then Valentina was sick all summer, and to cap off a truly shitty year, her father died in August. The two of them weren't close, but even so, I know it's taken a toll on my friend. As for Angelica, she's been having nightmares ever since her grandfather died.

And now this. My poor friend.

"How's Angelica doing?" I lean forward. "How are *you* doing?"

"I'm fine," she lies. "I'm putting her in a different school. A more international, diverse one." She stares morosely into her glass. "I miss you. Sometimes, I wish you were closer—" She cuts off whatever she's about to say next. "How's the job hunt going?"

"Miserable." My employment troubles are nothing new. I'm trained as a curator, but museum funding is highly volatile, and permanent positions are few and far between. I've spent my adult life hopping from one short-term contract to another and lived in eight cities in the last ten years. My last contract ended a couple of weeks ago. I've sent out some feelers, but it's getting close to the end of the year, so hiring is slow.

But that's not what's bothering me now. It's Valentina's despondent expression. Her uncharacteristic melancholy.

She's never once complained about the physical distance between us. Never once expressed discontent that I hadn't met Angelica in person.

Both her parents are now dead. They weren't much, but they're gone now, and she's spending her first Christmas without them.

I remember my first Christmas alone. The crippling loneliness and aching sense of loss. I would never wish that on my worst enemy. How can I do that to my best friend?

On impulse, I look at job listings in Europe. Then I go perfectly still.

Because there's a job opening in Venice. A four-month contract at the Palazzo Ducale to digitize their catalog.

Speaks fluent Italian? *Check.*

In-depth knowledge of Italian art? *Check.*

The pay is. . . well, I won't starve. And most importantly, I'll be there for Valentina.

Can you do it? Can you go back to Venice, the city you fled ten years ago?

My heart starts to race. I take a deep breath and order myself to calm down. It's only four months. I'm not going to stay forever.

Out of sight of the camera, I open my purse and fish out the business card I've held onto for a decade. It's faded. Dog-eared. I run my thumb over the handwritten note.

Call me.

I wonder if the number still works.

I'm tempted to call. *So tempted.*

It's been ten years, Lucia. He's probably married with a handful of children by now.

I tuck the card away.

Valentina says, "Lucia?"

"Sorry. I got distracted by something on my phone." I'm more than qualified for the Palazzo Ducale role. I should be a shoo-in for the job. I won't tell Valentina until I know for sure, but after ten years away, it looks like I'm finally returning home.

ANTONIO

Venice is my city. I head up her mafia, run her casinos, and rule her underworld. I know every dark alley and every narrow canal. All her secrets are mine. I started life with nothing, and I've fought my way to the top. Everything I've ever wanted is within my grasp.

And still, lately, I've been so fucking *bored* with it all.

I walk into our weekly meeting a good twenty minutes late. My second-in-command, Dante, glances pointedly at his watch as I enter. He's the only one who dares. My other lieutenants—Joao, Tomas, and Leonardo—ignore my tardiness and greet me respectfully.

"Sorry I'm late," I say crisply. "Let's get started."

Joao delivers an update on our smuggling operations. Leo goes next, and then it's Tomas, our numbers guy. As usual, his presentation is detailed and thorough. I normally find his briefings fascinating, but today, I have to work hard at faking interest.

"We're flush with cash," Tomas finally finishes. "Business has never been better. I have identified some investment opportunities. Padrino, I recommend—"

"Send me an email with the options," I say, cutting him off before he gets into the weeds. "Is there anything else?"

Dante, who's been silent all meeting, nods. "We have a problem," he says grimly. "The bratva has been spotted in Bergamo."

I sit up. Bergamo is only a couple of hours away. Too close for comfort. "Who?"

"A couple of foot soldiers of the Gafur OPG. Should I reach out to the Verratti?"

Salvatore Verratti runs Bergamo, and I can't see him forming alliances with the Russians. As far as I know, the family's finances are in good shape, and even if they weren't, Federico, Salvatore's father and the former head of the crime family, loathes foreigners.

And yet my instincts urge me to proceed cautiously. "Not yet," I reply. "Not until I have a better sense of what's going on."

"You don't trust Salvatore?"

I give Dante a dry look. "I don't trust *anyone,* as you should know by now. Get Valentina to intercept their communications." Valentina Linari is my most talented hacker. If she can't keep the Russians under surveillance, no one can. "If the bratva makes contact with the Verratti family, I want to know immediately."

"Yes, *padrino.*" My lieutenants look alert, almost excited by the prospect of a turf war. Not me. I just feel a headache coming on.

I look around the room. "Anything else?"

"One more thing." Dante opens the folder in front of him. Extracting a note, he pushes it in my direction. "You got a letter from Arthur Kirkland."

The name is vaguely familiar. I search my memory. "The art collector?"

"Yes."

That explains the letter. Arthur Kirkland is eighty and doesn't believe in computers. I scan the sheet of paper with a frown. "He's warning me about an art thief. Do you know what this is about?"

Dante has an answer, of course. He always does. My second-in-command is loyal, ruthless, and, above all, unfailingly competent. "Arthur Kirkland collects Italian art. Some of his collection has been acquired through dubious means."

"Most of his collection," I correct, remembering more of the details now. "The Third Reich looted Italy in 1943, and Kirkland's uncle, a Nazi sympathizer, mysteriously ended up with priceless paintings when the war ended." I glance at the letter again. "This mystery thief stole one of his pieces last year."

"I think I like this thief," Joao says. Dante glances at him, and he lifts his hands in an expressive gesture. "What? You expect me to feel bad for a Nazi looter?"

Can't say I disagree with Joao's sentiment. "Kirkland says his security people have put together a profile of the thief."

"Yes, there was a dossier enclosed with the letter." Dante reads from his file. "The thief's specialty is sixteenth-century Italian religious art. Ten major works have been stolen, all from that period. And all from private collectors. Interestingly, the targeted paintings were also all previously stolen." He pauses for effect. "And they've all been returned to their rightful owners."

That *is* interesting. "A thief who fancies himself a modern-day Robin Hood?"

"Herself," Dante corrects. "At least, that's what Kirkland's investigative team concluded."

"A woman?" A current of anticipation hums through me. "How did they determine that?"

Dante pushes forward a tablet. "One of the cameras from Kirkland's compound took this before it shorted out."

I play the video. The thief is wearing a faded sweatshirt, its hood obstructing her face. But it's definitely a woman. The baggy sweatshirt can't hide her curves.

There's something about the way she moves that tugs at my memory.

"Kirkland wants her caught, padrino," Dante finishes. "It feels personal. He's written to everyone who might be her next target."

"Has he now?" I have an extensive collection of Venetian art that was mostly bought in public auctions, but not all.

Not my Madonna.

Painted by Titian himself and valuable beyond measure, the *Madonna at Repose* was my first big job. I stole it from the Palazzo Ducale when I was sixteen. I should have fenced it immediately but couldn't bring myself to part with it. It currently hangs in my bedroom.

I play the five-second clip again. There's nothing here —nothing to identify the thief—and yet something continues to tickle the back of my mind. The way she moves feels familiar somehow.

Tomas is reading the file. "Weird," he says. "She targets people all over the world but always strikes between November and January. Every single time."

"Well, it *is* Christmas," Leo points out. "People are distracted during the holidays."

"You know what else is strange?" Tomas continues. "Look at her targets. Vecchio, il Giovane, Lorenzo Lotto. . .

These are all Venetian painters. But she's never struck in Italy."

I look at him curiously. "I didn't realize you were interested in art."

Tomas flushes. "I like to paint, padrino. It's a hobby of mine."

Dante takes the file from Tomas and scans it with a frown. "You're right," he says. "That is strange. There's plenty of stolen art in Italy, but it's almost as if she's avoiding coming here. You want Valentina to look into this?"

The puzzle pieces finally connect. I pull up my tablet and run a search to confirm my hunch.

Teresa Petrucci, died the seventh of December.

Paolo Petrucci, died the seventh of December.

And now I know why the woman seems familiar.

Teresa and Paolo were art thieves. And Lucia Petrucci, their only child, wandered the wharfs the night after she buried her parents, clutching a bottle of vodka and nursing raw grief in her heart.

Lucia, who graduated from the University of Chicago with a master's degree in art history.

The timing matches up. The thief stole their first painting ten years ago on Christmas Day. That would have been only two weeks after Lucia's parents died.

She's been stealing a painting every year since her parents died. A way of remembering them, perhaps?

Beautiful, *reckless* Lucia. Where is she now? I run another search, and the Internet provides me answers. After stints worldwide and ten years away, she's finally coming home. She starts as an assistant curator at the Palazzo Ducale next week.

Ten years, and I still remember the bottle green of her eyes. Ten years, and I still remember the hitch in her voice as she asked me to stay with her. *Don't go,* she whispered, her lips quivering. *I don't want to be alone tonight.*

She didn't call me the next day, and when I stopped at the hotel after dealing with the trio who accosted her, she wasn't there. She'd left for the airport. Flown out of Venice and out of my life.

Now she's back.

And she's an art thief.

I can't wait to see her again.

Venice is my city. I head up her mafia. I rule her underworld. Nobody steals in my city without my permission.

"I know who she is." Sharp hunger fills me, a hunger I haven't felt in years. "Don't involve Valentina; she has plenty of other things to do. I'll take care of this thief personally."

Dante studies me thoughtfully, but whatever he's thinking, he keeps to himself. "Yes, padrino."

ABOUT TARA CRESCENT

Get a free story from Tara when you sign up to Tara's mailing list.

Tara Crescent writes steamy contemporary romances for readers who like hot, dominant heroes and strong, sassy heroines.

When she's not writing, she can be found curled up on a couch with a good book, often with a cat on her lap.

She lives in Toronto.

Tara also writes sci-fi romance as Lili Zander. Check her books out at http://www.lilizander.com

Find Tara on:
www.taracrescent.com
tara@taracrescent.com

ALSO BY TARA CRESCENT

CONTEMPORARY ROMANCE

Venice Mafia

The Thief

The Broker

The Fixer

The Fighter

Hard Wood

Hard Wood

Not You Again

The Drake Family Series

Temporary Wife

Fake Fiance

Spicy Holiday Treats

Running Into You

Waiting For You

Standalone Books

MAX: A Friends to Lovers Romance

WHY CHOOSE / MFM ROMANCE

Club Ménage

Menage in Manhattan

The Dirty series

The Cocky series

Dirty X6

You can also keep track of my new releases by signing up for my mailing list!

Made in the USA
Middletown, DE
15 July 2024

57308748R00248